Praise for THE

"Poaching big game . . . check. A loveable yellow Lab . . . double check. Computer hackers from India . . . WHAT! That last item is the big checklist twist in outdoor writer Rob Phillips' latest novel, *Cascade Kidnapping*, the fourth in his Luke McCain series. As in all of Phillips' books, *Cascade Kidnapping* reinforces healthy respect for the outdoors and laws that protect it."
–Bob Crider, retired editor and publisher, *Yakima Herald-Republic*

"*Cascade Kidnapping* has Washington State game warden Luke McCain and his yellow Lab, Jack, arresting salmon poachers, investigating a serial elk killer, and dealing with administrative duties. . . . Phillips' writing displays a real knowledge of the outdoors, as well as the duties and responsibilities of game wardens. A very enjoyable book!!"
–Rich Phillips, book reviewer for the *International Game Warden Magazine*

"*Cascade Predator* is a well-blended stew of Northwest icons, a reflection of Rob's intimate knowledge of wildlife, outdoor realism, and page-turning curveballs that is just flat tough to put down. This latest edition to the Luke McCain series confirms Rob Phillips' standing as a skilled mystery writer. Already I want to read another."
–Terry W. Sheely, northwest author and writer

"This is crime fiction at its finest–the perfect blend of a compelling mystery, a fabulous setting, the best dog ever, and a very likeable hero you won't forget."
–Christine Carbo, award-winning author of the Glacier Mystery Series

"*Cascade Vengeance* takes readers on a thrill ride through the dual worlds of drug dealing and big-game hunting deep in Washington's Cascade mountains. Rob Phillips uses his extensive knowledge of the region to tell the fast-moving tale . . . on the way to the story's harrowing and heartbreaking conclusion."

–Scott Graham, National Outdoor Book Award-winning author of *Mesa Verde Victim*

"Rob Phillips delivers another page turner. *Cascade Vengeance* is full of murder, intrigue and suspense. And just when you think the case is solved, Phillips throws you a curveball. If you enjoyed *The Cascade Killer*, you'll love Phillips's latest in the Luke McCain series."

–Pat Hoglund, publisher of *Western Hunting Journal, Traveling Angler*, and *Salmon & Steelhead Journal*

"*Cascade Vengeance*, the second book in the Luke McCain series, is another hang-onto-your-hat, nonstop action episode with Luke, a Washington State Fish and Wildlife officer, his FBI girlfriend Sara, and Jack, his loyal yellow Lab. I felt like I was riding shotgun in Luke's Ford pickup, bouncing along forest service roads where very bad guys might be lurking."

–Susan Richmond, owner of Inklings Bookshop

"Another fast-paced, exciting chapter in the Luke McCain series that remains true to the Pacific Northwest. Phillips leaves readers with a splendid conclusion, helping us wonder when the next Luke McCain volume will be out. I am truly a fan of Luke and Jack!"

–Vikki J. Carter, host & producer of *Authors of the Pacific Northwest Podcast*

"If you're looking for an enjoyable read out in deer camp or for just sitting next to your fireplace, then *The Cascade Killer* is a definite winner."

–John McAdams, author of *The Big Game Hunting Blog* & host of The *Big Game Hunting Podcast*

"Real! Captivating! Once you start, you can't put it down! *The Cascade Killer* is VERY well done!"

–Scott Haugen, host and producer of *The Hunt* and author of numerous outdoor books

CASCADE
KIDNAPPING

A LUKE MCCAIN NOVEL

ROB PHILLIPS

LATAH
BOOKS

CASCADE KIDNAPPING

Book design by Kevin Breen and Jon Gosch
Cover image derived from Adobe Stock photos

ISBN: 978-1-957607-05-4
Cataloging-in-Publication Data is available upon request

Manufactured in the United States of America

Published by
Latah Books, Spokane, Washington
www.latahbooks.com

The author may be contacted at yakimahunter@yahoo.com

PROLOGUE

A thin ribbon of gray smoke was still rising from the dying embers in the fire pit when they came. They approached quietly, hoping to not wake the three individuals in the small green tent.

One of the campers, Skyler Sloan, was awakened when he thought he heard a twig snap. He wondered if a bear had stumbled into their camp, looking for food. He thought of waking the others but instead lay perfectly still and listened. If it were a bear, he reasoned, it would be making more noise. What he heard in his semi-consciousness was something, or someone, stepping on a stick. Or so he thought.

Sloan listened intently for one minute, then two. Finally, not hearing anything else moving, he put his head back down and closed his eyes. Later, he would kick himself for not waking Skip—not that it would have mattered much.

Seven minutes after Sloan thought he had heard something, the tent erupted with noise and light. A man was yelling, and bright lights were flashing in the camper's eyes. The young man didn't know what was happening, but he knew it was trouble.

CHAPTER 1

"**D**id I tell you Cale called me?" Luke McCain hollered down the hall toward the bedroom where his wife Sara was getting dressed for work.

Sara, a beautiful, tall, dark-haired FBI agent, was totally out of Luke's league. At least, that's what he believed. He had helped save her from probable death three years earlier, and somehow in the weeks and months that followed, she had fallen in love with him. And he with her. They were married a year later. McCain thanked his lucky stars every day. He didn't know it, but Sara thanked hers every day too.

"No, what's he up to?" she asked as she came out of the bedroom brushing her shoulder-length black hair. She already had her shield fastened to the left side of the belt on her black slacks, and a pistol in a belt holster sat on her right hip. A crisp, white blouse was tucked into the slacks.

"He wants me to go with him up into the high Cascades in September to do some hunting."

"That sounds like fun. Are you going to do it?"

"I wanted to check with you to make sure we're not doing anything, but yeah, if there are no conflicts, I would love spending a little time with him again."

Cale Harris had been Luke's best friend through most of his formative years—they'd gone to grade school, middle school, and high school together. After high school, Luke went off to Washington State University to try to figure out what he wanted to do with the rest of his life, and Harris, who was one of the smartest kids Luke knew, took an appointment to West Point. After college, he did two tours in Afghanistan and then went to work for the Washington State Patrol, quickly moving up the ranks to become a special investigator. The two stayed in touch via social media, but getting together for something was a rarity.

"I think you should," Sara said. "We have nothing going on that I know of."

"I might even be able to turn it into work and not have to take vacation days," Luke said. "I can check on hunters during the day, help Cale if he needs it, and we can even fish some of the lakes in the early mornings and evenings."

"I assume Jack will be joining you," she said.

Jack was Luke and Sara's big yellow Labrador Retriever. The dog was originally Luke's, but if you watched Jack closely, you would see he spent more time with Sara at home, often sleeping within feet of the lady of the house. Luke noticed it and was happy that the two had become so close. Of course, Jack being a true Lab, eating was extremely important to him, and Sara was always a sucker for the dog's big brown eyes and would sneak him a table scrap or other treat now and again.

"Geez," Luke said one evening after Sara gave in to a longing look from Jack, giving him a bite of a cookie. "If I looked at you like that, could I get anything I wanted?"

"It all depends on what you want there, mister," she said with a sly smile.

"Give me a couple minutes, and I'll think of something."

Jack was an excellent hunter and retriever, but he also had some other natural talents. He was a master at tracking, and more than once he'd helped track down humans who were either running from the law or lost. Because of his abilities, Jack often accompanied Luke during his days in the field as a Washington Department of Fish and Wildlife police officer.

"I wouldn't go without Jack," Luke told Sara.

At the sound of his name, the big yellow dog walked into the kitchen where Luke was just finishing up a bowl of Wheaties with sliced bananas.

"Sorry, boy," Luke said. "None left for you. You don't like bananas anyway."

Luke McCain was a big man. At 39 years old, with thick brown hair, he stood nearly six feet, five inches tall, weighed 227 pounds, and had about eight percent body fat. In his uniform, he oozed authority. A workout fanatic, McCain had wide shoulders, thick biceps, and a narrow waist. He liked being in shape for two reasons. First, he wanted to be able to climb around the Cascade Mountains without constantly sucking air when he was hunting deer and elk. And he wanted to look like someone who wasn't to be messed with.

McCain had been a WDFW police officer for fifteen years, during which he'd run into a few men who were of the mind to take him on. When they tried, it usually ended up badly for them.

Of course, being in good shape still wouldn't stop a bullet or a knife. Luke had learned over the years that if you can help it, you just don't put yourself in a situation where deadly force might be necessary. Walk away and deal with it another day was his philosophy. Sometimes, however, those situations were unavoidable.

The year before, a crazy guy living in a hovel in the mountains had attacked Luke with some homemade hatchet-type weapons made of cougar claws. Luckily, Jack had intervened, rushing in to bite the man in the ass and giving Luke time to get on top of the situation.

Luke rubbed Jack's ears and patted him on the side.

"Come on, boy. It's time to earn our keep. See you tonight!" he said down the hall.

"Have a great day!" Sara said.

At his state-issued, Ford F-150, four-wheel-drive pickup, Luke opened the back driver's side door. Jack leapt in and landed softly on the seat, his normal riding area. There, he could see what was happening, and when he got sleepy, he could lie down and snooze for a while.

It was late June, and Luke was on his way up into the Yakima River Canyon between Yakima and Ellensburg. The Region 3 office of the Department of Fish and Wildlife had received an anonymous tip the night before about some guys fishing illegally for spring Chinook salmon below Roza Dam.

Salmon had once been plentiful in the Yakima River Basin, but the construction of irrigation diversion dams and decades of habitat destruction in the higher elevations where the fish spawned had drastically reduced their numbers. To help restore the population, spring Chinook were planted every year in the river system by the Yakama Indian Nation. Some years, there were enough returning hatchery-origin salmon to open a sportfishing season. Other years, such as this one, the run numbers were so low, fishing for salmon was closed.

Still, the idea of catching a tasty Chinook salmon was just too much of a temptation for some folks, so they'd slip down to the river and try to catch one or two.

The caller reporting the poaching said two men were fishing about a half mile down from Roza Dam. State Route 821 followed along the Yakima River through the canyon, and the fishermen were supposedly catching the salmon in a portion of the river about six hundred feet below the highway. The walk down to the river was through a major rock field, and Luke wasn't looking forward to hiking down through it.

Before he made the hike, Luke pulled into a small gravel pullout, grabbed his binoculars, and walked across the highway to peek at the river. Below, two men wearing hip waders were throwing bobbers out into a deep slot in the water.

Catch-and-release fishing for trout was open on the Yakima all year above Roza Dam, and beginning in early June, the river opened for trout fishing below the dam too. As long as the men had a current fishing license, they could legally fish there. The question was what they were trying to catch.

Luke had been watching the two men through the binoculars for about ten minutes when one of them, a younger guy all decked out in camouflage, set the hook. The man's fishing rod doubled over and bounced up and down, indicating he had hooked a large fish—much larger than a rainbow trout. As Luke watched the man fight the fish, he could see what looked to be a silvery salmon dashing around in the river.

Three minutes later, the man brought the fish to the shoreline and slid it up on the rocks. As soon as the salmon was on land, the man pounced on it and took a large rock and smacked it on the head. He then stood up and looked around. Luke ducked down as the guy turned his head up to the road.

There were no rigs parked along the highway anywhere close, but Luke remembered seeing a small red sedan sitting about a mile down the highway in a large pullout. He figured that must be where the men had parked. If it was their car, it would take them a while to get back to the rig, so Luke decided to watch the men for a bit longer.

While the other man continued to fish, the man in the camo clothing started to hike downriver, in the direction of the car. Luke looked closely but couldn't see the fish. The man looked like he was limping, and Luke realized the poacher had stuffed the salmon down along his leg into his right hip boot. He had seen this little trick before. He once caught a man coming out of a catch-and-release lake with nineteen rainbow trout crammed into his hip boots.

While keeping an eye on the man walking downriver, Luke also watched the man who continued to fish. He was about to return to his truck to drive down to the red sedan when the second man set the hook on a fish. Just as his partner had done before, this man—dressed in blue jeans, a tan shirt, and a red ball cap—fought the fish for a while and then slid a fat salmon up on the shoreline. This time, McCain watched as the man slipped the salmon into his left hip boot, grabbed his fishing rod, and took off walking down the river.

With both men headed to what Luke believed to be their car, he jumped into his pickup, checked for traffic, and did a quick U-turn.

"I think we're going to catch us some salmon poachers," Luke said to Jack. The yellow dog was sitting dead center in the back seat, panting slightly. "Pretty exciting isn't it, boy."

Luke reached the red sedan quickly and parked as far off the road as he could. The salmon poachers wouldn't see his truck until they were breaking over the hill to step onto the highway. At that point, they would have nowhere to run if the thought crossed their mind.

Jack whined a bit from the back seat as they waited for the men to arrive. It did seem like it was taking them longer than usual to get to their car—if it was their car. Of course, it would take anyone longer to walk with a salmon in their boot.

Luke wondered if he should have kept an eye on the men all the way back to the car and then drive in on them, but that could end up in a car chase if he didn't time it correctly. He was just thinking he should walk across the highway and take a look when the camo-clothed man's head popped up on the other side of the road. As soon as he saw Luke's WDFW truck, he dropped down.

"Come on, boy. Let's go have a little chat with these guys," Luke said to Jack.

Luke got out, let Jack out and told him to heel, and they walked across the road to where he'd seen the man's head pop up. Luke couldn't believe it, but in the time it took to let Jack out of the truck, check for traffic, and walk across the road, the men had made it fifty yards back down the hill. They were both walking like one leg was shorter than the other.

"Hang on there, guys!" Luke yelled. "I need to talk to you!"

The men hobbled faster down the hill.

"I can send my dog down there if you'd like. He'd only bite one of you, but both of you will probably get knocked down in the rocks."

About that time, the man in the brown shirt and red hat tripped and went rolling through the rocks. The salmon slipped out of his boot and slid down the hill. His buddy in the camo clothing hobbled faster.

"Get him, Jack," Luke hissed.

It only took Jack about fifteen seconds to close on the man running down the hill. He didn't bite the man because he wasn't trained for that. He had bitten people before, but only when they were an immediate danger to Luke. Jack raced past the camo man who stopped and raised his hands as soon as he saw the big yellow dog.

When Luke got to the man who had fallen, Luke helped him up. The guy had some scrapes on his elbows and blood coming out of his mouth.

"I fink I bit my fung," the man tried to say, holding a hand over his mouth.

"You coming?" Luke asked camo man. "Or do I need to come down there and handcuff you?"

"Naw, I'm coming," the man said. "Just don't let yer dog bite me. I got bit in the ass by the sheriff's German Shepherd a few years ago, and that hurt like hell."

Luke patted his hip, indicating to Jack to come walk at heel, and he herded the two men back up the hill. Luke carried the salmon that had slid out of the one man's boot. Camo man still hobbled as he walked.

When they returned to the rigs, Luke dug some gauze patches from his first aid kit, poured cold water on them, and gave them to the man in the red hat with the bleeding mouth.

Luke then turned to the other man and said, "You might as

well pull that salmon out of your waders. I saw you put it in there."

The man dropped his head, reached into his left boot, and pulled the fish out. Then he reached into his right boot and pulled a second salmon out. Luke hadn't seen him catch that one.

Luke asked for the men's fishing licenses, and when neither could produce one, he asked for their driver's licenses. When he had those, Luke told Jack to sit and watch the men, and he went to his truck to run their information on the computer.

Eight minutes later, he had information on both men. Each had past infractions for fishing out of season, fishing without a license, taking more than the daily limit, and a few other violations. They also hadn't paid the fines for several infractions the year before.

"You fellas don't seem to learn, do you?" Luke asked as he walked back to the men.

After he read the men their rights, he handcuffed them, placed them under arrest for three outstanding warrants related to the non-payment of their fines, and put them in the back seat of his truck.

As they rode back to the county lockup in Yakima, the camo man said, "Why'd you have to go and arrest us for? We just wanted a coupla salmon for supper."

"Well, if this had been your first time, I would have let you go with a ticket," Luke said. "But you guys need to learn that when you keep breaking the laws, there are consequences. You don't pay your fines, and you seem to have no regard for the laws, so we're going to let the judge figure out what to do with you."

At that, the man in the red hat groaned and said "thit" and continued to hold the wet rag on his mouth.

CHAPTER 2

It had taken Skip Harvey a little over two years to get his outdoor survival school to be busy enough to hire a second instructor. He had groups scheduled throughout the summer and fall, and while there seemed to be interest in doing some winter schools, Harvey needed to upgrade his equipment before he tried to take a group of teens out into the wilds for a week of camping, hiking, climbing, and foraging for food in what could often be deep snows and freeze-your-ass-off temperatures in the high Cascade Mountains of Washington State.

Harvey was 29 years old and had the lean, muscular physique of someone who worked out daily. He wasn't a bodybuilding buff, but he looked like he could climb Mount Rainier tomorrow if he needed to. Right at six feet tall, Harvey wore hiker shorts and ankle-high hiking boots no matter if it was Christmas or the 4th of July. His face was covered in a scraggly brown beard, and his mop of long hair resembled the armpit of a yeti. People wondered if it had seen a brush anytime in this century. That didn't bother the wilderness instructor any. He wasn't out to impress anyone.

Surprisingly, his Grizzly Adams-meets-Bear Grylls look and vibe made him extremely attractive to the ladies. Not that Harvey had a lot of time for the opposite sex. He'd been dreaming about creating a survival school ever since he spent a summer guiding anglers on the Deschutes River in Oregon six years earlier. There, he and other guides had taken folks of all ages down the rapids, showing them where to throw their flies to hook redband trout or steelhead. At night in the guide tent, after all the chores were completed and they were ready for the next day, Harvey would talk to the others about different ideas for creating a life in the outdoors that would be meaningful and also pay the bills.

One of the guides, a man of diminutive stature but with arms like a butcher, nicknamed Shorty, came up with the idea for an outdoor survival school for teenagers and young adults.

"There's lots of money in Portland and Seattle," Shorty said one night as he, Harvey, and two other guides lay on their cots. "Millionaires by the hundreds, living in giant houses for as far as the eye can see. And most of those folks haven't spent a night in the outdoors. They've become city folks, like in New York or Chicago. If they were turned out into the wilderness, they'd be coyote turds in three days."

"Ain't that the truth," a tall, lanky blond guide named Sven said.

"The adults might not be interested," Shorty continued. "But they might be up for putting out some serious bread to get their kids out of the house, away from the computers and video games, to learn some real-life skills."

"Bread? Did you just say bread?" asked the fourth guide named Tim. "What are we, back in the 1970s. My old man grew up a hippy, and he doesn't even say bread anymore."

The other three guides ignored Tim. He had been a pain in their collective asses the whole week, shirking duties and complaining about most everything. Frankly, the other guides were hoping the outfitter might send Tim packing when they reached the takeout at the mouth of the river in a couple days.

"You might have something there," Harvey said. "I know there are climbing schools and schools to teach other outdoor skills, but having something that was specialized for teens, where they could go out and learn what it's like to live and survive in the outdoors for a week, might have some real appeal."

The guides talked more about it and threw out ideas on how such a business might succeed. Tim sat with a scowl on his face and didn't say another word.

✳

Harvey's business plan came together fairly quickly, but saving enough money to buy the equipment he needed to safely take four or five kids into the wilds of the Cascade Mountains took a little more time. Slowly but surely, he built up a survival school for teens to teach them some useful outdoor skills, while allowing them to have at least a little fun.

When he'd finally opened the doors to Wilderness Northwest Survival the summer before, he ended up with just a few older teens enrolled over a four-week period during July and August. It wasn't enough to live on by a long shot, but it was a start.

For the next six months, Harvey worked odd jobs—guiding anglers on various rivers around the Northwest and teaching some rock climbing in the Columbia River Gorge. And he worked hard at marketing his school.

While rock climbing, he met a woman who worked at the corporate headquarters of Starbucks in Seattle. He and the woman dated a few times and, as she learned more about Wilderness Northwest Survival, she became a big fan. The relationship ultimately sputtered out, but the woman helped spread the word amongst the other managers and co-workers at the big coffee company.

For three consecutive weeks in June, Harvey had groups of teens who all had parents who worked for Starbucks. From there, things blossomed as the kids told their friends, and the parents told their friends and so on. Soon, Wilderness Northwest Survival was getting groups from all around the Puget Sound, and he stayed busy throughout the summer and into the fall.

To help keep track of things, Harvey kept a giant calendar on a whiteboard on the wall in his small office in Redmond. It was August, and as he looked at the weeks ahead, he saw that the calendar was full through the end of September. He was reluctant to schedule much after that as the high country in the Cascades could go from summer to winter overnight, and he still wasn't quite equipped for that.

As he perused the calendar, he saw that he'd had four or five kids every week but one. Most of the classes were made up of young men, but there were a few others that were all young women. He had made an early decision to not do any co-ed groups. The last thing the kids needed during a trek into the wilderness was to think they were in love.

When Harvey took a group of young women, he brought along a female assistant who ensured there were no accusations of improprieties. Truth be told, while Harvey always enjoyed being with the young men, most of whom were full of piss and vinegar and ready to show one another up, he especially liked working with the girls. They were always eager to learn, listened to what he said, and followed directions very well. The boys, not always so much.

His assistant, Amy Graham, was a sprite 22-year-old with dirty dishwater blonde hair, cut shorter than his. When she wasn't on an outing with him and the young women, she helped with marketing the school, updating the company website, working social media and booking classes.

"What's up with the third week in September?" Harvey asked as they looked at the big whiteboard.

"Oh, that's a special deal," Amy explained. "Some guy at Starbucks has a son turning sixteen, and as a birthday gift he wants to send just him and one of his buddies with you. I told him you'd do it if he paid the full amount for a class of five."

"And he did it?" Harvey asked.

"He didn't blink an eye. Well, I don't think he blinked. I couldn't see him over the phone. But he gave me a credit card number before I could even ask. He said his son was going to be thrilled."

"Okay. Did he ask for any kind of special training?"

"Nope. He just said that anything you teach the kid will be more than what he could do. He said the boy loves the outdoors and is eager to learn it all."

"We can do that," Harvey said. "It'll be nice being able to work with a smaller group. That'll be the easiest week of the whole year and should be a good one to end with."

CHAPTER 3

It was a little after 2:00 a.m. when Jai Bakshi came up with the idea. Just short of six feet tall with short jet-black hair and a well-kept beard, Bakshi had been, without much success, trying to snoop around in the highly protected files of Microsoft, Oracle, Adobe, SAP, Intuit, and a handful of other top software companies in the United States. Bakshi, his cousin Darsh Patel, and longtime friend Rishi Singh had gone into the scamming-foolish-Americans business three years ago. While they were making decent money, they believed there had to be a way to make more.

As Bakshi nosed around in the personnel files of some lesser-known businesses in the United States, the idea popped into his head. He needed to talk to his cousin and friend, but he believed his idea was one that would make them wealthy—or at least wealthy enough that they'd never again have to talk to yet another old lady in Wisconsin, trying to wring a few hundred dollars out of her.

Bakshi kept thinking about the idea, and the more he did, the more he liked it. He searched through the files and found more of the information they would need to pull this off. He wanted to have his plan laid out before he talked with the other men so that they could clearly see his vision of how they could become quite wealthy with a little hard work.

Yes, they would most likely need to go to the United States, but all three had traveled there at least once with their families while growing up. And, like most educated people from India, the men spoke English fairly well.

After spending a few more hours rattling around in the mainframes at several companies that didn't have the latest in security systems, Bakshi kept thinking about his plan and all the ramifications and potential roadblocks. Then he pulled out his phone and texted Patel and Singh.

I have an idea that has some merit. We will meet to discuss. 1:00 p.m. my apartment.

It was 5:30 in the morning when he pushed send. He knew his cousin and friend would most certainly be sound asleep. Both probably had their simple-minded girlfriends in bed with them. He hoped the men wouldn't be too tired from their time with the women and would be up and moving by midday. He really needed to share his idea with them.

After sending the message, Bakshi climbed into his own bed. Alone as usual. When he became independently wealthy, then he would have time for a lady or two. And they most certainly would not be simple-minded.

Because his brain wouldn't shut down, he had trouble falling asleep. Bakshi thought of the timeframe for his plan and how they would complete it. And he thought about the money. He was counting the millions when he finally fell asleep.

Bakshi awoke with a start when his phone dinged a few minutes before eleven.

It was a text from Singh. *I'll be there.*

A few minutes later, Patel texted his confirmation.

Bakshi smiled as he read the texts. This time next year, they would hopefully be well on their way to retirement.

The two men arrived promptly at one, both looking a little haggard. They spoke in their native Punjabi language.

"So, you have come up with a grand plan?" Patel asked as he came through the door. "I am excited to hear it."

Patel, who was two inches shorter than his cousin and skinnier too, had a narrow face with sharp features. His longish black hair had some waves in it, and, because he thought it looked cool, Patel wore a perpetual two-day growth of facial hair.

"As am I," said Singh. "I hope it is better than breaking into the Royal Bank of England's computers and syphoning off a few pennies each day. That one would have taken years to pay out, and we most assuredly would have been caught at some point. We would have ended up in Arthur Road Jail where we would have taken beatings every day for the rest of our lives."

Singh, who also had shiny black hair but no hair at all on his more roundish face, was just an inch shorter than Bakshi. Sometimes Singh wore glasses, but at other times he wore contact lenses to correct his vision. When he wore contacts, he often seemed to keep his eyes open wider than normal, making him look like an owl, Bakshi thought.

"I believe this one has real potential," Bakshi said after cringing at the thought of a lifetime of beatings in the local prison in Mumbai. Sometimes at night, the residents could actually hear screams coming from within the walls of the penitentiary several miles away. "It is definitely going to take some planning and hard work, however."

As the three men sat down in the small room adjacent to the kitchen, Bakshi began. "We're all aware of the success the Russians and the Chinese have had in getting important information on companies and individuals and holding it hostage until a ransom is paid."

The other two men nodded their heads.

"Is that what your big plan is?" Patel asked.

"No, just listen," Bakshi scolded. "Most companies and individuals are now aware of this scheme. It is too late for us on that. But in looking into the computer systems at some fairly large companies in the United States, I have discovered a few cracks in some of their security systems and have found enough information to know who the really wealthy officers and managers of those companies are."

"So, we are going to scam all of them?" Patel asked.

"No. Please, just listen," Bakshi scolded again, getting more agitated.

"The information I have discovered also shows the private addresses of these individuals and who their family members are. It didn't take much searching once I knew an address to get into school computers in the area around their homes and have located where many of these children go to school."

"So, we are going to—" Patel started to say before being abruptly cut off when Bakshi held up one finger, giving his cousin an angry glare.

"I'm not exactly sure how we are going to do it yet, but I am most certain one of these rich Americans would be willing to pay millions for the safe return of one of their children. Kidnapping is a serious offense, but we are smart enough, I believe, to pull it off. We just need a foolproof plan."

"In the American movies, when a person is kidnapped, the victim ends up being killed," Singh said. "If your plan includes having to kill someone, I am out."

"Me too," said Patel.

"I am not proposing that as any part of this," Bakshi said. "But, if it meant taking someone's life to save mine, I would be willing to do so."

"I do not like the sound of this," Singh said.

"That is why our plan has to be worked out to the last detail," Bakshi said. "We need to start now and try to find the right person in the right situation."

The men talked more about the idea, and as they discussed it, they became more excited about the possibilities.

"You are right. It will work if we identify the perfect person in the perfect situation," Singh said.

The other two men agreed.

"We will go to work," Bakshi said. "We must look through everything. Check Facebook pages, Twitter accounts, TikTok, Instagram, all of them. We will find someone, I am sure."

*

A week after Luke caught the men poaching salmon on the Yakima River, he pulled his truck into the driveway of his home in Lower Naches when a bright red, four-wheel-drive, Chevy pickup came down the road. A horn blasted from the truck, and Luke looked up to see Austin Meyers' smiling face behind the wheel.

Meyers lived across the street from Luke and Sara near Gleed, on the outskirts of Yakima, with his mother Jessie and her boyfriend Charlie Tucker.

"Hey, Luke! Look what I just got," Austin said as he jumped out of the truck.

"Wow, pretty nice. Did you trade in your T-100?"

"No, I sold it to a buddy of mine. And Charlie helped me pick this one out."

"That's great. What year is it?"

"It's a 2015. Only has seventy-nine thousand miles on it."

Luke walked over and went around the truck, giving it a quick once-over.

"Looks to be in really good shape," Luke said.

"I can't wait to take it up in the hills and see how it does."

"I'm sure you checked to make sure the four-wheel drive is all working right. It should be a really good truck for you, Austin. I'm happy for you."

"Yep. Charlie and I checked it all out. And best of all, Charlie paid for the truck. Well, he paid for the difference in what I got for my truck from Chris, my buddy."

"Very nice," Luke said.

He was truly happy for the young man. Austin's father had divorced his mother five years earlier and was basically out of the boy's life. He'd visit maybe once a year, and it became obvious pretty quickly that he didn't want much to do with his son in Washington State.

Because Austin liked to fish and hunt, Luke had taken him under his wing after his father had left. He had helped the boy get his hunting license and had taken him fishing on the river near their houses many times over the years. Those outings had become fewer and fewer after Austin got his driver's license and had bought his first truck, an older Toyota pickup. With the freedom of being able to go with his friends, Austin didn't need Luke as much as he had when he was younger.

Luke understood that, but he still tried to stay in touch with Austin, and they would occasionally get down to the river to fish and talk. Now and again, they would also take their dogs—Jack, and Austin's yellow Labrador Retriever, Bear—out to chase pheasants or for a duck hunt.

There had been some concern about the new man in Austin's mom's life. He seemed to have plenty of money and treated Jessie and Austin well. But there was an air of mystery around the man. He would be gone for days and weeks at a time and then would just magically appear.

While Sara had gotten some strange vibes from Charlie, the little checking she did on the guy and his company, AM EX Imports, turned up nothing out of the ordinary.

"Looks like Austin may have a new pickup," Sara said when she walked through the door after work that evening.

"Yep, he was pretty excited about it," Luke said. "He sold his old truck to a friend and put that money in on the new one. Charlie paid for the rest."

"Good old Charlie," Sara said sarcastically. "There is just something about that guy."

"Yeah, well, Austin and Jessie sure seem to like him, so let's give them the benefit of the doubt."

"I will—at least for now. So have you heard any more from Cale?"

"Yep, I received an email from him today. We're planning on meeting in Chelan on the fourteenth of September and then we'll head into the high country that day."

"Any idea on how long you'll be up there?"

"Not sure. If Cale can get his buck fairly quickly, we'll be back in a few days. No more than a week is my guess."

"Jack will enjoy it too."

"Can't let him miss out on all the fun. If I was hunting deer, I couldn't take him. But since I'll be checking hunters, maybe with a little grouse hunting here and there, Jack will be good to have along."

*

The three men had met several times at Jai Bakshi's apartment in Mumbai. Bakshi had done a little tutorial for his cousin and his friend on how to beat the firewalls and security at a company in Kansas City, another in Austin, Texas, and yet another in Newark, New Jersey.

"Would it not be nice to get into Amazon," Rishi Singh said. "I am of the opinion their top managers make large annual salaries."

"I did some snooping there," Bakshi said. "Their systems are impenetrable as far as I can see."

"What about Starbucks, the big coffee company?" Darsh Patel asked. "I did some contract work for a company that was upgrading their payroll system last year. I might still be able to sneak into their personnel files. Would that help?"

As smart as his cousin was at some things, including code writing and computer hacking, Bakshi thought the man could be naive and very dense.

"Yes, that could be very helpful," Bakshi said.

They had decided early on that they would not attempt to break into some of the industry giants such as Microsoft because they knew that their security systems and firewalls were the best around. But if they had a way into Starbucks, that would give them another option.

Bakshi liked the idea of possibly locating a potential target or two in the Pacific Northwest, as he had read that the police there were not as good as in other parts of the country.

"From what I understand, Washington State is more lenient in policing their citizens," Bakshi told the men. "If we could find a suitable target there, we might get less resistance."

"There do seem to be plenty of very rich people living there," Darsh Patel said.

"I have heard there are still lawmen in that area who wear big western hats and ride horses," Rishi Singh said. "I have seen their election advertisements on YouTube."

"You mean, just like in the movies with John Wayne?" Patel asked. "I thought that was Texas where the lawmen wore cowboy hats."

"Yes, Texas, but in other parts of the Western United States too," Singh said. "Most look like posers. I wouldn't want to mess with John Wayne. But some of these men in their pointed-toe boots don't concern me much."

"Hopefully, we will not have to find out how tough any of them are," Bakshi said. "If we can find the right situation, we can grab the kid and be back in Canada before anyone even knows they are missing."

"I've been doing some research on the kidnapping laws in the United States," Patel said. "The laws are very strict. Taking someone across state lines, let alone out of the country, could lead to some very serious prison time if we were to get caught."

"That is just the point," Bakshi said. "If we plan this right, we will not get caught. You will see, and you will be very happy when we are lounging on the beaches of Goa with beautiful, half-naked women bringing us drinks and catering to our every whim."

Patel and Singh smiled at the thought of sitting on the white sandy beaches of Goa. Even though they had seen photos of this special place, just an hour by plane from Mumbai, they had never visited Goa.

"So, see if you can still get into Starbucks," Bakshi said to

Patel. "We will go from there."

Within an hour, Patel was on the phone to Bakshi.

"I am in," Patel said without saying the name of the giant coffee company.

"We should meet immediately," Bakshi said. "We can discuss our next steps."

The men met back at Bakshi's apartment, and Patel showed his cousin and Singh what they needed to do to sidestep Starbucks' payroll security and get into the personnel files.

"After I got into the files, I started looking for families with children," Patel said. "Already, I have found one or two that might work."

"Tell me about them," Bakshi said.

"Well, there is the daughter of one of the executive vice presidents who is taking a trip with a church group," Patel explained. "Evidently, the high school-age youth in their church will be going on a mission trip to Guatemala to help build homes for needy people. They are going in August. If we could get there and take the girl, there would be very little resistance, I believe."

"How do you know all of this?" Singh asked.

"Once I got the name of the Starbucks vice president, I looked into the personnel files, found the health insurance policies that show names of her children, and then I went into Instagram and found their accounts. The daughter mentioned the trip to Guatemala several times."

"Okay, that is a definite possibility," Bakshi said. "Although traveling to Central America might be more difficult than we want. What else?"

"The son of one of their on-staff attorneys is going for a week into the mountains to learn outdoor and survival skills. From what I can see, he will only be with the instructor of the school."

"How old is the boy?"

"He will be sixteen. The trip is a gift for his birthday."

"Okay, that is another definite possibility. When do they go?" Bakshi asked.

"According to the boy's Instagram, it will be in September. I will have to do some more research to find the exact dates."

"Do that. And see if you can find out where in the mountains they will be going," Bakshi said. "We will need that for our planning if we decide to try for him."

The men talked for a while longer. Most of the talk was about just how much ransom they might ask for and what kind of resistance they might receive. The more they talked, the more the beaches of Goa seemed like a real possibility.

Finally, Bakshi said, "Keep looking. Those are both good options, but we need more."

CHAPTER **4**

The summer was flying by, or at least it felt that way to Skip Harvey. Since late May, he had taken eleven groups into various parts of the North Cascades for anywhere from five to seven days as part of his survival school. And things had gone well. Oh, there'd been the occasional sprained ankle, and one young man had cut his hand with a knife that needed stitches, but for the most part things had gone along smoothly enough.

As the calendar had filled earlier in the year, Harvey had had the foresight to plug in what he believed would be a much-needed week off during mid-August. He figured that would be about the right time to recharge and gear up for the final month of his season.

"Did those new tents get here?" Harvey asked Graham as he was going through his gear at their office during his break. "I'm going to need one next week."

One of the things Harvey hadn't thought about when he'd started his school was the amount of wear and tear on his equipment. Even the finest tents and tools wore out quickly under continual use and abuse, especially by the sometimes awkward teen boys.

"That kid couldn't have hit the tent more perfectly with that hatchet," Harvey said. "Looked like a grizzly tore a hole in the side."

"Why did he throw a hatchet at the tent?" Graham asked. "That seems rather stupid. And where were you when all this happened?"

"They were supposed to be chopping some kindling," Harvey explained. "But a yellowjacket started buzzing the kid doing the chopping. He took a swing at the hornet and lost his grip on the hatchet handle. Luckily, he didn't hit one of the other boys."

"I have all the dried foods stocked for the next few weeks, and I'll check the other supplies to make sure we'll get through the rest of the season," Graham said. "We have that group of girls next week, you remember?"

"Yep, I remember. Five young ladies from Portland?"

"It looks like it might be just four. One of the girls believes she'll be on her period and doesn't want to be in the wilderness at that time."

"Okay, well, I understand," Harvey said, although he really didn't.

"Her parents think it would be best if she is not up there possibly around grizzly bears during her menstrual cycle," Graham said.

Harvey had spent the past three months in the high mountains and had seen no sign of grizzly bears living in the area. Biologists with the Department of Fish and Wildlife report the last confirmed grizzly sighting in Washington's North Cascades was in 1996. Still, nobody really knew for sure, so he always carried bear spray with him, and he made sure all his students carried it too.

"I've not seen sign of any bears," Harvey said. "And those reports of bears being attracted to the odors of a menstruating woman are all speculation. I think she would be fine. But better to be safe than sorry, I guess."

Harvey asked if there were any other changes to the final four groups. After the week with the young women, he was to have a group of five college-aged men and two groups of high schoolers, including the 16-year-old kid and his buddy on the last trip of the year.

"No changes that I'm aware of," Graham said. "The father of the birthday boy did ask if his son could bring a pistol."

"Absolutely not," Harvey said. "It's right there in the agreement—no firearms. The last thing we need is an armed teenager who has no idea how to handle a pistol."

"Actually, the father said his son is quite familiar with firearms, including how to shoot a pistol. He's been training at a local shooting range since his last birthday."

"That's good to know, but there is no reason for him to be carrying a pistol that week. I have my pistol, which should give us enough coverage in the rare event that we might need something for protection."

"Okay, I'll let him know," Graham said as she was heading to the front door. "I'm off to pick up a couple other items for next week. Holler if you can think of anything else."

"Will do," Harvey said and went back to checking equipment. As he did, he thought about the young man who he would be taking, with a friend, into the mountains in a month. He wondered if the kid was one of those spoiled rich kids or someone who really wanted to learn outdoor survival skills. And he thought about the boy's ability to shoot. Maybe he would take an extra couple boxes of ammunition for his Glock, and he and the two boys could do a little shooting one afternoon. Harvey made a note to add the ammo to his supplies for that week and went to check on the new tents.

*

It had been a crazy summer for Luke. There had been a sting operation to catch some anglers who were fishing for sockeye salmon in Cle Elum Lake during a closed season, and he was working on reports of a series of illegal elk killings in the forest above Bumping Lake.

Those two investigations, along with the major boon in fishing brought on by people not working during the COVID pandemic, kept Luke and the other wildlife enforcement officers busy checking licenses, writing violation tickets, and handling the never-ending request for reports from his bosses.

Washington State Fish and Wildlife police officers had become aware of the elk poaching situation when hikers found two dead cow elk with only the tenderloins and some of the hindquarter meat missing. The kills were fresh and hadn't been ravaged by coyotes or other scavengers when the hikers found them. After the hikers marked the site of the kills on a GPS and called 911, Luke was dispatched to check it out.

The call had come in mid-morning, and by the time Luke got out of the office, loaded his gear for the hike in, drove up to Bumping Lake, and made the hike up the hill, it was close to two o'clock when he found the dead elk. It had been a bit of a hike into the spot where the dead elk lay, but Luke—with Jack running alongside—was able to take a well-established trail to within a hundred yards of the carcasses. By then the birds had discovered the carcasses, and being that it was mid-July, the yellowjackets and flies were swarming the elk. The animals were just starting to stink.

Many times, there isn't enough evidence to determine who has killed an animal at a poaching scene, but Luke always did his best to gather what evidence might be there to identify and catch the poachers.

The first thing he did when he arrived at the two carcasses was to see if there were any identifiable footprints. If there was at least a partial print in soft soil, he would make a plaster cast of it. But a close look around the elk showed no identifiable tracks, which didn't surprise him given the dry and compact soil and the grassy sidehill on which the two elk lay.

As he searched for tracks, Luke looked for other evidence as well. There were cases where poachers had been convicted with the help of DNA found on cigarette butts near their kills, or by fingerprints on beer cans or cartridge casings. So, Luke looked for anything that might assist in identifying the killers, including anything else left behind. On two other poaching investigations, Luke had found a knife lying near the carcasses, left behind in a hurry by the poachers. Each time, good fingerprints were found on the knife handles that helped to identify and convict the perpetrator.

Luke found no knives or cigarette butts, but he did find a cartridge casing not too far from the first animal. It was from a .300 Winchester Magnum and it was fairly shiny, which Luke believed meant it had not been lying in the grass for long. He pulled some rubber gloves out of his pack, put them on, picked up the shell casing, placed it in a baggie, and put it in his pack.

The next task was to determine how the elk were killed. After finding the newish shell casing, Luke assumed the poacher had used a high-powered rifle. But even with the use of a bigger rifle, it was somewhat rare that the animals were both dead within a fifty-yard diameter. One elk, yes. But after the first shot, any other elk close by would have been running for cover, making it quite difficult to kill a second. Until he found a bullet hole in one, or both, he wouldn't know for sure how the animals had died.

Elk are big with tough hides, and often a bullet will stay inside of the animal. On some occasions, when he had investigated other suspected illegally killed deer, elk, or sheep, Luke had used a metal detector to try and locate the bullet inside the animals. But he hadn't brought the metal detector up the hill with him, and he hoped he could find the bullet without it.

On closer inspection, Luke found that the first elk had been shot in the head. The bullet hole right between the animal's eyes meant it had most likely died immediately. It looked to Luke like it was a small-caliber bullet hole, and if so, the bullet would most likely still be lodged in the elk's brain.

Seeing the small hole, Luke thought about the shell casing he'd just found. From his experience, not only would the .300

Winchester Magnum have made a much bigger hole in the elk's head, it might have blown the top of the head off completely.

He started thinking the casing may not have come from the poacher's rifle until he got a better look at the second dead elk. It had a much larger bullet hole in its side. From the placement of the bullet, it looked like the elk had been hit in the spine, just above the shoulder. While a bullet hitting an animal in the spine may not be instantly lethal, it will almost always put it down immediately.

With some effort, Luke rolled the elk over to see if the bullet had passed through the animal. Not finding an exit wound, he worked his hands along the hide of the elk to try and feel any bump or abnormality that might be the bullet. He felt slowly along, and within a minute or so, he discovered something small and hard just beneath the skin. Luke pulled out his knife, cut a small hole in the hide, and a mushroomed bullet popped out neatly.

Having the bullet might not solve the crime, but it could help to determine what kind of a rifle was used to make the kill, including the make and model of the firearm. By examining the bullet closely under a microscope, scientists can determine the number of lands and grooves and the twist that are imprinted in the bullet as it travels through the rifle barrel. Different rifles, and different rifle barrels, make unique grooves, and the markings on the bullet can be used to help identify the rifle used by the poachers. Doing so would definitely help in a conviction.

During his search of the area and the inspection of the animals, Luke took photos of what he had discovered. And after bagging the bullet, he took some samples of meat from the animal for DNA identification. The DNA could be used to possibly match meat found in someone's freezer or at a butcher shop. Luke then returned to the first elk and separated its head from the carcass. The head would provide DNA, and it most likely was carrying the fatal bullet. He would have to cut into the cranium of the animal to try and locate the bullet, and that would be much easier to do with a saw at his office versus out here in the woods with his knife. Luke bagged the head, placed it in his pack, and looked around to see if he was missing anything.

He had not paid much attention to Jack during his time investigating the dead elk scene, and now that he was done at the kill site, he stopped and looked around for the yellow dog.

"C'mon, you lazy mutt," Luke said after spotting the dog. "Let's go."

Jack had been sound asleep in the cool shade of a fir tree not far from the elk. When Luke called, the big dog jumped up and headed downhill for the truck.

Since the elk were far off the main road, someone had carried the meat from the elk to their vehicles, probably on their backs. Luke wondered if anyone might have seen them or the vehicle the poachers were driving. This time of year, hikers and anglers were in the mountains, and there was a good chance someone might have noticed something. The problem was trying to locate those folks. Before he headed back to his office, Luke took a drive up the gravel forest service road to see if he could find anyone who might have seen anything of interest near where the elk were killed.

About two miles up the road, he spotted a small orange SUV. Luke knew immediately that the car was a Subaru, as the only orange cars he ever saw were Subarus. Whenever he saw one, he wondered what type of person would really want to drive an orange car. He was about to find out, as two people—a young man and woman—came hiking down a trail toward the car with large packs on their backs. The young people were following two medium-sized dogs of mixed heritage—one brown and white with short hair, the other black and white with long hair. Each dog was wearing a red cowboy handkerchief tied around its neck.

"Yep," Luke said to himself as he pulled up behind the orange car. "That fits."

"How you folks doing today?" Luke asked as he climbed out of his pickup.

"Doing great," the young lady said. She was wearing over-the-ankle hiking boots, tan hiking shorts with about eleven pockets, a blue tank top, and a red handkerchief tied up on her head to hold her strawberry blonde hair away from her reddish, freckled face.

The young man, who had on the exact same boots and shorts as the woman, wore a yellow T-shirt and a tan hat with an REI logo on it. He smiled at Luke but said nothing. Luke figured the man was happy to let the woman do the talking.

"You on a day hike or up camping?" Luke asked.

"We spent the night," the woman said as she wiped sweat off her brow with yet another red handkerchief she had pulled from one of her pants pockets. "But we decided to come out. The mosquitoes up near the lake are the size of horseflies, and the yellowjackets are the size of sparrows. In fact, Bradley thought he saw a yellowjacket carrying off a chipmunk."

Luke laughed at the joke, but neither of the hikers even cracked a smile.

"I'm investigating the illegal killing of two cow elk a couple of miles down the ridge," Luke said as the woman brought her hand up to her mouth and gasped as if she was horrified.

"Did you happen to see a vehicle parked along the road a couple miles back or hear any gunshots while you were up the mountain yesterday?" he asked.

Bradley stood and thought, looking at the red-faced woman and waiting for her to respond.

"Actually, we did hear some shots yesterday evening. We just thought someone was target practicing."

"About what time was that?" Luke asked.

"About seven-thirty or eight. We were just finishing dinner," she answered, looking at Bradley for confirmation. Bradley nodded his head dutifully. "But I don't remember seeing any rigs parked along the road when we drove up here."

Again, she looked at Bradley who was nodding his head, confirming what she'd said.

"Do you remember how many shots you heard?"

"Hmmm, let's see. We weren't paying much attention, really. I was fighting a couple of yellowjackets for the last bite of my hotdog when we heard the first shot. There was more than one, but I can't remember if there were two or three. Can you remember, hun?" she asked as she turned to Bradley.

Bradley was just about to speak when the young lady cut him off. "It was three. There were two loud shots and one that was much quieter." She looked at Bradley, and he just shrugged.

Luke jotted a condensed version of what the young woman said into his pocket notebook, omitting the tussle with the yellowjackets, and asked, "Can I get your names?"

"I'm Brittney Cox, and this is my husband, Bradley. Our two dogs," she said pointing at the two canines with the red handkerchiefs, "are Martin and Louis."

"Like the comedy team?" Luke asked.

Brittney looked at him like he'd just stepped out of a UFO.

"Dean Martin, Jerry Lewis," he said.

Still blank stares.

"Never mind," Luke said, taking their phone numbers before handing her his card. "If you can think of anything else, please give me a call."

He climbed back into the truck and said to Jack, "Man, that Bradley was quite the motormouth."

Jack, asleep in the back seat, didn't make a sound.

A few minutes later, as he was driving back down the gravel road toward the highway, Luke said, "Dang. I forgot to ask them about their orange Subaru." But, as he thought about the couple and their conversation, he figured he probably knew all he needed to know about people who drive orange cars.

CHAPTER 5

Bakshi, Patel and Singh had spent hours on their computers, nosing through personnel files at Starbucks, monitoring Facebook, Instagram, and Twitter, and they had come up with five possibilities for their kidnapping-for-ransom scheme. They had had seven, but over the summer, two of the kids had changed their plans due to family situations or illness.

At some point, Bakshi knew, they would have to decide on one and start developing a plan. And not just any plan but a foolproof one. He decided that August 1st would be that point. On the last day of July, he called Patel and Singh and told them to meet him at his apartment at six o'clock the following evening when they would be moving into stage two of the operation.

"Stage two, what is this stage two?" his cousin Patel asked before Bakshi could hang up. "I didn't know we were at stage one."

Bakshi pushed the end button on his phone. Maybe he had been a fool for inviting his cousin to participate. He was a genius with computers but an imbecile in other ways.

"I certainly hope the imbecile side of him does not get us all killed," Bakshi said to himself after he had hung up.

The two men showed up promptly at six the next day, and after each retrieved a bottle of Kingfisher beer out of the refrigerator, they sat around the tiny table in the unbelievably small kitchen of Bakshi's incredibly small apartment.

"So, what is this stage two?" Patel asked after taking a long swig of his beer.

"Please be patient. We will discuss this shortly," Bakshi said. "First, we must come to a decision on our target. I want a primary target and a secondary target in case something should happen to our primary target."

"Good thinking," Singh said. "I know who I think we should make our primary target."

The three men had discovered three other teenagers, in addition to the girl going on the church mission to Guatemala and the boy who was taking the survival class in Washington State.

Their first choice was the daughter of a COO at Starbucks. She had just graduated from high school and would be traveling across the United States on a bike in early September with four other girls, one of whom would be in a van, following the riders, carrying food, tents, medical supplies and clothing. The cross-country bike trek, as the men found out, would be financed by the girl's father.

"Their travel route will take them along a major highway out of Seattle, through Idaho and southern Montana and into Wyoming," Singh explained. "There are very few people living in Wyoming with miles and miles between towns. Somewhere along there will be the perfect place to grab her."

Bakshi and Patel agreed.

"We can stay on the roads with a car, get ahead of them and pick just the right spot for an ambush," Bakshi said. "And then we can head straight north, through Montana, to the border crossing into Canada."

The other two possible kidnapping candidates included the son of a Starbucks vice president who was headed to southern Florida to start college at the University of Miami and a girl who would be going on a walkabout in Australia before starting college. Her mother was the highly paid Chief Financial Officer at Starbucks, and her father was a surgeon at one of the big hospitals in Seattle. The thought of trying to bag someone at a university didn't settle well with the men. And the idea of having to go to Australia was a red flag to Patel and Singh.

"Everything down there will bite you or sting you," Patel said in a whiny voice.

"Or eat you," Singh said.

"Okay, so we have settled on the biker girl," Bakshi said. "Now we must pick our second target."

"I think we should go after the boy at the survival school," Singh said. "It sounds like an excellent, remote place to grab someone. Although I'm not exactly sure how we're going to find him in the middle of a large state."

"I agree," said Bakshi. "We can figure out how to find him. He will most likely have a phone. We will be able to track him with that. What do you think, cousin?"

"I think that girl is crazy to ride a bike across the United States," Patel said. "I mean, how far is that? Would your ass not be raw after only a couple days? I know mine would be."

"So you agree on the boy at the survival school as our backup if something happens to the girl riding the bike?"

"Yes, I agree," Patel said, nodding his head. "I wonder what kind of bicycles they ride?"

Bakshi just looked at his cousin and shook his head. He probably had made an error in inviting Patel to join in, although the guy could write code like nobody's business, was an artist at hacking security systems, and had been invaluable in the search for possible targets.

"So now we must start developing our plan," Bakshi said. "We need to work out even the most minute of details. It is going to take time and much more research, but we must do it. The girl leaves on her bicycle trip on September 4th. The boy goes to the survival school on September 15th."

"Is this stage two?" Patel asked.

"Yes, this is stage two," Bakshi answered. "And it is the most important stage. It will mean the difference between enjoying cocktails on the white beaches of Goa or spending the rest of our days in a prison."

"I wonder if they give daily beatings in the prisons in the United States?" Singh asked.

They all thought about that for a minute and then Bakshi said, "Probably. That is why we must do everything we can to not find out. Now, here is what we need to do next."

He laid out a duty list that each man was to have completed when they met again in a week. They all agreed and left to go to work. As Patel was walking out the door, he was rubbing his buttocks with his hand, like it hurt just from thinking about riding a bike across the United States.

It had taken a bit of scrounging around in brain matter, but after sawing the top off the elk's head, Luke found the bullet. It looked to him to be a .22-caliber rifle bullet—awfully small to be shooting at an animal as big as an elk. But with a precisely aimed shot, like right between the eyes, a small-caliber bullet can be every bit as deadly as an elephant gun.

As he looked for the bullet, Luke was reminded of one day when he was at a friend's house during high school. The friend lived on a small farm, and on that particular day, a man was there to kill and prepare two steers for butchering. The family called it "slaughtering day," which to Luke sounded a bit grisly, but he was interested to see what happened.

Luke was surprised when the butcher pulled a small .22 rifle out of the cab of his butchering truck, loaded a single bullet in it, walked over to within ten yards of one of the steers set for slaughter, and shot the bovine right between the eyes. The thing was dead before it hit the ground.

In the right hands, in the right situation, a .22-caliber bullet is deadly, and Luke believed many deer poached in Washington and around the country were killed with small-caliber rifles. The ammunition is less expensive, the rifles don't make much noise in comparison to large-caliber rifles, and in many cases, the bullet is so damaged, it provides very little evidence.

That was the case with the bullet Luke dug out of the brain of the elk. The bullet was so deformed, he believed the lab techs wouldn't learn much about it. Even so, Luke bagged it and put it, along with the large-caliber shell casing he'd found near the elk carcasses and frozen samples of meat, in an overnight box for the Fish and Wildlife Laboratory in Ashland, Oregon for DNA and other forensic analysis.

For years, the Washington State Department of Fish and Wildlife had used the Washington State Patrol's forensic lab to analyze evidence, but it had switched to the lab in Ashland because the technicians there specialized in wildlife cases, and because they weren't so backed up all the time. Still, it would take a few weeks to get any information back from the lab in Ashland, and even then, Luke felt there wasn't enough information to point the finger at someone. But at least the evidence was filed properly and could be used for making a case against the poacher—if they could find that person.

To make sure he crossed all his t's, Luke made contact with the meat shops in the area, including those shops that made sausage and other specialty meats out of wild game, to see if any of them had received any elk meat in the past day. All but one of the shops hadn't received any elk meat since December or January, so they were of no help. One shop had received some elk meat the day prior, and Luke thought he might have a hit. Unfortunately, the elk meat was from a hunter the previous fall who'd shown his license and tag. The butcher knew the guy well and vouched for him. The hunter had brought in nearly 150 pounds of meat to make into burger and sausage and to be cut into roasts and steaks.

Luke did a quick calculation, and he was confident no more than 70 pounds of meat had been removed from the two poached elk above Bumping Lake.

Two days later, as Luke was patrolling near Rimrock Lake, he received another poaching call from dispatch. The dispatcher told him that a fisherman had found the carcass of a dead elk not far from Clear Lake that had some meat removed. With the coordinates from dispatch punched into his GPS, Luke headed that way.

He'd been told the angler was still at the animal's carcass and would wait for a game warden if it didn't take too long.

"Tell him I'll be there in fifteen to twenty minutes," Luke said into his truck's radio microphone. "If he can't wait that long, get his contact information and I will call him."

"The man's name is Ben Allard, and he said he'll wait for you," the dispatcher's voice crackled over the radio a minute or two later.

"Ten-four. Wildlife 148 out."

Luke parked next to a late model Chevy Tahoe at a trailhead close to where the caller had discovered the elk. He hopped out of the truck, let Jack out the back door, pulled his pack on, and started hiking. From what he could tell, the dead elk should only be about a half mile up the trail.

Almost to the blue pin mark on his GPS map, Luke saw Jack stop and stare off to the right, with ears perked. A second later, he heard a person whistle. Luke searched for a second and then caught the movement of a man waving at him amidst a thick stand of young pines.

As he approached, Luke said, "Mr. Allard?"

"Yessir."

"Thanks for calling this in. Geez, down in these trees, how'd you even see the carcass?"

"I wouldn't have, but a bald eagle flew up out of the trees, and I saw a coyote running away up the hill. That almost always means something is dead. I decided to check it out. I don't think the elk has been dead all that long, although in this heat it is starting to stink a bit."

Luke looked at the carcass and was amazed—the elk looked just like the other two he had seen a couple of days before. Only the backstraps and some meat from the hindquarters had been removed. Yes, the eagle and coyotes had eaten some, but not enough to distort or disguise what the poacher had removed.

As Luke considered the scene, he caught his first good whiff of the decaying elk. He'd definitely smelled worse, but it was not pleasant. Some wardens carry a small jar of Vicks in their packs and will put a little bit on their upper lip, just under their nose, to help cover the putrid smell, but Luke never remembered to bring any, so he would just breath through his mouth.

The elk had been dead at least a day, so Luke assumed the fisherman hadn't been in the area when the animal was shot, but he asked him if he'd seen or heard anything anyway.

"No, sir," Allard said. "I fish at a couple of high lakes this time of year, but the last time I was up here was about a week ago. I was just heading up to fish when I saw the eagle."

"Okay, well, thanks again. I don't want to keep you from your fishing any longer," Luke said as he handed the man his card. "If you see anything else, or think of anything else, please give me a call."

The man had turned and was walking back up to the trail when he said, "You know, when I was up here last week, I met a couple of guys in a pickup, driving slowly along the road below. I thought they looked like road hunters, you know, like you'd see in October."

"Did they have any guns that you could see?"

"You know, come to think of it, I did see a rifle with a scope hanging in one of those gun racks that you used to see in the back window of about every pickup in the 1970s."

"Can you describe the truck?"

"It was a gray and white Ford, I believe. Maybe from the mid-90s. And it had a crease at the top of the tailgate, like a small tree or a steel bar or something had fallen on it."

"Anything else?"

"I remember the driver was wearing one of those denim shirts with the sleeves torn off right at the shoulder. And he had a tattoo on his left arm, up on the bicep. I looked at him and said hello as our trucks were passing on the road."

"That's great, Mr. Allard. Thank you. It's probably nothing. There are all kinds of folks up in these parts during the summer, but I'll make a note of it. Good luck fishing."

After Allard was up the trail, Luke once again started working the scene around the dead elk. The first thing he noticed was that this elk had been shot right between the eyes, like one of the elk had been near Bumping Lake.

Otherwise, there was very little evidence—no cigarette butts, no discarded shell casings, no footprints, no knives left behind accidentally. Luke once again took a few photos, then removed the elk's head for the DNA and the bullet, if it was still inside the skull. He bagged the head, loaded it into his pack, called Jack, and headed back down the trail.

As he walked, he thought about the three dead elk. He was convinced they were killed by the same person or persons. He wondered if any others would be found anytime soon.

CHAPTER 6

I t was four minutes after ten when Luke's phone started buzzing. He had been asleep all of about twenty minutes. Out of habit, he had switched the phone off ring, so that when he got a call at night, it wouldn't disturb Sara.

"Is that your phone?" Sara asked groggily as Luke reached to pick it up off the nightstand.

"Yeah, sorry. Hello?"

"Mr. McCain, this is Brittney Cox. We talked to you up on the mountain near Bumping Lake a week ago. I was with my husband and two dogs."

"Oh, yes, Ms. Cox. What can I do for you?"

"Well, we're not sure it's anything, but we heard three more shots just a few minutes ago. We're camping near Bear Lake, up Oak Creek. It was kinda the same except for this time we heard two quiet bangs and one pretty loud one."

"Okay. Can you give me your exact location and what direction you think the shots came from?"

"We're right at Bear Lake. Camped right on the shoreline. The mosquitoes don't seem to be as bad here, but I'll tell you, the yellowjackets are just as fierce."

"And which direction did the shots come from?"

"Just to the north, I think. What do you think, Bradley?"

Luke could just imagine Bradley shrugging his non-opinion.

"Yes, we think it was to the north. Do you think it is something? I mean, the shots certainly sounded the same, except there were two quiet ones and one loud one. You know, just the opposite of what we heard the other time."

"It could be something," Luke said. "I'll head up that way first thing in the morning. You have a nice night, and I'll see you tomorrow."

"Okay. So, you don't want us to go looking around for a car on the road, like you asked about last time?"

"No, you just enjoy your camping, and I'll see you tomorrow. And thanks for the call."

Luke clicked the phone off and put it back on the nightstand.

"What was that all about?" Sara asked.

Luke described the call and told her it was probably nothing, but he'd go check it out in the morning. Then he put his head on his pillow and immediately fell asleep.

Sara was still asleep as Luke headed for the door the next morning.

"You headed to Bear Lake?" she asked after he whispered goodbye to her.

"Yep, it's worth checking out."

"Good luck," Sara said before rolling over for a few more minutes of sleep.

Luke occasionally got work calls at night. Some were from people he knew that had hit a deer or elk with their vehicle and wanted to know what to do with the animal. Sometimes, if it was still alive, he would go to where the animal had been hit and have to put it down. Once in a while, he and Jack would have to track the animal before putting it down.

Other nighttime calls came from dispatch telling him that someone had called in about possibly seeing poachers spotlighting and shooting at deer or other game animals. He would almost always head out right away after receiving those calls, but most of the time he was unable to catch the poachers. They were always very quick in their crime. They would shoot the animal and have it in the back of a truck or trunk of a car and be out of the area within minutes.

Sometimes he would find tire tracks or blood in the dirt or snow where someone had parked and shot an animal, but it was never enough to catch the perpetrator. Most of the times when he or his fellow officers were successful in catching a poacher, someone would have seen a vehicle and had taken down a license plate number.

The other way poachers were typically caught was when someone dropped a dime on them. Either a family member or friend, or maybe a disgruntled girlfriend or ex-wife, would call and tell officers what the person had been up to. Some made the call out of vengeance. Others called because they just felt what the poacher was doing was wrong. And some called to collect the bonus points offered by the Department of Fish and Wildlife to be used on future special hunt draws. Whatever the reason, most poachers were caught because someone saw something or knew something and made a call.

Luke was thinking about that as he was driving up the rough road to Bear Lake. The little lake in the Cascades was a popular fishing hole and camping spot in the summer. Evidently, the Coxes and their dogs enjoyed camping on weekends. Even though she'd complained about the bugs the week prior, Brittney Cox was right back up there amongst all kinds of insects again.

When he'd left his house in Yakima, Luke had called his captain to inform him of the call the previous evening and to let him know what he was up to. The captain gave him the 10-4 to go check it out, and with that Luke headed up State Route 12.

When he came over the rise to Bear Lake, Luke immediately

spotted the orange Subaru. He drove down and stopped next to the little car.

As he was climbing out of his truck, Brittney Cox walked over from a small campfire. She again had her reddish blonde hair tied up in a red handkerchief and was wearing the same hiking boots and shorts, this time with a purple tank top. The two dogs, Martin and Louis, were right by her side, both adorned with their red cowboy handkerchiefs tied around their necks.

"Hi, Mr. McCain. We didn't know if you were going to show up or not. I mean, when you think about it, the bangs we heard last night could have been anything. And how are you going to find who made the noise?"

"I think it's worth checking out. Now, which direction do you think the shots came from?"

Bradley popped out of the tent near the campfire and walked over.

"They came from that way," Brittney said, pointing to the north. "Don't you think, Bradley?"

Bradley looked in the direction his wife was pointing, thought for a second, and said, "Yes, believe that is correct."

The sound of Bradley's voice almost made Luke jump. It was a high, squeaky voice—almost cartoon-like. Not quite Mickey Mouse high, but getting there.

"Okay then. I'll go have a look," Luke said. "I know there are a couple of trails over that way. I'll grab my dog and my pack, and we'll go see what we can see."

With that, Luke went back to his truck, opened the passenger door to let Jack out, and then grabbed his pack out of the bed of the truck. Jack immediately went to meet Martin and Louis, sniffing butts and raising hackles, but within a few seconds, all tails were wagging.

"C'mon, Jack. Let's leave these nice people to their camping."

Jack turned and followed as Luke headed up the trail in the general direction of where Brittney Cox had pointed.

If there was a dead animal somewhere up ahead, Luke figured

he had a chance to find it. Just as Ben Allard had done earlier, Luke most likely wouldn't see the actual animal at first, but he might see scavengers on or near the animal. Occasionally, he had found dead animals—and once, a dead person—when he had spotted turkey vultures circling overhead. And there were almost always golden eagles, bald eagles, ravens, crows, or magpies at a carcass.

Not to mention the coyotes. One or two always seemed to be lurking somewhere close to a dead animal. Luke had also seen cougars and bears working on a dead deer or elk. If any one of those carnivores was around, it wouldn't take them long to get a dead elk or deer or cow eaten down to nothing but a pile of bones.

As he walked the trail, Luke listened and looked for birds or other animals that might be reluctantly leaving the area.

His other tool for finding a downed animal was Jack. The big yellow dog had a great nose, and because Luke had used him to track injured animals after they had been struck by a vehicle, Jack knew what he was looking for if Luke gave him the command to search.

They walked about a mile and a half down the trail with Jack crisscrossing the terrain above and below the trail when the dog suddenly froze, ears perked, staring forward. Luke peered in the direction Jack was looking and caught a glimpse of a cougar slinking away through the trees.

Over the years, Luke had seen a good number of mountain lions, but he knew that in his time in the woods, way more big cats had seen him without him seeing them. Most would disappear at the first sound or smell of a human. This one clearly hesitated, meaning it may not have wanted to leave a kill or a found carcass. If the cougar was on a dead animal, it was a good bet it had kept every other scavenger away. Luke watched as the cat disappeared over the hill and then looked around. He spotted a golden eagle sitting atop a tall, dead pine tree.

"Good dog," Luke whispered to Jack. The dog was still standing where he had been when they first spotted the cougar.

"Let's go see what that cat was up to."

They had only gone about sixty yards when Luke spotted the velvet-covered tip of an antler sticking up out of the brush. He walked over toward the antler and saw it was attached to a very dead bull elk.

The cougar had clearly been feeding on the back end of the big animal. The rear hindquarter was almost gone, and so were the back straps, obviously cut out of the animal by a knife. It was basically the same scene Luke had seen two other times in the last two weeks, only this time the elk had a small five-point rack, still in velvet.

Cougars are mostly deer hunters, but they will kill an elk now and again. Most of the time, it will be a calf or a sick or aging mature animal. This bull was no more than three years old, maybe only two, and while Luke couldn't tell if it was injured, he was pretty sure the animal was dead when the cougar arrived on the scene.

A few minutes later, when he spotted not one but two small bullet holes in the elk's forehead, he knew he was dealing with the same poachers.

"These guys are starting to piss me off," Luke said quietly.

Jack, who was standing nearby, watching up the hill where the cougar had run, wagged his tail a couple of times.

As Luke pondered who might be killing these elk, he thought about how poachers like them are not hunters. They are criminals who steal from the people who pay the license fees and taxes on sporting equipment that the state uses to protect wildlife habitat, game animals, and all the other creatures that live in the wilds of the United States. Hunters hunt, within the laws, to feed their families. Most often, poachers are killing animals for profit, and they do so while ignoring every law there is to protect the animals that they kill.

Once again, Luke went into investigation mode. He took photos of the elk's head and where the backstraps had been removed. He looked for tracks and anything else in the area around the elk that might help in identifying who was doing this.

He remembered Brittney saying on the phone they had heard two quiet shots and one big one. If the big shot came from a larger, high-caliber rifle, there might again be a shell casing nearby. Before he looked, Luke removed the elk's head and placed it in a garbage bag he removed from his pack.

Then, with some effort, he rolled the carcass over. He looked for any obvious bullet holes in the elk's body but saw none. Why would someone shoot at an animal with a high-powered rifle after shooting it with a .22 or some other small-caliber rifle, he wondered. Maybe the high-powered rifle shot was first. Luke made a mental note to ask Brittney Cox what shot she had heard first, the quieter ones or the louder one.

Luke threw his pack over his shoulders—much heavier now with the elk head and antlers on board—and started looking around the area for anything else that might be evidence. He was about to head back up the trail toward his truck and the campground at Bear Lake when he caught the glint of something in the sunlight. He walked over to discover a bright brass shell casing sitting in the grass. With gloves on, Luke picked up the casing and read the etchings on the bottom. It was a .300 Winchester Magnum, just like the one he had found at the scene of the two dead cow elk above Bumping Lake.

After placing the casing in a plastic bag and putting it in his pack, Luke whistled for Jack, and they headed up the trail.

Back at the campground, Luke found Bradley Cox sitting on a stump next to the fire, poking it with a stick. Brittney was nowhere to be seen.

"Looks like you found something," Bradley squeaked.

"Yes, I did, thanks to you and your wife. I was thinking, though. Your wife said there were three shots, two that were quieter and one that was louder. Which of the shots was first?"

"One of the quiet shots was first, then the loud shot, and finally, a few seconds later, another quieter bang."

"Hmmm," Luke hummed, then said. "Okay, thanks again,

Mr. Cox. And please tell your wife, thank you too."

"Will do," Bradley said in his high-pitched voice. "Hope you catch whoever is doing this."

"Me too," Luke said with a wave. Then he loaded the pack into the back of his truck and opened the back door for Jack.

As he drove back down the bumpy forest service road, he thought more about the sequence of shots. They were definitely dealing with at least two shooters. But what were they doing with the elk meat?

CHAPTER 7

It was about a week after the men had decided that their number one target in America would be the girl riding her bike across the country that they found out she had called off the trip.

"She announced on her Facebook page that the cross-country bike trek is off," said Patel as he sat with Bakshi and Singh at the tiny table in Bakshi's apartment.

"I wonder why?" Singh said.

"Probably because she did not want to have blisters on her bottom," Patel said. "Why would someone not want to drive a car across country? It would be much more comfortable."

"It doesn't matter," Bakshi said. "Now, we must concentrate our efforts on the boy who is going to the wilderness school. We need to learn everything we can about this school, about its personnel, and about the boy."

"I saw his grades from his high school," Patel said. "He gets all high marks and seems to be very bright."

"What is his name again?" Bakshi asked. He had heard it

before, but since they were putting all their efforts into planning the capture of the girl, he had forgotten it.

"His name is Skyler Sloan," Patel said. "His father is the corporate attorney at Starbucks. The father is very well-compensated. The boy is his only son. He will not want any harm to come to him."

"That is good," Bakshi said. "And what about this survival school? Do we know anything about it?"

"I have looked into it," Singh said. "It is run by a man named Skip Harvey. They do weekly schools for young men and women. The reviews I have found online about the school seem very favorable."

"Do we know when the boy will be going into the wilderness with this school?" Bakshi asked.

"No, not yet," Patel said. "A post he made on his Instagram mentioned going for his birthday, but his date of birth was two weeks ago."

"So, did he already go?" Bakshi asked.

"No, I do not believe so," Patel said. "His earlier post mentioned going in the middle of September."

"I've been thinking about this some," Singh said. "While we were concentrating on the girl, it seemed we could be well-equipped to take her on our own. We could drive a car along the interstate highways and grab her and be gone. But what do we know about the wilderness of Washington State? We are city people. I know I couldn't walk a mile through the wilderness or mountains. I don't think any of us can."

"So, what are you saying?" Bakshi asked. "Do you think we should target one of the others?"

"No, I think the boy is still a good target," Singh said. "I just think we might need some help."

The other two men sat in silence for a couple minutes.

"I agree," Patel finally said. "We are ill-equipped to be out there searching through the wilderness trying to find this boy. And I have read there are bears and mountains lions and even wolves in that part of the world. I do not wish to fight off a bear or a lion."

"I believe we will need to hire someone to help us," Singh said. "A friend I went to school with moved to the United States several years ago. I could make contact with him and see if I could come for a visit. There, I could start looking for someone who might be interested in making some good money for only a day or two of work."

"I don't know if I like this," Bakshi said. "The more people we get involved, the higher our chances of failure and getting caught."

"That is the nice thing about hiring someone," Singh said. "If we give them false names, there will be no way for them to identify us."

"Let me think about this," Bakshi said after a bit. "In the meantime, let us find out more about the boy, Skyler Sloan, and when he is to go to this survival school. We will meet again in three days."

*

As the days drew nearer, Skyler Sloan was getting more and more excited about his week-long adventure in the Cascades. He and his buddy, Tory Green, were going to be out of school for a week. That made it worthwhile by itself. But the best part was that they were going to be out in nature, living off the land, learning to survive without computers, televisions, and cellphones. Yes, he liked all those things, and relied on them almost every waking moment of every day, but the idea of being away from all the technology was thrilling.

Skyler knew he would like the outing. He believed he was the type of person that would love the outdoors. He felt the need to be outdoors. Something deep down inside of him was pushing more and more, trying to get out. He'd done some kayaking in Puget Sound and he skied with friends, but he was jealous when other school buddies told tales of going waterfowl hunting or deer hunting in Eastern Washington or in other states.

His dad was always too busy with his job to want to do any

outdoor things like fishing or hunting. Supposedly, he had grown up fishing with Skyler's grandfather and uncles, but once his father was admitted into law school and then joined a law firm, it was like all he did was work. When he took the job as the lead in-house attorney at Starbucks, he was even busier than before.

Skyler had once asked his dad if he missed going fishing. He said he did, and that once work slowed down, they would go out— but work never seemed to slow down.

When his father asked what Skyler wanted for his birthday, he told his dad about the wilderness survival school. A couple of his friends had done the school and loved it. Skyler had received the certificate for the school on his sixteenth birthday in August. As an added bonus, his dad had paid for his best friend Tory to go too. It would only be the two of them and their instructor at the camp. They would be heading into the Cascades for a week on September 15th.

"This is going to be so cool," Tory said as the two young men were talking after Skyler's birthday. "I can't believe your dad paid for me too."

"Yeah, he's pretty cool with that. I think he's feeling guilty about not being able to spend the time with me, so he wanted me to be there with someone I know and like."

"The other nice thing is we get to be out of school for a week. My mom wasn't too excited about that, but once I told her it would be a chance of a lifetime, and that I'd probably learn more life skills there in a week than I have in all my high school years, she caved in."

"My mom said the same thing. She thinks it's great that we're going to learn some stuff that could help us later on in life."

"Did you ask about bringing your pistol?" Tory asked.

"Yeah, my dad asked the lady at the school. She said, 'No way.'"

"Did he tell them that you've trained with a shooting instructor for a year on gun safety and how to shoot?"

"Yep, didn't seem to matter. But the lady told my dad the main instructor said he'd bring his pistol, and one of the days we'd get to do some shooting, so I am cool with that."

"That'd be awesome. I can't wait."

*

When the three men reconvened in Bakshi's tiny apartment, Singh had some good news.

"My friend who moved to the United States has a sister and brother-in-law who own a convenience store in Washington State," Singh explained. "I have called the brother-in-law and talked with him about hiring some men to help us. I did not tell him what we were doing but indicated that we might want to keep some things discreet."

"What did he say?" Patel asked.

"He said he knows a couple of men who might be willing to help. They have done some odd jobs for him, and they have indicated they would do whatever was needed to make some money. The brother-in-law thought the men had spent some time in jail."

"Where is this store and how would we reach these men?" Bakshi asked.

"The store is in a town called Ephrata. It is in the eastern part of the state. We would most likely have to travel there to meet the men and discuss what we would expect of them."

"That is an unusual name for a town," Patel said. "Is it a big city with skyscrapers and palatial homes? Is it close to where Skyler Sloan lives?"

"I do not know," Singh said. "But we need to go there soon and find these men. If they are not willing to participate in our plan, then we will need to find someone else."

"I agree," Bakshi said. "I will make arrangements for us to travel to the United States right away."

"Will we be coming back here before we take the boy?" Patel asked.

"No," Bakshi said. "We will go there, talk to these men, learn more about the country, and continue to develop our plan."

"We will need some money," Singh said. "These men will want to be paid in cash."

"I have that all worked out," Bakshi said. "Now, let us figure out our flights and make preparations for our stay in America."

CHAPTER 8

Two days after Luke had been at Bear Lake, the wildlife forensic lab in Ashland, Oregon emailed the test results of the first bullets he had sent in. The information was very basic. The cartridge casing was indeed a .300 caliber, as was stamped at the bottom of the brass casing. It was made by the Federal Cartridge Corporation.

The bullet Luke had extracted from the side of the elk was a 180 grain Nosler AccuBond. Based on the grooves in the bullet, it was most likely shot from a Savage rifle, probably a model 110.

The smaller bullet taken from the other cow elk's brain was a .22 caliber long rifle, and based on the metallurgy, it most likely was made by CCA. There were not enough markings to determine what kind of a rifle was used to shoot the elk.

After reading the report, Luke printed it out and put it in a file. You had to start somewhere on a poaching case, and now at least he had a little information on who might be killing the elk. The bigger question in his mind was why.

Poachers kill animals for a variety of reasons. Some, who have fallen on hard times, will kill a deer or elk to help feed their family. While killing animals out of season was never excusable, Luke always understood when he caught someone who had shot an animal out of desperation, driven by hunger. He couldn't imagine ever being in the situation where he couldn't feed his family but thought if it ever came to that, he too might kill an animal for meat.

Other poachers killed for fun. Those were the ones Luke never understood, and frankly, he despised those who did it. Over the years, he had occasionally come upon scenes that just about made him sick.

At one poaching scene he'd investigated, someone had fired on a herd of Roosevelt elk near Mount St. Helens. The poachers had killed six cows and calves and wounded five others with AR-15s, indiscriminately shooting at the elk. When they ran out of bullets and elk to shoot at, they just drove off.

When Luke and another wildlife officer got to the scene, they were tasked with tracking the wounded animals and putting them down. It took Luke the better part of the day to track one wounded spike bull that had hobbled over three miles. The animal was not losing much blood but would have died at some point because its lower front leg had been blown off at the knee by one of the shots.

Ultimately, the men were caught and lost their hunting rights for ten years. They were fined twelve thousand dollars each, and both did some prison time. After Luke testified at their trial, he was left with the feeling that the men enjoyed killing things just to be killing things, and they would most likely be out doing it again when the spirit moved them, laws be damned.

Other poachers did it for the money. Three years earlier, Luke and Stan Hargraves—a fellow WDFW officer—had run down a father and son who were killing black bears out of season and selling their paws, claws, and gall bladders on the black market. The men had killed seven bears before Luke and Hargraves caught them.

As he thought about the two men who had been poaching the

bears, Luke wondered if whoever it was that was killing the elk was also doing it for money.

Finally, the last category of poachers were the ones who were trying to be hunters, but they just had trouble staying between the lines. It was like the two guys Luke had caught fishing illegally for salmon earlier in the summer. The men liked to fish for salmon, knew there were salmon in the river, and even though there was no open season for salmon, they went and fished for them anyway.

Over the years, Luke had nabbed several hunters who had opened the season a day or two early or had killed an extra elk or deer during the hunting season. Most would justify breaking the law because they paid for their license and tags, and they just wanted to get their money's worth.

There was always some excuse, but no matter how you sliced it, it was poaching. With some of the herds of deer and elk in Washington State in serious decline, every single animal taken illegally mattered.

As he reflected more on the elk poaching case, Luke pulled out a legal pad and jotted down some notes. First, he wrote the word "why" followed by a question mark and an arrow pointing to a money sign and another question mark.

Then he wrote the word "how" followed by a question mark and an arrow pointing to two numbers: 22 and 300. Behind the 22, he wrote "close range."

Next, he wrote the word "who" followed by a question mark and an arrow pointing to the words "two people" with another question mark.

And finally, he wrote the word "when" followed by a question mark and an arrow pointing to the words "night time" with another question mark.

He tore the sheet off the pad, went to the copier and made a copy, then placed one of the pages in his newly created elk-poaching file, folded the other copy, and put it in his back pocket. He would bring it out and talk it over with Sara at dinner. Luke and Sara often discussed cases they were working on. Sara always brought fresh thinking to the cases Luke was working, and he'd been a big help on a couple of her cases as well.

Next, Luke went and chatted with his captain, Bob Davis. The captain was a large man—not fat or obese but more like a guy who had played lineman for a Division I college football team, which Davis had. His brown hair was graying by the month, and he had a big bushy mustache à la Wilfred Brimley.

Luke gave Davis a quick recap of what he knew about the four elk that had been killed, and Davis said, "Not much to go on."

"No, there isn't," Luke said. "I have a gut feeling there are going to be more dead elk. This seems like something that is planned, and there is a purpose to it all."

"Well, stay after it," the captain said.

"I will," Luke said. "Right now, I'm heading up to check on anglers at some of the lakes on White Pass. That'll give me a chance to look around a bit more."

"Sounds good."

"Oh, and I wanted to clear something with you. I'm planning on heading up into the high Cascades next month to go with a friend who will be hunting deer. I won't be hunting deer myself—just going along to keep him company and maybe do a little grouse hunting. I can take it as vacation days, but I could also make it a work week by checking on other deer hunters, grouse hunters, and anglers in the high lakes if you would approve that."

"Will you be in our region?"

"No, I'll be up in region two. Chelan County, probably."

"Let me coordinate with John McCarthy up there. I'm sure he'd be okay with you working in his region, but let me check. If he's good with it, I'm okay with making it a working deal."

"Great. Thanks."

On his drive up into the mountains, Luke thought about his upcoming trip into the high Cascades with his buddy Cale Harris. As young men, the two used to fish and hunt together almost every weekend and whenever they had a day off from their summer jobs. Harris had the use of his grandfather's fourteen-foot aluminum boat, which got them out on most any water they wanted to fish. And Luke's 1985 four-wheel-drive Chevy pickup would get them pretty much wherever they wanted to go come hunting season.

The two, with some of their other friends, spent days in the Cascades, hiking, camping, hunting, and fishing. Harris was an excellent shot with a shotgun and a rifle, and he seemed to always be in the animals. The other guys said Harris was lucky, but Luke knew differently. Yes, he almost aways shot the most ducks and got his deer every year, but Harris worked harder than the rest of the guys. He was always thinking and would put himself in a position to be successful. It was a trait that Luke loved about his best friend and tried to emulate. Frankly, working hard, thinking ahead, and getting into the right position had helped Luke be successful in his job too.

In the early days of their hunting adventures, Luke believed he was a better shot than Harris or any of their buddies, but now he believed Harris to be the best. Because of his ability with his deer rifle, and because Lucas McCain was the name of the main character on the old 1960s TV series *The Rifleman*, several of his high school hunting friends had nicknamed Luke "the rifleman." He wasn't fond of the nickname, but he put up with it. Thankfully, Harris always called him Luke.

In recent years, a few of Luke's colleagues in the Yakima County Sheriff's Office caught on to the likeness from the TV show, and they too called Luke the rifleman. As much as he tried, Luke couldn't shake the nickname, and it only got more prevalent after he had taken down what the media dubbed "the Cascade Killer" with a long cross-canyon shot from his favorite deer rifle three years earlier. The shot hadn't killed the serial killer, but the man was probably never going to walk the same again. After what the killer had done to the women he had murdered, Luke didn't really care how the guy walked.

With the high mountain hunt less than a month away, Luke had stepped up his exercise regimen. He had always kept himself in good shape, working out three times a week on weights and cardio, but knowing what some of the elevations were in the country Harris wanted to hunt and how long the hike would be to get there, Luke wanted to be ready.

The extra work was paying off. He had dropped a few pounds and he seemed to have more energy. He was really looking forward to the week with his old friend.

Harris could have gone to any college in the country, probably on a full-ride scholarship. He was a four-point student in high school, got a 1570 on his SAT, and was a National Merit Scholar. All of this led him to be recruited by Stanford, MIT, Yale, and several other prestigious universities. But when it came down to it, he decided to go to West Point.

Coming out of West Point as an officer, Harris did a four-year stint with the Army where he trained to be a sniper. During two deployments to Afghanistan, he led a team of six sharpshooters that spent their entire time providing cover to help keep troops on the ground safe.

After his time in the Army, Harris could have taken any number of jobs, but wanting to get back home he took a position in a newly formed special unit of the State Patrol. The small group in the special unit did investigative work, concentrating their efforts on human trafficking, drug smuggling, and high-profile murder cases around the state. With the freedom to work autonomously, and with the full support of the governor, the special unit had been successful in taking down some serious criminals, lowering the rate of disappearing young women, and cutting into the drug cartels. Harris had tried to recruit Luke into the special unit, but Luke liked being a game warden and especially enjoyed traveling the waters and mountains of Central Washington.

Luke's first stop was at Dog Lake, where a few small boats bobbed in the green water. The lake, which sat at the base of a giant shale rock mountain, was planted with trout a couple times a year. Dog Lake drew anglers in late summer because it was always much cooler at the higher elevations than the towns in the valley floors below.

Luke stopped his truck in the shadows of some evergreens and grabbed his binoculars to watch anglers fishing off the bank. As he scanned the fishermen, he came across a couple of familiar faces. Jim Kingsbury and his buddy Frank Dugdale sat in lawn chairs at the water's edge, holding their fishing rods and waiting for a bite.

The two men were mainstays in the town of Naches, and they loved to fish and hunt. Luke ran across them often, and he always got a kick out of chatting with them. Kingsbury was known for wearing shirts with weird or funny sayings on them, and in all the times that Luke had seen him, he had never seen Kingsbury in the same shirt.

The man was a bit too far away for Luke to see what his shirt said today, but he figured it would be a good one. Rumors around town were that Kingsbury had boxes of the slogan shirts. According to the grapevine, he would wear each shirt once and then donate it to a charity that helped clothe people in South America.

Luke watched the anglers for twenty minutes or so and saw a few fish caught, but it looked like the fishing was slow. He decided he'd go have a chat with Kingsbury and Dugdale. He drove around to the small campground along the highway, got out, and walked down to where the men were fishing.

"I thought that was you over there watching us," Kingsbury said as Luke stopped just above them on the rocks. "Don't think you'll catch any perpetrators here. The fishing is real hit and miss."

"Kinda what I was seeing," Luke said. He looked at Kingsbury's white shirt that read in bold red letters: FISH FEAR ME, WOMEN WANT ME. "I guess your shirt is right, huh?"

"Well, half of it is right," Dugdale said. "Although I don't think the fish fear him as much as he is just a crappy fisherman."

"At least the women still want me," Kingsbury said.

Dugdale broke out in a laugh, which made Luke laugh too.

Just then Kingsbury set the hook on a bite, and in short order he was working a foot-long rainbow trout up onto the rocks at the edge of the lake.

"There's supper," Kingsbury declared. "If I can catch another,

I'll invite you to dinner, Frank."

"Screw you," Dugdale said. "Save it for one of those women who supposedly want you."

"You guys have fun," Luke said as he turned and started walking back toward his truck. "I gotta go try to catch an elk poacher."

CHAPTER 9

Bakshi, Patel and Singh made it to Vancouver International Airport in British Columbia at five o'clock in the morning. The men had to change planes in London, and with the layover, they had been traveling for almost a full day.

"What day is it here?" Patel, yawning and scratching his head, asked his cousin as they headed from the terminal to baggage claim.

"It is Tuesday. We need to get our bags and go to the car rental check-in. We have a long drive to this Ephrata. I would like to be there by dinner time."

"Speaking of dinner," Patel said, "can we please get some food? I am starving. The airline food was just short of inedible."

"I am hungry as well," said Singh, who was running to catch up to the other two men as they weaved their way through a couple hundred people, also on their way to baggage claim.

"Yes, we will eat," Bakshi said. "As soon as we are issued a car and we are on the road."

The car-rental process took another forty-five minutes, but once they had everything loaded into the Ford Explorer, it didn't take them long to get on the freeway headed south to the United States.

"Maybe we should eat before we get to the border crossing," Patel said. "I heard sometimes the wait there can be very long."

Bakshi was hungry too. But this whining from his cousin was getting on his nerves.

"We will eat when we finally get into the United States. Now, please, no more talk of eating."

When they finally arrived at the border, they sat and waited for twenty minutes, then the line of cars began moving. As they approached the crossing, Bakshi made sure they all had their passports ready. When it was their turn, the Border Control officer asked for their identification, and the men handed her their passports.

"What is the purpose of your visit into the United States today?" the officer asked.

"We are here to visit family," Bakshi lied.

"Where do your family members live?"

"They live in Seattle."

"You couldn't fly directly into Seattle?"

"Yes, but we also have family in Vancouver. We plan to visit them on our return."

"How long will you be in the United States?"

"We will be here a month," Bakshi said.

The officer asked them to roll down their back windows, and she looked around the back seat and in the rear area of the SUV.

"Not much luggage for a month's stay," she said as she kept looking.

"We plan on purchasing some clothing while we are here," Patel said.

After asking a few more questions, the Border Patrol officer handed them their passports and waved them through.

"Now can we look for someplace to eat?" Patel said.

They stopped at a small café in Blaine, and because it was morning, the three men ordered pancakes and eggs. Patel asked for a double order.

After a quick meal, they were back on the road and traveling south through an ever-growing number of homes, apartment complexes, shopping centers, fast food restaurants, gas stations, and car dealerships.

"Just like on TV," Singh said. "All of these auto sales stores, one after another. Who buys all of these cars?"

"Look around," Bakshi said. "There are cars on the highway for as far as the eye can see."

"And the fast food restaurants," Patel said. "Do Americans not eat at home anymore?"

"I have read these places selling unhealthy food will be the downfall of America," Singh said. "Obesity, heart disease—it all comes from eating these Big Macs and Whopper burgers."

It was a clear, sunny day in the Pacific Northwest, and from the freeway the men could see Mount Baker standing tall in the mountains to the east.

"I'm glad we are going to hire the men to go into the mountains," Patel said, nodding toward the snow-covered mountain. "I don't think we would do well up there."

"I must agree," Singh said. "Is this close to where we will meet the men and the boy?"

"No, it is not," Bakshi said. "We will meet them on the other side of those mountains."

Both men looked at the dark fir trees of the mountains to the east. They wondered what it looked like on the other side.

As they got closer to Seattle, they could see the skyscrapers and the Space Needle standing tall near Elliott Bay. Everywhere they looked, they saw signs for Starbucks.

"It seems Starbucks are very plentiful here," Singh said. "And somewhere in one of these suburbs, a young man named Skyler Sloan is preparing for an excursion into the wilderness."

"We need to get a couple of burner phones," Bakshi said.

"Look for the sign for a Walmart. We can purchase them there."

In one of the strip malls right off the freeway, Singh spotted a Walmart sign. They pulled in, and all three men went into the store.

While Bakshi was back in the electronics department, Singh and Patel shopped for some clothes. They wanted more "American"-looking attire to somewhat blend in. After purchasing the phones and the clothing, they quickly got back on the freeway, looking for the exit that would take them to eastern Washington.

"Now, help me watch for a sign to Spokane," Bakshi said.

"Are we going to Spokane?" Patel asked.

"No, but that is the biggest city on the east side of the state. The signs will take us that direction, and we will find our way to Ephrata from there."

Soon, they saw the sign to Spokane and Interstate 90 and merged onto the freeway headed east. The men continued to look in wonder at the buildings, the shopping centers, and yet more auto dealerships.

"I believe we are about two hours from Ephrata," Bakshi said as they drove past Issaquah, headed up the freeway that crosses the mountains to the arid side of the state.

After descending from Snoqualmie Pass and approaching Ellensburg, Patel looked at the temperature gauge on their SUV. It read ninety-eight degrees.

"Everything you see about Seattle is it is raining all the time. This is not rain. This heat could compete with Mumbai," Patel said.

"We have arrived in an area that is called high desert," Singh said, "I read about it in a book. The eastern part of the state receives very little rain and can get very warm in the summer."

"I thought we would be away from the heat," Patel said. "I was looking forward to the coolness of the summer rain."

All three men decided they needed a break to urinate. Plus, Patel was hungry again. They pulled into Ellensburg and looked for a place with a bathroom where they could get something to eat.

"Take your choice," Bakshi said as the men looked down the road at dozens of brightly colored signs for every fast food known to mankind.

"Let's see if their McDonalds is the same as ours," Patel said.

"Please no," said Singh. "Their food gives me instant diarrhea. I will be shitting every five minutes from here to Ephrata."

"We can't have that," Bakshi said. "I will choose."

He pulled the rig into Arby's and parked.

"This will do. We will urinate, order our meal, and come back to the car so that we can keep going. Rishi, you call the friend's brother-in-law at the convenience store and let him know we will be arriving in a little over an hour. Find out if he has the men lined up to meet with us."

The men grabbed fish and chicken sandwiches, French fries, and soft drinks, then climbed into the Explorer and started back to the interstate.

"Have you noticed all the beautiful young women here?" Patel asked.

"This is a university town," Bakshi said. "That is why. We need not be thinking about them. We have work to do."

"Yes, we do," Patel agreed. "But when we have the money, I may very well come back here and meet some of these young women. I especially would like to meet a blonde."

Bakshi ignored his cousin and, in between bites of his chicken sandwich, asked Singh what the convenience store man said on the phone.

"He has the men lined up to meet us in two hours. He says they are quite intrigued with the chance to make some good sums of money."

"We will see how excited they are after we discuss what it is we are hiring them to do."

*

Rod Fredricks and Bart Rogers had been friends all their life. They had grown up in and around Ephrata, Washington, doing the kind of things country kids do. The two had been smart enough to do well in school, but neither of them cared enough to try.

Fredricks' parents had divorced when he was seven, and his mother worked two jobs to keep him and his big sister fed. She didn't have time to be checking on whether her son had done his homework.

Rogers had some issues with dyslexia, which made reading a pain in the ass, so he just didn't read. His parents had gotten married because they were pregnant with him during their senior year of high school, and they dropped out before graduating. Neither his mother nor father cared much if Bart was passing his classes. They'd done just fine, thank you, without a piece of paper telling them they now could go to work for the rest of their life.

During hunting season, Fredricks and Rogers would often miss at least their morning classes, as they chased ducks, geese, pheasants, and quail until noon many days of the week. If the ducks were really coming into a nearby corn field, they might miss all day. During spring, fishing caught their fancy. There were all kinds of lakes around the area where they could catch trout, bass, perch, and walleye.

Their first run-in with the law came early in life. As fifteen-year-olds, they had "borrowed" one of Fredricks' neighbor's old Chevy pickups. The two needed the truck so they could get up into the dryland wheatfields northeast of Ephrata to hunt mule deer.

The neighbor, who probably would have let the boys use the truck if they had just asked, didn't even realize it was gone from his back pasture until he saw the pickup rattling up the gravel road to the double-wide mobile home where the Fredricks lived. When he saw his truck, with a large mule deer buck in the back, driven by a boy he knew wasn't old enough to have a driver's license, the neighbor decided that it might be something the sheriff should deal with. He had watched the Fredricks boy grow up and knew he was ditching school many days because he often saw him and the Rogers kid wandering up the road on a weekday with a shotgun or a fishing pole slung over their shoulders. The neighbor knew that Fredricks wasn't getting much parental guidance and that if the boy got a scare from the sheriff now, maybe it would steer him back onto the right road.

Ultimately, the sheriff gave both boys a stern warning, especially after the neighbor said he didn't want to press charges. The bigger issue, as the sheriff saw it, was that the boys had taken the mule deer buck without a valid tag. So, the local game warden was called, and there were more stern warnings. And of course, the deer was taken from the boys.

"That really pisses me off," Fredricks had said to Rogers at the time. "I had a hunting license."

That day would be the first of many go-rounds both young men would have with the local game wardens through the years. And they'd have several more issues with the sheriff's office as well, including being arrested for breaking and entering into two homes in the area. Both the houses had security cameras which showed Fredricks and Rogers clearly wandering through the homes.

After Fredricks and Rogers turned twenty-one and could legally visit the local taverns, they often ended up in fights with other patrons. Fredricks had been shorter than average all his life. Now, as a grown man of only five feet, five inches, he was inflicted with what some would call "little man's syndrome." Boosted by a few drinks, he often bit off more than he could chew, picking fights with men much bigger than he. Luckily, Rogers stood almost a foot taller than his lifelong friend, and with a natural strength that only heredity could account for, he would have to wade into the fight and save his buddy. Soon, because of Fredricks' temper and affliction, both men were banned from most of the drinking establishments in the area. Their barroom brawls had also landed them in the local hoosegow on several occasions.

The men were gainfully employed off and on. Rogers worked with a local landscaping company, doing odd jobs like mowing lawns and building rock walls and walkways, among other tasks. He liked the job because about the time things slowed down with cold temperatures arriving in the fall, he was laid off, giving him more time to hunt.

Fredricks worked as a cashier at one of the mini-marts at the end of town. In addition to selling giant soda pops, corn dogs, and beer to customers, he had built a decent little business selling pot out the back door. Fredricks worked the graveyard shift at the store, which gave him time to do some hunting and fishing during the daylight hours.

It was Fredricks' boss who first approached him about doing a side job for some men coming in from out of town. The boss had been contacted by the owner of another mini-mart in town, and when his boss broached the subject with Fredricks to see if he and his hunting buddy might be interested, Fredricks said they would do it.

Fredricks had talked it over with Rogers, who was still paying off some fines and could use more cash. Rogers was agreeable to at least talking to the men. He liked the idea of making some extra money.

"I assume it means we might possibly be tiptoeing the line between legal and not," Rogers said when his friend approached him about meeting with the strangers from out of town. "Not that I am totally against that."

"I'm not either. But I ain't into killing anyone or anything," Fredricks said. "Unless they paid me some huge amount of cash," he continued with a sly grin.

Rogers smiled too, but he didn't like the sound of killing anyone.

"Let's see what these men are proposing before we get too committed," Rogers said.

CHAPTER 10

Luke and Sara were just finishing up a quick dinner and were about to take a walk down to the river when their doorbell rang.

"I'll get it," Luke said and headed to the door. Jack didn't even raise his head from a lengthy afternoon nap that was turning into early bedtime.

Luke opened the door to Austin Meyers' smiling face.

"Hi, Austin. Come on in!" Luke said as he opened the screen door.

As soon as Jack heard Austin's voice, he was up and moving quickly to the neighbor boy's side.

"Hey, Jack," Austin said as he petted the big yellow dog. "Mom told me to bring this over to you guys."

Austin handed a foil-wrapped paper plate to Luke.

"It's peach cobbler," Austin said. "Mom made it from the peaches on our tree and thought you guys would like some."

"Wow, thanks," Luke said.

"We had it after our elk steak dinner. Everything was soooo good."

Sara came into the living room and said, "Hi, Austin. How are you?"

"Fine. Mom sent over some cobbler."

"That was very nice of her. How is she doing? I haven't had a chance to talk to her in a while."

"Oh, she's doing great. Charlie is keeping her busy, going on out-of-town trips to here and there."

Sara asked the young man about school and football practice and if there were any new girls in his life.

Austin answered each question, blushing a bit at the question about girls.

"Okay, no more interrogations," Luke said. "Let's let Austin get back to his family. Tell your mom and Charlie hello and thank your mom for us."

After they said their goodbyes, Luke put the cobbler in the refrigerator. He would definitely enjoy a small piece, maybe with some vanilla ice cream, when they returned from their walk.

"C'mon, Jack," Luke called. "Time to get a little exercise."

Jack came running, blowing past Luke and Sara as they headed out the door, walking down the road to the river.

"That was nice of Jessie to send over that cobbler," Sara said. "I know you love it. I guess I should learn how to make it."

"No need, unless you want your husband to be a fat boy. I'd eat every bite and certainly don't need it."

"I guess you didn't marry me for my cooking."

Over the three years they'd been married, Luke had actually prepared most of their meals. He loved to fix the venison and fish that he brought in during the year, and although Sara was a bit of a skeptic at first regarding the deer and elk meat, she had learned to really like it. She especially loved the fish. Everything was healthy and tasty, but the spring Chinook and sockeye salmon Luke caught were her favorites.

As they walked, they discussed a case Sara was working on that involved yet another missing woman on the Yakama Reservation. It was a continual issue, and when another woman went missing, it just added to the fear and frustration felt by the Yakama Tribe and its members.

As Sara talked through the case, Luke offered her an outsider's view of things, though he was feeling a bit distracted. He was trying to get at whatever it was when his cellphone rang. It was his old friend Bill Williams, a deputy with the Yakima County Sheriff's Office.

"Hey, Bill. What's up?" McCain asked, putting his phone on speaker so Sara could hear too.

"We just got a call about a dead cow elk up in the Ahtanum. Looks like it was shot with a rifle, and some meat was removed."

"Okay, you have a location?"

"Yeah, the guy who called it in said it was up in Carpenter Gulch. I'll text you his phone number, and you can call him and get zeroed in."

Luke looked up at Sara, who was reading his mind.

"Go," she said.

"Let's go, Jack," Luke said, and then to Sara, "See you sometime."

Luke ran back to the house, geared up, and headed across town to the road that would take him into the area known locally as the Ahtanum. As he drove, he called the man who had found the elk. He had a similar story as the two men who had discovered the other elk carcasses. He had been up on one of the forest service roads in his side-by-side ATV and had seen three coyotes run out of a stand of fir trees. There were several magpies and crows in the trees too. He figured something was dead and thought that if it were an elk or deer, and it had antlers, he would go grab them.

"Someone took the backstraps and a hindquarter," the man said after giving Luke the exact location of the animal. "Definitely was poached, and it had to be today. The coyotes were working on it, but they hadn't eaten much."

Luke thanked the man and drove a bit faster out of town,

wanting to get to the elk before the coyotes and birds did much more destruction. Although it was mid-summer and stayed light late into the evening, he might be fighting darkness and wanted to get to the dead animal while he still had light to see.

When he arrived at the spot where the man told him to park, Luke got out of his truck and immediately heard the magpies chattering. That pretty much told him where the elk carcass was. He let Jack out of the truck, and they worked their way over to the group of trees where the man had said the elk would be.

The light was starting to fade, so Luke hustled. He took photos and checked around the animal for usable human tracks or anything else that might have been left behind by the poacher. Then he searched for a bullet hole. Eventually, he found an entrance hole in the center of the neck with a large hole exiting on the other side. He would have no bullet this time to send to Ashland. The neck shot would have been as fatal as a bullet to the brain, taking out the spine and most likely the major arteries from the brain. The elk had probably died in its tracks.

The caller had been correct. As was the case with the other four poached elk, the backstraps had been removed from this elk, and most of one hindquarter had been removed.

Luke tried to figure out where the person might have shot from based on where the elk lay, but that was tough. It was a huge open area around the trees, and if the poacher had shot from some distance, he'd only be guessing where the shooter had been. Still, he looked for any brass that might have been left behind.

This elk, unfortunately, offered no evidence. No bullet in the head. No bullet in the body. No brass in the weeds. Nothing other than the fact that Luke knew, just by looking at it, that it had been killed and partially butchered by the same person or people.

It was just getting dark as Luke and Jack walked back up to the truck.

"We need to figure this out," Luke said to his canine traveling companion as he started the pickup and turned around, heading back to town.

Luke called Sara to let her know he was on his way back home, and then he turned the radio on and switched the dial to the local country station. As he listened, he started thinking about the piece of peach cobbler waiting for him in the fridge. He did love peach cobbler made from local, tree-ripened peaches. It was very nice of Jessie Meyers to think of him, sending the dessert over with Austin.

As Luke thought about his brief conversation with Austin before Sara had come into the room, he tried to recall whether Austin had said they had eaten elk steaks for dinner. Yes, that's exactly what he had said.

Luke often shared his game meat with the neighbors, but last fall he hadn't killed an elk, so he had no elk steaks to give to the Meyers. Austin hadn't had any success hunting elk last year either. Of course, they could have received the venison from any number of other friends or family, but it wouldn't hurt to ask where they had gotten the elk steaks. He didn't think the Meyers had obtained the elk meat illegally. Luke knew they wouldn't do anything knowingly against the law.

Yes, people ate game meat all year long. Many preferred moose, elk, and deer meat because it was much healthier than other meats. Venison was leaner than beef and had virtually no hormones. And venison was much lower in cholesterol. Some people found the taste of deer to be a bit gamey, but the flavor of elk and moose venison was preferred by many folks.

Someone who preferred wild game to grass-fed beef but didn't hunt, or someone who wasn't successful during the previous hunting season, might just be in the market for some fresh elk meat. The more Luke thought about it, the more he was convinced someone was killing the animals to sell the prime cuts of meat. He wondered how many other animals the poachers might have killed, now out in the mountains feeding the coyotes and eagles with the meat left behind.

Luke would talk to Austin in the morning, and he would talk with his captain and the other officers in his office. It was time to start pushing some of the habitual poachers in the area to see if they, or someone they knew, might have any idea who was selling game meat, poached or not.

He was just about back down to the paved road when he passed an older gray and white Ford pickup going up the hill. Luke glanced at the two men in the truck, trying to get a good look at them as his headlights briefly illuminated the cab of the truck. The driver was a big guy with the sleeves torn out of a denim shirt and, while Luke wasn't positive, he thought he glimpsed a tattoo on the man's upper left arm. The passenger looked to be smaller but about the same age as the driver. He was wearing a camo baseball cap and a white T-shirt.

Luke thought about the description of the driver that Ben Allard had seen near the site of the first poached elk, and it seemed to match the truck and driver he had just passed.

He quickly turned his truck around, hit the switch for his blue lights, and headed after the truck. He had no real reason to detain the men, but he wanted to do a quick check on them. If nothing else, he could ask them if they might have seen anything at the first poaching site—if, in fact, they were the men Allard had seen.

The Ford pickup slowed as soon as the driver saw the blue lights coming up from behind, and the man pulled the truck off the road when he found a wide spot. Luke turned the spotlight on and shined it into the cab of the truck. The driver put his hand up to shade his eyes from the bright light reflecting from the rearview mirror.

Before he got out of his truck, Luke rolled the back driver's side window down which would allow Jack to get out and come to his assistance if need be. He told Jack to stay, then climbed out of the truck and walked slowly toward the back of the Ford. Normally, Luke would approach a stopped vehicle from the passenger side, but since the truck was pulled off the road alongside dense brush, there was no easy path to that side of the truck. So, he kept moving slowly to the driver's side window.

In the back window of the truck, there was a scoped rifle hanging from a rack. Luke looked quickly into the bed of the pickup and only saw a few discarded soft drink cans and a five-gallon gas can. There was a dark stain on the bed's metal, but in the dark, he couldn't tell if it was oil or blood or paint or something else.

As he approached, Luke watched for any sudden or unusual movements by either of the men in the truck.

"Good evening, officer," the driver said out the window before Luke could see the man's face.

"How we doing tonight?" Luke asked.

"Doing good. What's up?"

"Well, I had a report earlier that a truck that matches yours was seen near where some elk have been poached. I saw the rifle in the back of your truck and just thought I'd check things out. Can I see your driver's license?"

"It's not against the law to have a rifle in the truck driving down the road," the man said.

In the light, Luke could see that the man did have a tattoo on his upper bicep, maybe a bald eagle on a shield of red, white, and blue.

"No, it's not. Unless it's loaded. Can you please hand it to me?"

The man dug his wallet out of his back pocket, pulled the driver's license out and handed it to Luke. Then he reached back and grabbed the rifle. Luke recognized it as a Ruger 10/22 because he had one just like it.

Luke took the license from the man and then grasped the rifle as the big man handed it butt-first out the window. Luke took the rifle, removed the magazine, then pulled the cocking handle of the little semi-automatic to make sure there wasn't a cartridge in the chamber. The clip was empty, as was the chamber.

As Luke was handing the rifle back to the men, he asked if they had any other weapons in the truck.

"I am carrying a pistol," the driver said. "It's loaded, but I have a concealed weapons permit."

Luke looked at the man's license in the light of the spotlight, still turning night into day in the cab of the truck. The driver's name was Oxford Smythe. Luke glanced at the photo on the license and then at the man in the truck.

"Everyone calls me Ox. And no, I am not English. But my granddaddy was, and my folks handed his name down to me."

Smythe was a man of ample size. Luke couldn't tell just how tall he was because he was sitting in the truck, but his driver's license listed him as six-foot-seven with a weight of 310 pounds.

"Okay, Mr. Smythe. It seems everything is in order. What are you doing up here this evening?"

"Just call me Ox. My buddy and I are hunting rattlesnakes. They like to slither out and warm themselves on the road on these hot summer days. We make hatbands out of the skins."

As he was explaining, he pointed to his buddy's straw cowboy hat encircled by a rattlesnake skin. It took Luke a second, but he could see that the snake's head was still attached to the skin, sitting right out front, its mouth open like it was going to strike.

"And sometimes we'll get the odd coyote crossing the road," the man in the passenger seat said. "We're getting forty bucks for a good coyote hide."

"Do you have your hunting licenses with you?" Luke asked.

Both men did, and they handed them to him. The other man's name was Duke Mackey. Luke took out his notepad and wrote Smythe's and Mackey's names and addresses and license numbers.

"So, would you have been up above Clear Lake about ten days ago or so?" Luke asked.

Smythe thought about it for a minute or two and then said, "Yep, we was up there around that time. Why?"

"Well, we're investigating a series of illegally killed elk in the area, and someone said they saw a person who looked like you, driving a truck similar to yours, up near where one of the elk was killed."

"No, sir. It weren't us. Check my license and record. You won't find anything bad under my name. I hate people who break the law. It ruins it for all of us."

"I appreciate that, Mr. Smy . . . er, uh, Ox."

"And Mackey here couldn't hit a bull in the butt with a banjo. He's about half blind and can't see three hundred yards down the road."

"I can take the head of a rattler at six feet though," Mackey said with a smile.

"So, in all your travels in the mountains around here, have you noticed anything that might be out of the ordinary?"

Both men thought about it for a bit.

"Not really. We'll occasionally see a car parked off of one of these roads, all steamed up from folks enjoying themselves if you know what I mean. But mostly we just mind our own business."

"Here's my card," Luke said as he handed it to the big man who was still blinking and moving his head, trying to avoid the bright light's reflection. "If you do happen to see anything, would you please give me a call? Whoever is killing these elk out of season is stealing from you and me and every other person who enjoys having the elk around."

"Yessir, mister," Ox paused as he tried to read Luke's card. "Mister McCain. We will do that. Yes indeed."

"Okay, have a good evening and don't get bit by a diamondback. I hear it hurts."

"I'll say it does," Mackey said, pulling his hat off his head. "This'n here got me in the arm. I shoulda shot his head off, but I wanted a hat band with the head on it."

Ox chuckled, dropped the Ford into gear, and they slowly pulled back onto the road as Luke turned to go back to his truck.

CHAPTER 11

Bakshi could see two men standing next to a green Chevy Suburban parked alongside an old barn when they turned up the gravel drive at the address they'd been given by the man at the mini-mart.

Until he'd arrived in America, Bakshi didn't know there were so many of these large vehicles being driven. In India, a truck that size would not make it through many of the crowded streets. Bakshi wondered how Americans could afford to keep such large vehicles full of petroleum.

The three men had decided on the drive to the old farmhouse to use the names Dinesh, Raj, and Anup. They had read some American newspapers, spent time on Hollywood gossip sites on the internet, and found some well-known actors and political commentators from India with those first names.

"I hope I can remember who is who," Patel had said after they decided on their fake names.

"We will practice as we drive," Bakshi said. "Don't you think that is a good idea, Anup?"

Patel and Singh both said "yes" simultaneously.

"I am Anup," Singh said. "You are Dinesh."

"No, I am Dinesh," Bakshi said. "Darsh is Raj."

It took them a few minutes, but soon they were calling each other by their new names.

The men standing next to the green Chevy Suburban were quite different in physical size, Bakshi noticed. They were both wearing blue denim pants with baseball caps and T-shirts—a white one on the larger man, and a blue one on the smaller man.

"Good afternoon," Bakshi said in Indian-accented English as the three men climbed out of the Explorer. The heat of the August afternoon hit them smack in the face. "I am Dinesh, and these are my partners, Raj and Anup."

All three men extended their hands.

"I'm Rod," the shorter man said as he and Rogers shook the men's hands. "And this is Bart. Glad to meet you fellas."

The men eyeballed each other for a few seconds, and then Fredricks said, "Well, hell, let's get out of this furnace. We got some beers in a cooler inside the barn. We can sit and talk in there."

Rogers pulled the rickety, weather-beaten door open, and the three men from India walked into the darkness of the barn. Fredricks and Rogers followed.

"Have a seat," Fredricks said, pointing to a couple of cloth folding camp chairs next to three metal folding chairs. A white Coleman cooler sat in the middle of the chairs, arranged in a semi-circle.

"Hope you like Keystone," Fredricks said, opening the cooler and handing each of the men a chilled can of beer.

"That will be fine," Bakshi said as he opened the beer. "It was a long drive. A cold beer is quite welcomed."

"Yeah, that's what I always say," Rogers said after taking a big swig of his beer. "Quite welcomed."

"So, what do you fellas have in mind for us?" Fredricks asked.

Bakshi would never tell the men exactly what they were

planning, but since they were going to need to kidnap the boy, he wanted to test the water to see what they might be willing to do. So, he told them a vague story using hypotheticals to see what kind of response he might get.

"What if you were the divorced father of a child that has been taken to another country by his mother, and the father is concerned about the health and treatment of the child. Would you be willing to come and take that child away from the mother?"

Rogers and Fredricks looked at each other and thought about it for a minute.

"So, you are talking about kidnapping?" Fredricks asked.

"I would not like to call it that," Bakshi said. "It is more like giving the child the opportunity to reunite with a father who has had his rights taken away by a vengeful and conniving mother."

"Still, in this country it'd probably be called kidnapping," Fredricks said. He paused for a few seconds, looked at Rogers, then said, "But I could see where a father might be so interested in getting his child back that he would be willing to pay someone to, let's say, rescue the child, for a fee."

Rogers smiled.

"Yes, yes," Bakshi said. "Now you understand. Do you have children?"

"Not that I know of," Fredricks said with a laugh.

Rogers laughed too. Bakshi, Singh, and Patel did not.

"What kind of a fee would you suggest?" Singh asked, saying what Bakshi and Patel were thinking.

"Now, that depends on some of the other circumstances," Fredricks said. "We need to know all of the particulars. Where? When? How much time might be involved? What the chances might be that the local police will catch us and not care about how vengeful and conniving your wife is?"

"I did not say it was my wife," Bakshi said.

"Okay, but what about the answers to our other questions?"

"We believe the best opportunity to, as you say, rescue this child will be three weeks from now, in mid-September. We do not know the exact date yet, but will soon. And we do not know the exact place, but it will be in the Cascade Mountains where there will be very few people around."

"Okay, that helps a bit," Fredricks said. "How many days do you think this rescue might take?"

"We hope no more than two or three. One day to find the child, and one, or possibly two, to get him out of the mountains and to a meeting point."

"So, it is a boy?"

"Yes, a teenage boy. His father misses him dearly."

"And how dearly does he miss him? Maybe five thousand dollars a day dearly for each of us?"

Bakshi looked at Patel and Singh. They had talked about how much they would be willing to pay these men to hike into the mountains and grab the boy. This requested amount was actually less than they thought they would have to pay. With the ransom they were going to request, paying these men twenty or thirty thousand dollars was very reasonable. But before they agreed to a price, they had decided in advance they would tell the men they needed to check with the father before making a deal.

"Let us go and talk with the father," Bakshi said. "Can we meet tomorrow to give you his answer?"

"Sure," Fredricks said. "Same time, same place?"

"That would be agreeable to us. Thank you for the beer."

With that, the three men stood, shook hands with Fredricks and Rogers, and headed out the rickety door. The heat again blasted them in the face.

When they got into the car and started the engine, Patel said, "Was that not the worst beer you have ever tasted? I thought Americans were beer connoisseurs?"

"Yes, it was bad," Bakshi said as they drove down the gravel drive to head to Moses Lake where they would be staying for the near future. "What did you think of their fee request?"

"I thought it was very reasonable," Singh said.

"Yes, I did too," Patel said. "Can we stop someplace on the way to our hotel so that I can buy something to get that foul beer taste out of my mouth? I wonder if any stores here carry Kingfisher."

"My guess is no," Singh said. "But we will need to eat dinner soon. That will help with the bad taste. We will find a restaurant in Moses Lake."

As the three Indian men headed to their hotel, Fredricks and Rogers sat in the camp chairs and cracked another Keystone.

"So, what do you think?" Rogers asked.

"I think they'll go for it. I was watching their faces when I mentioned the money. The guy who did all the talking didn't seem surprised or worried."

"This dude who wants his kid back must have deep pockets. Maybe an oil magnate or something?"

"I don't think they produce much oil in India. But yes, he must have money to be sending lackeys here to do his bidding. Maybe we should've asked for more. I don't like the idea of leaving money on the table."

"I'm perfectly happy with five grand a day," Roger said.

"Yeah, I guess I am too. Maybe we should be like those guys on TV and ask for the fee plus expenses."

"That's not a bad idea. And we need some cash up front. Maybe half to start and the other half when we deliver the kid to his old man."

"Exactly what I was thinking. We'll make that part of the deal. And listen, Bart, we can't tell anyone about this. I know they want us to think this is some sort of a rescue mission, but it is a kidnapping any way you look at it. We get caught, and that's some serious time in the big house."

"No kidding. That's the last thing I need. But the money is good and worth it, I think."

"Okay, so when we get more information about where this kid is, we'll know what we need to prepare. If it is in the mountains, we might need some supplies."

"I'm not in the greatest shape," Rogers said. "Hope we don't have to hike some of those mountains."

"You'll do fine. It'll be my ass dragging if there's a bunch of hiking. We'll figure that out later. Now, let's go get something to eat."

*

Bakshi, Patel and Singh arrived precisely at the same time as the day previous. But, when they drove down the driveway, there was no large green SUV sitting next to the old barn.

"Do you think they are having second thoughts?" Singh asked.

"No, they are most likely just running late. Maybe getting more beer."

"I hope not," Patel said. "I cannot stomach any more of that swill."

The three men got out of the Explorer, walked up to the barn door, and opened it. No one was there, so they got back in the vehicle, started it, and sat in the cool air conditioning.

"I thought Mumbai was hot," Singh said. "The temperature gauge says it is a hundred and four out there."

"Will it be this hot in three weeks?" Patel asked.

"I don't know," Bakshi said. "But most likely it will be cooler in the mountains."

"We have a great deal of work to do between now and then," Singh said. "We need to determine how we are going to track the boy. And we have to build the plan for how best to take him. I don't trust that our two friends have the capacity to create such a plan. We will make it and ask them to follow it. We can make it part of the specifications for getting paid at the end."

The previous night, the men had agreed that Fredricks and Rogers would be paid one third of the fee requested in advance and two-thirds upon the successful delivery of the Sloan boy.

"We will need to get phones and a GPS unit so they know where they are and where they need to be," Bakshi had said at dinner the night before.

"It would also be good for us to have some way to track them," Singh said. "Maybe without them knowing."

"That is an excellent idea," Bakshi said. "I do not think they will run with our money before the job is complete, but this will be a way to assure we can find them if they do."

They sat in the vehicle's air conditioning for a few minutes before they heard tires crunching on the gravel road behind them. The green Suburban pulled up, parked next to them, and Fredricks and Rogers got out, waved at them, and headed into the barn.

Again, they all sat in a semi-circle, each man in the chair they had occupied twenty-four hours earlier. There was no offer of beer this time, which made Patel very happy.

"So, before you tell us if you have accepted our fee request, we have a few items to discuss," Fredricks said, finally breaking the silence.

"Certainly," Bakshi said. "We have some items to discuss as well."

Bakshi spoke first, telling Fredricks and Rogers that they would pay the daily five-thousand-dollar fee, but to assure the men completed the assignment, they were only willing to pay for two days and would only advance one-third of the fee.

Fredricks counter-offered, saying that one-third of the fee up front was fine, but they wanted four days pay and all their expenses covered.

"Gas, food, and equipment if we have to hike into the mountains," Fredricks said. "We'll keep sales receipts and expect to be paid back when we deliver the kid."

After thinking about it for a minute, Bakshi said, "That is agreeable to us. We will also purchase you new telephones and a GPS unit. These will help us stay in touch with you before and during the exercise. We hope to know exactly where the boy is at all times, and we will be able to get you very close when the time comes."

"Sounds good," Fredricks said. "So, when do we get our initial payment?"

"Three days before you are to move on rescuing the boy. That will give you time to purchase any gear you need and make any other plans for being gone from your work."

"Okay, when do we meet again?"

"One week from today. Right here at the same time."

"And since you brought the beer last time, it will be our pleasure to reciprocate," said Patel.

CHAPTER 12

Luke was in a staff meeting at his office listening to one of the biologists as he droned on about his research into the strange disappearance of jackrabbits in the region. Luke was actually quite interested in the biologist's research, but sometimes he thought the science folks liked to talk just to hear themselves talk—and to impress the regional director. As if talking more about something would make them more valuable.

The biologist was heading into the second half hour of what should have been a ten-minute presentation when Luke's cell phone started buzzing in his pocket. He looked at the phone and saw it was Cale calling. He probably wanted to discuss the details of their upcoming trip. Luke wanted to chat with Cale, but taking personal calls, even if he did so after walking out of the meeting room, was frowned upon. Instead, Luke found the pre-loaded text message on his phone that said, "In a meeting, will call back" and pushed send.

He was thinking about his high-mountain hunt with Cale when

one of the secretaries stuck her head in the door, looked straight at Luke, and gave him a "come here" with a curved pointer finger.

"Ah, thank you SOOO much," Luke said to his savior after he got out of the room. "I was about to fall asleep."

"There's a call for you. Someone has found another elk."

"Crap. Okay. I'll take it at my desk."

Luke walked to his cubicle, pushed the button on the flashing line, and said, "This is Officer McCain. How can I help you?"

"Yeah, this is Owen Wilson," a man's voice crackled over the phone.

"Yessir, Mr. Wilson. You found a dead elk?"

"No wise cracks about me calling from Hollywood or anything?" Wilson asked.

"Long story, but I would never do that to you. Now, where is this elk?"

Wilson explained that he and his wife had been huckleberry picking near Copper City, not far from the William O. Douglas Wilderness when they ran across the freshly shot cow elk. "We saw a black bear working on something," Wilson said. "It ran off when we walked over the hill. We went down to check out what it was doing there and found the elk."

"How do you know the elk was poached?"

"I'm a hunter, so I know what a rifle shot looks like in an animal. Even though the bear had started in on the belly, pulling the entrails out to eat, I could see a bullet hole in the neck. And, if I am not mistaken, the backstraps were removed by someone, not an animal."

"I don't think you're mistaken, Mr. Wilson. That would be the fifth elk poached in the past two weeks that we know of, all with the backstraps and some of the hindquarters removed."

"You know, this one was missing a good chunk of hindquarter. I just thought the bear or a coyote had chewed it up."

"Did you happen to see anyone else up there in that area? Any vehicles that you can remember?"

"As we were driving up the road, we did see a couple of other rigs heading down. One was an older white Toyota pickup—I don't know their models—and the other was a big silver Dodge dually, maybe a 3500."

"Remember anything about the drivers?"

"No, not really. There were two guys in the Dodge. I think there was a man and woman in the white Toyota, but if I had to pick them out of a lineup, I couldn't do it for a million bucks. You know how it is—you look at a face, and then ten seconds later it's gone because you figure you'll never see them again and who cares?"

"I do. Well, if you'll give me a better description of exactly where the elk is, I'll try to get there before that bear totally destroys the carcass."

Wilson gave him the location, and after Luke asked, Wilson told him the size and type of his shoe so that Luke could eliminate it from the scene—if there were any tracks there at all. The two men exchanged phone numbers, and Luke thanked Wilson for calling.

"Hope you can find out who is doing this," Wilson said.

"Me too," Luke said and hung up.

He really didn't want to drive all the way up to the site of the elk kill. It was going to take a couple of hours, and he believed the black bear would return to the carcass and could have it half-eaten or even dragged off and buried in a pile of brush and leaves by the time he got there. On the other hand, everyone else was still in the marathon meeting. That was the last place he wanted to be.

"Will you please let the captain know that I took that call, and I'm on my way up to another elk carcass near the Douglas Wilderness?" Luke said to the receptionist as he was heading out the door. "I'll call him when I get back down to let him know what I've found."

On his way out of town, Luke stopped by his house, changed quickly into more appropriate hiking attire, grabbed his bigger backpack, loaded Jack into the back seat of his truck, and headed for the highway.

With a bear in the vicinity, he always felt a bit safer with the big yellow dog at his side. Jack always either heard or smelled a bear before Luke saw them, and it gave him more time to be prepared. Black bears almost always ran from humans, but occasionally, when protecting cubs or guarding a kill, they had been known to charge.

As was the case with all state wildlife officers, Luke carried a state-issued sidearm. His was a Glock semi-automatic pistol in .45 caliber. In addition to the holstered pistol, his utility belt also carried pepper spray, a Taser, a flashlight, handcuffs and an ASP collapsible baton. His backpack included just about everything a person might need to survive a night or two in the mountains—raingear, an extra couple layers of polar fleece, a waterproof stocking hat and gloves, some freeze-dried food, three bottles of water, a backpacker's stove, a few energy bars, and some special dog bars for Jack. For safety and communication, he carried a GPS unit for marking and tracking his movement, a handheld radio, and his cellphone. In the storage bin in his truck, McCain always kept a sleeping bag rated to minus 20 degrees, a packable one-man waterproof tent, a down vest, and a heavy coat. If he ever thought he was going to need that extra gear, there was room in his pack for it too.

In his truck, Luke also had a state-issued Remington Model 870 12-gauge shotgun and a Springfield Armory .223 rifle with a suppressor. Depending on the situation, Luke would sometimes carry one or the other long gun into the field. If he had to put an injured animal down, and it was likely going to be in close quarters, Luke preferred the shotgun, loaded alternately with buckshot and slugs. Otherwise, the rifle was more precise and could be used at longer ranges. He doubted that he would need to carry anything other than his pepper spray and pistol while doing his investigation around the newly found elk, but at least he had the option if he felt it was necessary once he arrived on the scene.

Before Luke got too far up the highway, he called Sara to let her know he might not make it down out of the mountains before late in the evening.

"I have Jack," he said. "So don't worry about us for dinner."

"I never do," Sara said. "Besides, I have a late afternoon meeting, and I might just grab dinner with the other agents in town."

The FBI had brought two additional agents into Yakima to work with Yakama tribal police and other agencies in the area on the issue of the missing and murdered indigenous women. State and federal legislators had finally started recognizing the situation and were putting up funds to help try to figure out what was going on.

Sara had been successful in helping close a few of the cases over the four years she had been in the local office, but still there were over two dozen open cases where the family members rightfully were hoping to learn what might have happened to their loved ones.

"Okay, that works," Luke said. "Jack and I will probably just grab a bite at Whistlin' Jacks as we come down the hill."

"I'd much rather be up there with you," Sara said. "But duty calls."

"Ditto," Luke said. "Have a good meeting and dinner."

"I will. Love you." And she was gone.

He'd driven out of cell service by the time he remembered that Cale had called him. Oh well, he'd call his buddy tonight or tomorrow. He was definitely looking forward to accompanying Cale into the high Cascades. It had been several years since he had been up into the northern part of the mountain range. It was incredible country—peaceful and beautiful one moment and unbelievably treacherous and deadly the next.

What Luke loved most about the North Cascades was that because of its remoteness, very few people ever ventured up there. At times, it was like it was his own private wilderness.

He especially liked seeing the wildlife that made that part of the state their home, for at least part of the year anyway. From his studies, Luke knew that the high Cascades, particularly the northern part of the range, was home to at least seventy-five species of mammals and two hundred species of birds that either passed through or used the North Cascades for a breeding area. Luke had once seen a wolverine up high in the mountains, and he'd seen several wolves, a few cougars, a dozen or more black bears, and a handful of bobcats. Biologist reports indicate there are a few Canada lynx summering in the region too. Luke hoped they might spot one of those on this trip.

The high mountains were also great summering grounds for mule deer. Hunters with the gumption had a great chance at a mule deer buck with a rack of three-point or better in the short season in September. This was the hunt Cale was looking forward to with great anticipation.

It seemed Luke had driven forever up the Forest Service road. He checked his GPS and saw that he was getting close to the pin that he'd put on the map after talking to Owen Wilson.

Luke chuckled to himself as he thought about the phone call with the man. With the same name as a current Hollywood movie star, Wilson surely got plenty of comments about the coincidence. Luckily, *The Rifleman* was so old, not many people made the association with Luke McCain. Although in recent years, with the unbelievable number of channels on cable and satellite TV, reruns of the old black and white TV show seemed to be popping up almost daily.

When he found a place to pull off the dirt road near his mark on the GPS map, Luke stopped and looked around. According to Wilson, the elk carcass was to the north about six hundred yards from the road. Luke climbed out of the truck, let Jack out, and then pulled his pack out of the back of the truck and put it on. He decided that since there was a good chance the bear had been back to the elk carcass, he would take his metal detector with him this time. It might save him from having to dig through a bunch of blood and hair while looking for the bullet.

The climb up the hill wasn't too tough. In fact, Luke was hardly breathing heavy. It was evident that his extra cardio work in advance of the hunt in the high Cascades was paying off. Once he topped the hill, he stopped and looked around. Wilson said the elk was in a small aspen grove, but as Luke surveyed the area, he spotted three different patches of aspen. But only one of the groves had a large black bear standing in it.

With the pepper spray in his left hand and the .45 pistol in his right, Luke slowly walked down toward the aspen grove. The bear hadn't smelled Luke yet, as the slight breeze was blowing back uphill on the rising currents. Finally, the bruin heard him, or more likely, the bear heard Jack running around in the trees near Luke.

Luke whistled softly, then said, "Jack, come."

The dog ran back to Luke and stayed by his side.

As Luke and Jack approached, the bear didn't look happy to be giving up the ready-made smorgasbord for a second time in a few hours.

"Hey!" Luke yelled and waved his arms. "Get outta here!"

Jack started for the bear, but Luke said the dog's name and told him to heel.

"Don't go picking a fight with that thing," Luke said. "One swipe from a paw, and you'd be toast."

As he said that, he noticed the hackles were up all along the yellow dog's back. Jack was growling a low, rumbling snarl.

They kept slowly walking toward the bear, but the animal just looked at Luke and Jack like they were of no real concern.

Luke yelled and waved his arms several times as they got closer. The bear didn't budge. Luke thought about trying to give the bear a shot of the pepper spray, but it had a limited range, and with the breeze blowing back at him, Luke might just end up spraying himself. Having watery eyes with a black bear within charging distance would not be healthy.

Luke considered his options and decided to fire a shot into the ground from his pistol. At the sound of the shot, the bear stood up on its hind legs and stared daggers through Luke who fired the pistol again. Finally, the bear turned and loped off through the aspens, up the hill and out of sight.

"Let's go, boy."

They headed to the elk carcass, and, as Luke had feared, the bear had eaten quite a bit of the animal. It hadn't gotten to the neck yet, however. Just as Owen Wilson had said, there clearly was a bullet hole in the neck. Before he got any closer to the dead animal, Luke looked around the ground for footprints or anything out of the ordinary. He saw plenty of tracks in the torn-up dirt, but they were all from the black bear.

When he got to the elk, Luke lifted its head and looked at the other side of the neck. There was no exit wound, so he pulled the metal detector out of his pack, turned it on, and ran it over the elk's neck. The gauges moved, and the clicking quickened as he passed the search coil over the bullet hole. The bullet was in there somewhere. Instead of taking the time to dig around in the neck right there, Luke pulled out his knife, severed the elk's neck and head from the body, pulled a large plastic bag out of his pack, put the head and neck in the bag, and placed it in the pack.

Finally, he took a closer look at the back and hind end of the elk, but the damage the bear had done made it practically impossible to see what meat had been taken. He would have to take Wilson's word for it that the backstraps had been removed.

As Luke worked on the elk, Jack stood close by, staring off in the direction that the bear had run. Luke could see the dog's nose working in the breeze. His hackles were still raised.

"C'mon, boy. Let's leave this elk to that big ol' bruin."

When they got back up to the top of the hill, Luke turned around and looked into the aspen patch where the carcass was. It didn't surprise him to see the black bear right back where it had been, gorging itself on the fresh elk meat.

CHAPTER 13

Skip Harvey's wilderness school was as busy as it could get through the summer, and even though he was tired from all the trips into the mountains, he was glad to have been so busy.

"I am really looking forward to getting the last two classes over with," he said to Amy Graham as he was running through a list of two hundred and eighty-seven emails. "Geez, how do these things build up so fast?"

"If you'd check your emails each day, they wouldn't build up. Most, you can probably just delete."

"I think I can delete all of them, but just as soon as I do, I'd miss something important."

"The group next week is made up of some young men who are about to head off to college in a couple weeks," Graham said. "I think this is just a getaway and some male bonding time for them."

"Good to know. I guess I won't push them too hard. And the last group is the two boys from Bellevue?"

"Yes. And I called that boat operator in Chelan. He's all set to haul you guys up the lake, drop you off, and shuttle you back."

"Perfect. It'll be a fun boat ride, and it will be good to see some new country, for them and for me."

Harvey had been thinking about doing something special for the boys. Since there were only two of them, he thought they might like to see Lake Chelan and then spend their time hiking and camping in the Lake Chelan-Sawtooth Wilderness.

"Sounds like fun," Graham said. "Wish I could go with you."

"Maybe on the next group of all women, we'll give it a try. Once I get it scouted out, it should be a nice addition to our offerings."

"Looking forward to it," she said.

"Now, why am I getting emails in whatever this foreign language is?" Harvey asked in a frustrated tone, pointing at the computer monitor. "I can't read this."

"You probably need to upgrade your security," she said. "I'll take care of it next week when you are gone."

"Thank you. Now, let's go over the supplies for the college-bound boys. And no, we aren't packing any beer."

*

The closer the trip got, the more excited Skyler Sloan became. He talked with his buddy Tory Green every day, and they had gone over the list of items that they were supposed to bring again and again.

"Did your sleeping bag come?" Sloan asked.

The boys had ordered special mummy bags from Amazon that were guaranteed to keep them warm if the temperatures dropped below zero.

"Yeah, it came yesterday," Green said. "I pulled it out and climbed into it. There's not much room to be rolling around in them. I felt like I was in a coffin."

"I know, I'm worried I might not be able to sleep in mine. It's so confining."

"My mom said not to worry about it. We'll be so tired, we should be able to sleep in anything. Plus, she said we might be glad we have such a warm bag."

"I guess. I've been putting stuff into my backpack too. But I think I'm going to take just a few things and stick to the list the school sent over. I think they're going to load us up with food and other stuff. I don't want it to be too heavy."

"Good thing they told you not to bring your pistol. That would be added weight too."

The boys talked about other things such as what boots they were going to wear, clothes they were going to take, and how far they were going to be hiking each day.

"My mom got me one of those GPS deals that allows short texts to be sent via satellite," Green said. "She's read that there are grizzly bears up in those high mountains and wants me to check in every day to let her know I haven't been turned into bear crap."

Sloan laughed. "I can use it too, to contact my folks, although they don't seem to be as worried about me."

"Have you been to Lake Chelan before?" Green asked.

The boys had learned just two weeks earlier that they were going to meet up with Skip Harvey in Chelan, their starting point for the week in the wilderness.

"Yeah, we went there for a family reunion when I was in the seventh grade," Sloan said. "It's a really cool place. The lake is so clear, and when we were there, there were about a thousand jet skis running around. We rented some for the day, and it was a blast."

"Whoa, that would be cool. Maybe the dude with the school will let us try that for a day."

"I don't know," Sloan said. "It sounds like we're going to be taking a jet boat ride up the lake to where we'll be dropped off to start our hike. I'm guessing there won't be enough time."

"It's cool that your dad is letting us drive there to meet the guy."

"Yeah, I think my folks didn't want to make the drive. Ever

since I got my driver's license, they've been really cool about me driving places, just so they don't have to. I'm constantly having to run to the store for stuff my mom needs."

"Me too," Green said. "But I don't mind. I like finally being able to drive."

✳

While they waited for the next meeting with Fredricks and Rogers in Ephrata, the three men from India had been hard at work trying to get as much information as possible on the wilderness school and where it was the boy was going to be.

"I've been following the emails between the school owner and the boy's parents," Patel said. "It has been agreed that the school leader will meet up with the boys and the father in a town called Chelan. From there, the boys and the leader will ride in a boat up a lake and be dropped off to begin their school experience."

"Where is this Chelan?" Bakshi asked.

"Actually, it is not far from here. I looked it up. It seems to be a resort town on a large lake only sixty-one miles from Ephrata."

"That is good news," Singh said. "Fredricks and Rogers probably have been there and know where they are going."

"Yes, but that is just the starting point," Bakshi said. "We need to figure out where might be a good place for the abduction."

"Maybe we should leave that up to them," Singh said.

The three men thought about that for a minute and then Bakshi said, "No, I want to have at least some idea where this will take place. There can be no witnesses."

"There is no way of telling where in the mountains they will be," Patel said. "From what I can tell, there is very little phone service in that remote country, so tracking a cellphone will be next to impossible."

"Maybe the men should take the boy in Chelan before they get into the remote country," Singh said.

"I have considered that," Bakshi said. "But I fear there are too many people there. And if the boy is with his father, that will not work. I still think it needs to be while they are on their excursion."

"Let me keep monitoring the emails to see what else I might be able to find out," Patel said. "There is still time to learn more that might help."

"Yes, do that," Bakshi said. "And we will tell Fredricks more about what we want them to do when we meet again. I am going to check on our money to see if it has arrived."

CHAPTER 14

The digital mileage screen read three-point-two miles when the phone started beeping. Luke was jogging at a good pace, and while he was breathing harder than normal, he felt like he could keep going for a while. He really wanted to ignore the phone, but when he looked at the caller ID, he pushed pause on the treadmill and answered the phone.

"Hey, Cale. I was going to call you last night, but I was working in the mountains and didn't get home 'til late."

"No problem, buddy. I just wanted to confirm a few things before we head out for the mountains. Sounds like you're breathing heavy. I didn't catch you in bed, did I?"

"I wish. Sara left for work an hour ago, so I'm getting some miles in. I know you, you'll run up those hills, and I don't want to get totally left behind."

Harris wanted to confirm where and when the two would meet and double-check who was bringing what supplies. He had prepared a list of items he wanted to have during the backcountry hunt and had sent it to Luke two days earlier. After discussing it, they decided that each man would bring their own freeze-dried foods, backpacking stove, and water. Instead of packing a larger tent for two, they decided each man would carry their own tent, along with their sleeping bag, pad, and other necessities. Luke would need to make sure there was enough food for Jack, too.

Water wouldn't be an issue for Jack, but the men would need to have water purifying equipment to help eliminate the need to pack a bunch of water. Boiling the water each day or adding iodine were ways to make sure the water taken from a lake or stream was free of giardia or other harmful parasites and bacteria, but that took time and often made the water taste flat or unpleasant.

Water purifying pumps were another option, and that is what most backcountry hikers, hunters, and anglers used. Luke had purchased a Katadyn water filter the year before and found that the filter system worked great. It was light, and while it only held ten ounces of water, he had taken a couple of other empty plastic water bottles and filled them from the filter to make sure he had enough.

"We need to leave enough room in the packs for your deer meat," Luke said. "And I'm going to pack my shotgun to see if I can get a grouse or two for dinner."

"That sounds good," Harris said. "Hopefully I can get my buck in the first day or two, and we can get you off the mountain and back home to that beautiful wife of yours."

"Don't worry about that. I think she actually likes having me and Jack out of the house for a while. Besides, she's really busy at work."

The two men discussed Sara's work with the Yakama Nation for a bit, and Harris told Luke a little about some of the things he'd been doing with the WSP special unit.

As he listened to Cale describe one of his recent investigations—a case involving trafficking girls and young women out of the country to be sold as sex slaves—Luke wondered if he could do what Cale was doing.

"Man, it sure was good you found those girls before they were gone out of the country," Luke said.

"It was crazy, and unfortunately, we've just scratched the surface. We can talk about all of this more in a couple weeks," Harris said. "We should have plenty of time to catch up. I'm looking forward to it."

"Me too," Luke said. "Talk to you soon."

After hanging up, Luke decided to bag out on the rest of his workout, as he needed to get to work. Three miles was good enough for today, although he was sure he'd still end up dragging behind Harris who was one of those people who was always in top shape.

His friend was not quite as tall as Luke, probably six-foot-two, and while Cale looked like he might weigh a hundred and eighty pounds, it was more likely that he was pushing two hundred. There was very little fat there and plenty of muscle. Cale's chiseled facial features and strong jaw gave him the looks of a matinee idol, which always drew attention from the girls in school.

When Luke last saw his buddy, he still had his hair cut short and tight, probably from his days in the Army. Old habits were hard to break. And, while his friend was not married, Luke knew he had had a couple fairly serious relationships since he'd returned to Washington. Cale had told him that in his line of work it was difficult on the women. They always worried whether he'd be coming home each night, so the relationships never seemed to last.

Before the phone call, Luke had been thinking again about what Austin had said to him the previous night about the elk steaks. He looked out the window, saw that Austin's truck was there, changed into some dry shorts, a T-shirt and flip-flops, and walked across the street.

Austin's mom Jessie answered the door.

"Hi, Luke."

"Hi, Jessie. I'm looking for Austin. Is he around?"

"Yes, he is. Let me go get him."

"Thanks, and thanks for that peach cobbler. It was fantastic!"

Fifteen seconds later, Austin came to the door.

"Hey, Luke," he said with an inquisitive look. "What's up?"

"Last night when you brought the cobbler over, I think you said you had eaten elk steak for dinner."

"Yeah, that's right. It was really good too."

"I don't mean to be nosey, but do you know where it came from?"

"Geez, I don't know. Mom said Charlie brought it home."

"Did you see it when he brought it in? Was it frozen?"

"No, I didn't see it. Want me to ask Mom?"

"No, that's okay."

"Are you thinking he maybe got it from someone who killed it out of season?"

"I don't know what to think. I'm working a case with at least five elk poached around here in the last two weeks, and when I heard you had steak for dinner last night, I started to think more about it. I know you didn't get one last season. Do you remember anyone else giving you some elk meat last fall?"

"Not that I know of. If we'd gotten some, I'm sure we would have eaten it by now, and that's the first elk we've had in over a year."

"I'm starting to believe that whoever is killing the elk is doing it to sell the meat. Charlie might have gotten it totally on the up and up, but it would be good to know."

"How about I ask him tonight? You know, kind of like, 'Wow, Charlie. That was really good elk steak last night. Where'd you get it?' and see what he says."

"I guess it's worth a try. Don't let him know about my investigation though, please. I don't want him to think I suspect him of anything, because I really don't."

"Sure," Austin said. "I'll let you know."

Luke thanked him and headed to his truck. His hunting trip with Cale was coming up quickly, and he really wanted to get this elk poaching thing solved. He'd sent the bullet from the elk's neck to the lab in Ashland but was still waiting for the results. Just by the looks of it, he believed it to be from a larger-caliber rifle. His guess was that if the lab had enough to work with on the mushroomed bullet, it would be a match to the bullet taken from the first elk he had investigated.

Today was going to be an in-town day for Luke. He had some meetings at the regional office in the morning, and then he had to be in court to testify in the case against the two men he had nabbed poaching spring Chinook salmon in the Yakima River. The men were facing jail time because of their bad habits of fishing out of season, catching more than their limits, and not paying their tickets and fines. The prosecutor had asked that Luke be there to tell the story of arresting the men.

Many times, in cases like this, there would be a last-minute plea arrangement between the court-appointed public defender and the prosecutor, and there would be no need to testify. This meant that Luke, and any other officers or witnesses who had been called to testify in court, would not be needed, in effect wasting a whole lot of their time.

Luke understood the importance of being there and had been through it many times. But still, he always felt his time would be much better spent up in the woods or on the water, checking hunters and anglers.

So, when, after sitting in a waiting area for almost an hour, Eric Severson, one of five attorneys in the county prosecutor's office, came to Luke and said he wouldn't be needed, it didn't surprise him.

Severson was a small, trim, bespectacled man who always wore a dark suit, stiff white shirt, and a bow tie. Today his tie was bright yellow with blue spots.

"Sorry to waste your time, Officer McCain," Severson said. "The men have agreed to serve six months of jail time in order to have a couple other charges dropped."

"At least you got 'em for something," Luke said.

"They will also be losing their licenses for the next three years, so keep an eye out for them. Once they're out of jail, my guess is not having a license isn't going to stop them from fishing."

"Will do," Luke said, and he headed for the door.

Severson was right. Luke had seen it many times during his career—once a poacher, always a poacher. At least, he believed it to be the case with the hardcore ones. Which got him to thinking he should go back through the hundreds of poaching arrest records and see who had been arrested in the past ten years for poaching elk. Maybe their suspect would be among those names.

When he got back to the office, he checked in with Stan Hargraves. A fellow WDFW enforcement officer out of the Region 3 office, Hargraves had a few years seniority on Luke and had worked in the area longer.

"How's it coming on catching that elk poacher?" Hargraves asked as Luke wandered over to Hargraves' cubicle and plopped down in the chair next to his desk. A stout man in his mid-50s with black hair and '70s-style sideburns framing his round face, Hargraves looked like he'd be more comfortable sitting in the driver's seat of an 18-wheeler or an International Harvester combine rather than having a badge pinned to his chest.

"Not great. It's like pushing a tank down the road. Making a little headway, but it's really slow going."

Even though Luke had been taking the calls, it wasn't just his case. All five officers out of the Region 3 office were responsible for trying to catch the poachers, but each of the others was patrolling other areas and working other cases in the huge region for which they were responsible.

"Well, let me know if you need a hand," Hargraves said. "I'm just doing some checking of boats down on the Columbia."

"I'm thinking the poacher, or poachers—it most likely is a team—are selling the meat. Can you recall arresting anyone in the past that was killing elk and selling the meat?"

Hargraves thought about it a minute and then started tapping keys on the keyboard in front of his monitor.

"There were a couple of guys I arrested, probably ten years ago, that were shooting elk and selling the meat. But I think they learned their lesson after a hefty fine."

"Names?"

"Buzz Seifert and Eddy Cruz."

"Thanks. I'll look them up and maybe go have a chat with them."

"I'll keep thinking too, and anything comes to mind, I'll text ya," Hargraves said.

Luke found addresses for both men, still in the local area. There were phone numbers attached to the electronic file too, so he decided he'd try calling them.

The first number, for Seifert, rang and rang, and then an automated voice came on and said that the number was no longer active. So, he hung up and punched in the number for Cruz.

"Hello?" a man's voice answered after the third ring.

"Mr. Cruz, this is Officer McCain with the Department of Fish and Wildlife. Do you have a couple minutes to chat?"

"Yeah, I guess so. Listen, Officer McCain, I've done nothing wrong. I learned my lesson a long time ago and I got kids now. I'm teaching them the right way to be a hunter."

"I appreciate that, Mr. Cruz. I'm not calling because we suspect you of any wrongdoing. I just want to chat."

"Okay. What about?"

"Some elk being killed out of season."

"See, there you go. You do suspect me, don't you?"

"No, not at all. Just wondering if you have heard anything about any elk being killed recently, or anyone selling any elk meat."

There was a long pause on the phone. Luke knew he had struck a nerve with the man.

"Have you talked to Buzz Seifert?" Cruz asked.

"No, I tried the only phone number we had for him, and it said the number was no longer active. I planned to drive over to his place and talk to him too. Listen, Mr. Cruz. We're just trying to get anything that might help. We don't suspect you or Mr. Seifert."

"I haven't seen Buzz in five years or more. Frankly, he was the one that was the brains behind our deal, as stupid as he is. I just followed along, which makes me even stupider, I guess. But if there was a man who liked to kill things just to kill them, it would be Buzz. I saw him shoot the neighbor's cat one time, just to watch the thing start jumping around. He laughed and laughed. It was sick, man."

"Is he still living in Union Gap?"

"Last I knew he was. He lived with his old lady and her parents, kinda down there behind the Peppermint Stick drive-in."

"You wouldn't have a phone number, would you?"

"No, sir. After we got in trouble for shooting them elk, I decided my life would be a lot better without Buzz Seifert in it."

"Probably a smart move. Okay, well, thanks, Mr. Cruz. I appreciate your thoughts. If you happen to hear anything, please give me a call at this number, any time. And good luck to you and your kids this hunting season."

"Thanks," Cruz said. "I will."

Luke checked the time on his phone. He still had time to run down to the last known address of Buzz Seifert.

On the way to Union Gap, Luke thought about the conversation with Eddy Cruz. If Seifert was one of those people who liked to kill things just for the fun of it, chances were good he was still doing that. Sometimes, if they started out at a young age killing small animals for the fun of it, those people would move on and up, killing bigger animals. Some, as history showed, would even turn into serial killers.

Luke wondered what Seifert had been up to the past decade. His file showed no more arrests, and his only contact with any law enforcement was for a couple of traffic violations. Maybe, like his ex-partner, Cruz, Seifert had seen the error in his ways and started walking the straight and narrow.

Luke arrived at Seifert's last-known address in Union Gap and appraised the small 1950s rambler. The roof of the house was at least a decade past needing to be re-shingled, and the teal paint on the horizontal siding was chipping away at the edges, showing cracks here and there. A window shaker air conditioner groaned in one of the smaller windows at the end of the house, while the other windows were lined on the inside with silver reflective insulation in an effort to keep the summer sun from heating the house to triple digits. In front of the house, the lawn was almost dead, and a long-neglected rose bush sat next to a crumbling concrete path to the front doorstep.

Luke looked up and down at the other houses in the little neighborhood. All were similar in size and shape, but most were being kept up much nicer than the home that once, and maybe still, housed Buzz Seifert. Next door, an orange cat lay in the grass in the shade of a big maple tree.

"I guess Buzz hasn't killed all the neighbor cats," Luke said to himself as he parked his truck, put his hat on, climbed out and walked to the front door.

Luke could hear muffled voices inside the house, probably from a television. He rang the doorbell, but it didn't seem to be working, so he knocked. A little dog started yapping, and a woman with an aged, gravelly voice started yelling, "Shut up, Tinker!"

A few seconds later, amongst the shrill yaps of Tinker, Luke could hear footsteps slowly plodding to the door.

"Dammit, Tinker. Quiet!"

Yap, yap, yap, yap, yap, yap.

The door slowly opened, and a lady who could have been 68 or 88—Luke couldn't tell—with a little pot licker brown and black dog standing next to her, looked at him and said, "He doesn't live here no more."

Luke started to say something, but she cut him off. The woman had longish, gray, scraggly hair and was wearing a big pink and purple floral house coat. Or maybe it was a muumuu. If she had any teeth left in her mouth, Luke couldn't see them.

Yap, yap, yap, yap, yap, yap.

"That's who you're looking for, isn't it? That idiot ex-son-in-law of mine?" She had a scowl on her face, lips sunken in without the necessary teeth to keep them in their natural place.

"I'm looking for Buzz Seifert," Luke said.

Yap, yap, yap, yap, yap, yap.

Looking at the little brown and black dog, she hollered, "Tinker, shut up!" Then she turned back to Luke and said, "That's the idiot. Haven't seen him in a coon's age. Glad for it too. Worthless piece of shit."

"Any idea where he might be?"

Yap, yap, yap, yap, yap, yap.

"Tinker, I swear to God, I'm going to kill you if you don't shut up!"

For some reason, that worked. The little dog stopped barking, turned, and scurried back into the darkness of the house.

"Last I heard he was a livin' up in the mountains in some cabin. My daughter said the stupid bastard was a livin' off the land."

"Would your daughter know where this cabin is?"

"Don't know. Need to ask her yourself."

The lady gave Luke her daughter's phone number and then quickly closed the door.

Luke hated to do it, but he knocked on the door again.

Yap, yap, yap, yap, yap, yap.

"Tinker! Shut up!"

The woman opened the door. The little dog was again standing next to her.

Yap, yap, yap, yap, yap, yap.

"I'm sorry, ma'am. I didn't get your name, or your daughter's."

Tinker kept yapping as the lady gave Luke her name and her daughter's.

"Is that everything?" she asked.

Luke thanked her again and told her it was.

As she was closing the door, she said to the dog, "Tinker, you little asshole."

When he got back to the truck, Luke fired it up, turned the AC on high, and waited for the inside of the cab to cool. Then he pulled his cellphone out and dialed the number the woman had given him.

The daughter's name was Jolene. Luke didn't know if she had

kept Seifert's last name or not. The old lady had only given him her first name, and he wasn't going to go knock on the door again.

The phone rang four, then five times, and Luke was about to hang up when a very tired-sounding woman answered.

"Hull-oh."

"Jolene?"

"Yeah, who's this?"

"My name is Luke McCain. I'm an enforcement officer with the Department of Fish and Wildlife."

"What'd that dumb sumbitch do now?"

"Are you asking about your husband, Buzz Seifert?"

"He ain't my husband no more. After he got caught killing those elk and costing us all our savings, I got rid of his sorry ass. What'd he do?"

"Nothing that we're aware of. I just would like to talk to him. Do you know where I can reach him?"

"I don't think he has a phone, or if he does, he's not given me the number. Not that I want it. Last I knew, he was living in an old cabin up in the Nile. One of his friend's grandparents used to live there, but when they kicked the bucket, Buzz and his buddy moved in. Rent free, I guess."

"You wouldn't happen to know the name of his buddy, would you?"

"Yep. His name is Lawrence Wilburn." She yawned a very audible yawn. "But everyone calls him Tiny."

"I'm sorry to have bothered you. Sounds like I woke you."

"I work the graveyard shift at the apple-packing warehouse. I need to get up and get going anyway. Gotta get some groceries and dog food to take to my mom. She worries about that little dog of hers. He's about the only thing that keeps her going."

"I met Tinker," Luke said. "Yes, you can tell she loves him dearly. Thanks, Jolene, and again, sorry to have woken you."

They hung up, and Luke headed back to the office. He needed to locate a cabin owned by someone named Wilburn.

CHAPTER 15

Bakshi, Patel and Singh had been busy during the week between meetings with the men in Ephrata. They were now able to track Skyler Sloan's cellphone, and they were working on being able to track the phone of Skip Harvey, the owner of the wilderness school.

It had taken Patel some time and serious computer skills, but Bakshi knew if anyone could do it, it would be his cousin.

"That is outstanding," Bakshi said after learning that Patel had figured out how to track the phones. "This will help immensely."

Their surveillance, which included following texts on the boy's phone, confirmed that everything was still a go. Sloan and his friend would be meeting Harvey in Chelan, where a hired boat would take them to a place called Stehekin, forty-three miles up-lake. That is where they would start their wilderness journey.

"At the meeting today, we need to make Fredricks and Rogers aware of this," Bakshi said. "But we must continue the charade that we are just getting the boy for a reunion with his father."

"I agree," said Singh. "I believe that if those two realized we were doing this for a ransom, they might just go rogue and do the deal on their own."

"I have thought of that," Bakshi said. "It is a concern."

The cash they would need to give the men for their supplies and the initial part of their operation had come in by wire to a Bank of America branch in Moses Lake three days earlier. After Bakshi retrieved the cash, the men had obtained some other surveillance equipment, including three tracking devices and two receivers. They planned to put one of the tracking devices on Fredricks' big Suburban and hoped to place a second device in one of the men's backpacks just before they left to follow the boy. With the devices placed strategically, they could keep track of the two men until they went after the boy and ensure they didn't disappear with their down payment. Plus, they could go find Fredricks and Rogers in the mountains if need be.

"We certainly do not want to have to do that," Patel had said as they discussed placing one of the tracking devices in Fredricks' or Rogers' equipment. "We are not prepared at all for that."

So that they could purchase the items in anonymity, the three Indian men had made the two-hundred-mile round trip to Spokane to get the equipment they needed. At the electronics store, they also purchased a GPS unit and two cellphones for which they pre-paid for four hours of call time. One phone they would give to the two men, and the other they would keep. All communication going forward would be via these phones.

On the GPS unit, Patel had loaded a map program of Washington State that included all National Forests, wilderness areas, boat launches, public roads, rivers, creeks, and, with a touch of the screen, would give contour lines indicating elevation changes. The men had studied the maps on where the boy and instructor would be dropped. They had determined they would instruct Fredricks and Rogers to take the boy on the first night they were in the wilderness. From there, the two men would be instructed to take the boy northeast to the closest Forest Service road, which was an estimated eleven miles from the drop-off point.

Bakshi and Singh would be waiting in the Explorer for Fredricks, Rogers, and the boy near the campground. From there, Bakshi's plan was to drive the boy north to a border crossing into Canada near Oroville. They would cross the border and take up refuge in Penticton, British Columbia, where they would negotiate the payment from the boy's father. Once the money was wired to a bank in India, the men would leave the boy and head east to Alberta, working their way back to Mumbai.

As he reviewed the plan again, Bakshi knew that it would not go exactly as he hoped it would. There were many moving parts and many unknowns. He believed the men, Fredricks and Rogers, would do their part as best they could because they were motivated by the money. What he didn't know, or could not know, was what kind of resistance they might be up against when they took the boy.

The other unknown was the country in which all of this was to take place. He could see it on their GPS map, and on satellite photos, but those were static images. He knew that wild animals, and possibly other people, roamed those same mountains. What challenges might they create?

"I am going to go get the beer for our meeting," said Patel as he grabbed the keys to the Explorer and headed out the door. "And it will be no more of that cheap American swill."

When he was gone, Singh turned to his friend and said, "So, Raj, now that we are about to put the plan in motion, what, honestly, do you think our odds are for success?"

"I have been thinking about that. There are many unknowns yet. Still, I believe we have a very good chance. Eighty to ninety percent is what I am thinking."

"That is good. Because if it were fifty-fifty, I would opt for shutting it down and going home. I will not speak for Darsh, but I believe he is of the same mind. I know he fears being in this wilderness alone, and even more, he fears prison."

"Yes, I know he does. I do as well. Let us hope it does not come to that."

When Patel returned with two six packs of Heineken in a cheap Styrofoam cooler packed with ice, the men gathered up everything they would be giving to Fredricks and Rogers, loaded it into the SUV, and headed to the barn outside Ephrata.

The green Suburban was sitting in front of the old barn when the three arrived precisely at six o'clock. In one quick move while the Explorer was still slowing to park next to the big Chevy, Patel swung out of the back seat and quickly placed the tracking device, which was affixed to a heavy-duty magnet, under the rear quarter panel on the driver's side of the green rig.

"It is done," he said to the other two men as they were exiting the Ford SUV.

"Do you have the money?" Singh asked. He already knew the answer, but he just wanted to double-check.

"Yes, but I do not want to give it to them until we have discussed the plan and reviewed the equipment."

Patel grabbed the white cooler full of ice and beer, and the three men entered the barn.

"Welcome!" Fredricks said. The short man stood behind one of the folding chairs and made a waving motion for the three men to sit down.

In the days since they had met last, the daytime temperatures had dropped down into the 80s. Still, the two men from Ephrata were sweating, and Patel thought they stunk of body odor and bad beer.

"We have brought some beer," Bakshi said, pointing to the cooler. "Help yourselves. We have much to discuss."

The men all grabbed a beer and sat in the folding chairs.

After he popped the top and took a swig, Fredricks said, "Why'd you pay extra for this stuff? Beer is beer, you know."

"Yeah, but it tastes pretty danged good," Rogers said.

"You are welcome," Bakshi said, even though he didn't think there had been a thank you in that short discussion. "Now, here is what we would like you to do."

He pulled out a map and laid it open on the cooler. Then, he

CASCADE KIDNAPPING

started walking the men through the plan.

"If the kid and the instructor are going to be taking a boat to the end of the lake, how are we going to get there?" Rogers asked.

"We were hoping you would have access to a boat and could follow them," Bakshi said.

The two men looked at each other for a minute, then Fredricks said, "Ernie Borsman has that twenty-foot Hewescraft he might let us borrow. It would help if we offered to pay him a little something for his trouble."

"We certainly would pay for the use of a boat," Bakshi said.

"Okay, let's just figure we'll get the boat. What next?"

From there, Bakshi led the men through the plan, pointing out where the boy and instructor would be taking off from at Stehekin.

"We are not sure exactly which direction they will be going from there, but it has to be either north, east or south. It looks like there is a trail that goes to the northeast. That is most likely the direction they will be going."

The two men looked at the map and agreed.

"So, after we grab the kid, you want us to take him here?" Fredricks asked, pointing to the small campground symbol on the map. "That's a pretty good hike."

"Yes," Bakshi said. "But doable, no?"

"It might take us a day. What do you want us to do with the instructor?" Rogers asked.

"That is up to you," Bakshi said. "Tie him up. Leave him without shoes. We would not want you to kill him. If that is the only option, then abort. No one must be hurt. Is that clear?"

Fredricks and Rogers nodded their approval.

"Now, here is the equipment we have purchased for you," Patel said.

They looked at the tracking device and receiver. Fredricks took the cellphone.

"Your phone is already loaded with the number to our phone," Patel said. "Use your phone to call only ours, and no others."

Again, Fredricks and Rogers nodded their approval.

117

Patel walked them through how to use the tracking device and receiver.

"It might be difficult to get the receiver in the boy's pack ahead of time, but do the best you can. If not his, maybe the instructor's pack?"

"We'll handle it," Fredricks said, although he wasn't sure how.

"You have all the other items you need?" Bakshi asked.

"Oh, yessir," Fredricks said. "Brand-new packs, sleeping bags, and other necessities for a safe hike through the wilderness. Would you like the receipts for all that now?"

"Will you be armed?" Singh asked, ignoring the question.

"Yes, we will," Fredricks said. "Me and Bart will both be carrying pistols. We figured it would help persuade the boy to be rescued and would be nice to have along if we run into any angry bears or wolves or cougars."

The three men from Mumbai sat and thought about that for a few seconds. No one they knew in their country carried pistols or owned firearms of any kind. In America, it seemed that every private citizen owned guns. They did have some dangerous creatures in India, but they never feared them enough to want to carry a weapon.

"Yes, very prudent," Singh said.

"Would you be able to arrange a firearm for each of us?" Bakshi asked. "We would be happy to pay whatever is necessary."

Fredricks looked at Rogers and then said, "I think we can arrange that. It will cost about a thousand dollars apiece to find the right guns."

"That will not be an issue," Bakshi said. "You can give the firearms to us when we meet next."

"Will do, boss," Fredricks said. "Hope you don't need to use them."

The men all opened another beer and went through the plan again. Occasionally, either Fredricks or Rogers would ask a question, usually something hypothetical like, "What happens if the boat conks out as we are following them?" or "What if the instructor has a gun and starts shooting?"

Usually the answer was, "We will address that issue at the appropriate time."

Finally, after going through the plan one more time, and with no more Heinekens left in the cooler, the men stood and walked to the barn door.

"How about our fee?" Fredricks said.

"We have it in the vehicle," Bakshi said.

They walked out to the trucks where Bakshi opened the door to the Explorer and pulled out a manilla envelope holding two stacks of hundred dollar bills. There were fifty bills in each stack.

"And the money for the gear?" Fredricks asked, handing Bakshi the receipts. "It's right at two grand, plus the three thousand for the pistols."

Bakshi reached into his pocket and pulled out another wad of hundreds, counted out fifty, and handed them to Fredricks.

"We trust we will see you in Chelan on Saturday morning," Bakshi said. "Ready to go to work?"

"You can count on it," Fredricks said and walked around to get into the Suburban. "We're looking forward to it."

At about the same time, Skyler Sloan and his buddy Tory Green were sitting at a Dairy Queen in Bellevue, eating peanut buster parfaits and talking about their trip to the mountains near Lake Chelan.

"I can't wait," Green said. "I think I have everything ready. My mom's all worried about me going, but I keep telling her we'll be fine."

"I'm ready too," Sloan said. "I guess we can get everything loaded the night before, and if you want, you can spend the night at my house, and then we can take off early. We have to be at the boat dock at ten o'clock."

"That sounds good. My mom has bugged me every day about taking that satellite texting deal she got me."

"I'm sure our phones won't work, so it probably is something that will be good to have, just in case."

"Yeah, I told her I would text her every day, so she knows we're all good."

About that time, two cute girls from their school came into the restaurant, and all thoughts and discussion about the wilderness school suddenly disappeared.

CHAPTER 16

It had taken a bit of searching through the county records, but Luke found a title for a cabin sitting on ten acres of land west of Yakima, owned by a Marvin Wilburn. The address for the cabin was in the area known as the Nile, so Luke assumed it was the cabin that Jolene Seifert had mentioned.

Before he ran up to the cabin, Luke checked in with his captain to let him know what he'd learned about Seifert.

"It may be nothing, but it's worth checking out, I think," Luke said.

"I agree," his captain said. "Good work. Let me know what you find out."

On his way up to the Nile, Luke stopped by his house to get Jack. Just as he was letting Jack into the back seat of the truck, Austin came out of the house across the street.

"Hey, Luke. I talked with Charlie about that elk meat. He was pretty vague. Said he got it from a friend and left it at that. I didn't want to push it."

"No, that's good. Don't push it. Do you know, was there any of the meat leftover, or any more in the refrigerator or freezer to cook?"

"Geez, I don't know. Do you want some to eat?"

"No, but I'll take a small piece if you can find one. Cooked or not, doesn't matter. Even if you can find some scraps from the garbage."

"Want me to go check now?"

"Just when you get a chance. Jack and I are headed up the highway. I'll check with you when we get back."

If he could get a piece of the elk meat that Charlie had brought into the house for dinner, Luke could send it to the lab in Ashland to see if they could match it to the DNA from any of the five elk that had been poached. Even if it was some of the cooked meat, the lab techs could get DNA from the meat as DNA is quite thermostable. In flesh that has been cooked or burned, the strands will pull apart from one another some, but that's about it. There was effectively no degradation at all below two hundred and twenty degrees Fahrenheit.

It took Luke some looking around to find the cabin. It was set way back off a gravel road and was surrounded by trees and brush. Luke could just see a roof top and a stone chimney with a ribbon of gray smoke curling up from it. Someone was clearly home.

Instead of just driving up the driveway, Luke decided he'd do a little checking around first. He left Jack in the truck and walked cross-country to the trees near the cabin.

Behind the cabin was a small outbuilding Luke thought might be a garage or a shop. Near the front door, an old yellow International Scout was parked in the gravel with a silver, '90s-model Buick LeSabre parked next to it. He wrote the license plate numbers for both vehicles in his notepad and then moved around to see if anyone was in the house. The windows were covered with curtains, but they were just transparent enough that he could catch the movement of at least two people inside.

Before going and knocking on the door, Luke decided to go

back to his truck and run the tag numbers on the two vehicles. After punching the numbers into the Department of Motor Vehicles site on his on-board computer, he learned that the Scout was registered to Lawrence Wilburn, and the Buick was registered to a Doris Mason—Seifert's mother-in-law.

"Well, isn't that interesting," Luke said to himself. Jack's tail started thumping in the backseat when Luke spoke. "Hey, boy. Almost forgot you were in here."

"She must have forgotten her worthless son-in-law was driving her car."

Jack's tail thumped again.

"I'm blaming Tinker. She was too busy yelling at him. So, let's go see if we can have a chat with Mr. Seifert."

Luke drove his pickup down the gravel lane and parked it so that neither of the cars next to the house would have an easy way out. When he stopped the engine, he saw the curtains in the front window move and someone peering out at him.

As he walked up to the front door, he heard shuffling and murmured voices. He knocked on the door and waited.

The door opened, and Luke, for the first time in a long time, looked up. The man in the doorway was huge. He was at least five inches taller than Luke and he completely filled the space in the door jam.

"Are you Lawrence Wilburn?" Luke asked.

"People call me Tiny," Wilburn said. "What can I do ya out of?"

Luke was trying to get a glimpse around the giant to see what might have been going on inside the cabin, but the mass of the man blocked everything.

Wilburn, who was wearing what must have been a size XXXXL gray T-shirt and the largest pair of blue denim bib overalls Luke had ever seen, noticed Luke trying to look around him. Folded across his chest, Tiny's forearms were as thick as an average man's legs. A mop of brown hair sat on top of Tiny's head, looking like it was trying to do everything it could to grow long enough to cover his massive scalp.

"I'd invite you in, officer, but the place is a mess."

"My name is Luke McCain," Luke said, wanting to be as cordial and non-threatening as possible. "I'm trying to locate Buzz Seifert. I've been told he lives here with you."

"Oh, you have, have ya?"

"Yes. It's nothing urgent. I just want to ask him a couple of questions."

"Well, he ain't here right now. Can I give him a message?"

"I'd just as soon talk to him in person," Luke said, handing Wilburn his card. "Could you have him call me? Again, I just have a couple of questions for him."

Wilburn plucked the card out of Luke's hand. In the hand of the giant, the card looked like a miniature card from a kid's game. Tiny looked at it, stuffed it into one of the front pockets of his huge overalls, smiled at Luke, and closed the door.

Luke thought about knocking on the door again but decided against it. He walked back to his pickup, jumped in, fired up the rig, and turned around. He figured Seifert was in the house, but there wasn't much he could do about it.

With nothing better to do, Luke decided he would drive back down the road, tuck his rig into a little side road, and just watch. If he saw the silver LeSabre go by, he'd pull it over.

Once he was in place, Luke pulled out his phone and dialed up Jolene Seifert.

"Hello, Officer McCain. Didn't think I'd be talking to you again anytime soon."

"Sounds like you got some sleep."

"Yeah, sorry for being so groggy yesterday. My work schedule is the shits."

"I won't keep you long. Does your ex-husband drive your mother's Buick LeSabre?"

In an instant, she was hot. "That son-of-a-bitch! Is it still registered in my mom's name? He was supposed to change the registration two years ago."

"Yes, it is. I just saw it at Tiny Wilburn's cabin. I ran the plates, and it came back as registered to Doris Mason."

"I'll kill him," she said. "Mom doesn't drive anymore, and when Buzz heard she was going to sell the car, he came and bought it from her. I wasn't involved in the transaction or I would have told him to beat it. She gave in."

"Well, just so you know. If he gets in an accident or does anything stupid in that car, your mom might be on the hook since it's still in her name."

"Did you talk to him at Tiny's?"

"Nope. Tiny said Buzz wasn't there. I'm leaning on the idea that the big man was lying."

"Yuh think? Every time that overgrown pile of turds opens his mouth, he's lying. Or he's taking a bite of something."

Luke tried not to laugh, but he couldn't help himself.

"It isn't funny, Officer McCain. I've dealt with that giant, gross thing and my no-good ex-husband for way too long. I know you said you just wanted to talk to Buzz, but I hope to hell you catch him doing something that will put him in jail."

"Well, I'm pretty sure he was in the cabin, and really, all I wanted to do was ask him a couple of questions. But when he's avoiding me like that, it sure makes me think he's up to something."

"Something no good," Jolene said. "I can just feel it. If he gets my mom into hot water, I will, I'll kill him."

"Just for my information," Luke asked. "Is Tiny a violent man?"

"Oh, I think he'd have no trouble hurting someone. The problem is, he's so big and fat. He can't move fast enough to catch anyone. I think my eighty-year-old grandma could outrun him."

Luke thought about what her old grandmother might look like if her mother looked like she was eighty-eight.

"Just stay away from those giant hands of his, and you should be fine," she advised.

"Good to know. I'm going to try to catch up with Buzz as soon as I can, and when I do, I'll give him the message to get the registration changed or you are going to—"

"I'll kill him," she finished his sentence. "Tell him that."

"Will do," Luke said. "Have a good day."

The last thing he heard her say before he pushed the end button on his phone was, "How can I have a good day? That dumb son-of-a—"

Click.

Luke looked at the clock on his dash. It was almost noon. He'd give it until two o'clock, and if he didn't see the Buick roll by—or the old yellow Scout, for that matter—he'd head back to the office.

At precisely one fifty-nine, a silver car zoomed by on the gravel road, a large cloud of dust boiling up behind it. Luke wouldn't have been sure it was Seifert's Buick except there was a giant man sitting in the passenger seat.

"Here we go," Luke said to Jack.

He fired up the F-150, pulled out onto the road, and punched it. He caught up with the silver car quickly, and as soon as he did, he turned on the blue lights in the truck's grill. As he drove behind the car, he noticed through the clouds of gray dust that it was leaning severely to the passenger side. Luke followed the Buick for a quarter mile until the driver finally pulled the car to the side of the road. Luke worried that if the car got too close to the bar ditch, it might just roll over into it.

Luke parked right behind the Buick, climbed out, and walked slowly up to the driver's window. He could see Tiny Wilburn's fat head sitting on large, rounded shoulders in the passenger seat. The driver, presumably Buzz Seifert, was not rolling the window down.

Luke tapped on the window, but the man just sat there.

"Mr. Seifert," Luke said loudly enough that the man in the car could hear him. "I really just want to ask you a couple of questions."

He finally rolled down the window.

"I assume you are Buzz Seifert? Can I see your driver's license, please?"

"I thought you just wanted to ask me two questions."

"I need to verify who you are first. So, can I see your driver's license? And while you're at it, let me see the registration and insurance on this car."

"Aw, man," Seifert said as he pulled his driver's license out of his wallet. "I don't have the registration or insurance."

"I ran the plates earlier, and it shows this car is registered to a Doris Mason. Can I assume this is a stolen vehicle?"

"No, no, it ain't stole. Doris is my mother-in-law. Or, she was. I bought it from her. Paid her cash and everything."

"So, when did this sale occur?"

"About two years ago."

"You realize that's way too long to not register a vehicle in your name?"

"Oh, I guess. I just never got 'round to it."

"What about the insurance?"

"I guess it lapsed. I've been outta work for a while. Damned insurance people are all a bunch of crooks."

"Nonetheless, it is against the law to be driving without proper insurance and registration. Frankly, I could run you in right now for driving a stolen vehicle."

"I didn't steal it. I paid that old hag twenty-five hundrit dollars for this thing."

"Okay, here is what I am going to do, Mr. Seifert. I am going to write you a warning ticket. And I am going to come check on you in a week. If this car isn't registered in your name, and insured, I'm going to write you a real ticket with a hefty fine. You understand?"

"Yes. Now, whadaya wanna know?"

"I'm investigating some elk being killed up this way over the past few weeks. I have no reason to suspect you are involved, but since you've dabbled in this little pursuit in the past, I wondered if you might know of anyone who could be involved."

"Did you talk to Eddy Cruz?"

"I did. He gave me some names."

"Probably mine, right?"

Luke didn't say anything.

"I'll do some thinking on it. Nobody comes to mind right off."

"How about anyone who might be buying the elk to resell?" Luke asked.

Seifert hesitated slightly before saying, "What? Someone is selling elk meat? Now that ain't right."

"Think about that too if you would. If you do think of someone I should talk with, or you hear of anything, would you give me a call? Tiny there has my card."

Luke finished writing the warning ticket and handed it to Seifert.

"Don't forget our deal on the registration and insurance, Buzz. Oh, and if my ability to write you a big ticket isn't motivation enough, Jolene says get it done or she is going to kill you."

Seifert turned slowly and looked at Luke. There was just a little fear in his eyes.

"You boys have a good day," Luke said with a smile and turned to go back to his truck.

CHAPTER 17

Austin Meyers brought a piece of elk steak to Luke's house that evening.

"I remembered there were a couple of bites left from dinner the other night, and so I looked in the refrigerator, and there they were, wrapped in aluminum foil."

"That's great. Thanks," Luke said. "I'll get it ready to send to the lab tomorrow morning."

Luke explained to Austin what the lab would do with the meat, extracting DNA from it and then running it against the DNA from the elk that had been poached.

"You don't think Charlie poached them, do you?"

"No, I don't. But if it is a match, I'm going to want to talk with him about where he got the meat. That should lead us to who is killing them."

"Okay. Geez, I hope Charlie hasn't done anything wrong. He's a pretty good guy."

"I know he is," Luke said. "But just in case, can you not say anything to him or your mom about any of this just yet?"

"Sure," Austin said. "I guess."

Luke could see the concern in the young man's eyes.

"Listen, it's going to take a few days for the lab to find anything out, but when I hear, I will let you know. Chances are Charlie just got the meat from a friend or someone who killed the elk legally last fall."

"Okay. Thanks, Luke. Talk to you later."

"You know," Sara said after listening to Luke and Austin chat, "Charlie has that importing-exporting business. Maybe he is bringing in elk meat from some farm in Texas or someplace and he's selling it to a local restaurant."

"Could be," Luke said. "Or maybe he's importing it from New Zealand. If so, I'm guessing he has all the necessary paperwork from the U.S. Ag Department."

"Or maybe," Sara said, "he's exporting elk meat to Europe or someplace."

"He'd need a license and permits for that as well."

"Unless he's buying it from a local poacher," she said. "Then he wouldn't need any paperwork."

"Let's not go down that path right now. Like I told Austin, he probably was given a package of elk steaks from a friend."

"You'll know soon enough. I sure hope for Austin's sake Charlie isn't involved."

*

Luke was driving into the office the next morning when his phone rang. He looked at the caller ID and saw that it was Oxford Smythe. Luke pushed the answer button on his steering wheel to talk via the Bluetooth hookup and said, "This is Luke McCain."

"Yeah, Officer McCain. This is Ox Smythe. We met a few days ago up in the mountains."

"Sure Mr. Sm . . . er, Ox. What can I help you with today?"

"You may not believe this, but my girlfriend's daughter swears on a whole church full of Bibles that there is an alligator living in one of them ponds down by them apartments just off of the highway."

Luke had heard of all kinds of exotic creatures being released into the wild when they got too big to be kept as pets, including everything from goldfish to pythons. But an alligator was a first.

"She doesn't have a photo of the thing, does she?"

"I don't know. She called all excited that there was a gator sunning itself by the edge of the lake. I'm on my way down there to see if I can see it, but I just thought you or someone from the game department should know about it."

"Thanks, Ox. Give me the address, and I will meet you there."

Luke was familiar with the lakes. They were basically gravel pits dug out by the state highway department back in the 1960s when the highway was built around the town. The lakes were fed by underground springs and stayed full all year long. Someone with a little imagination and foresight had purchased the land, and over the next couple decades, office buildings, apartments and some really nice homes were built around the lakes.

In the 1990s, the state-record catfish had been caught in one of the lakes, which surprised everyone. Since they were private lakes, the Department of Fish and Wildlife had not planted any fish in them. Occasionally, property owners would plant some trout, and as was the case with just about every gravel pit and pond in the region, sooner or later someone would throw some live bass, perch, or sunfish in the water, and they'd quickly multiply.

Luke had checked anglers fishing on the lake by the apartments a time or two over the years, and most of the people would report catching a few sunfish or bass. So, he knew fish were in the lake. And if fish were there, and an alligator got dropped into the lake, it would most assuredly find something to eat.

As he drove to the apartments to meet Ox and his girlfriend's daughter, he wondered just how big this gator might be. He pulled in, parked, and was just getting out of his truck when he heard a yell.

"Officer McCain!"

Luke recognized Ox standing in a group of people. The big man waved.

"They just seen the gator again, right over there." Ox pointed back toward the lake. "But it dove down."

"Okay," Luke said as he walked up to the crowd of people. "Does anyone have an idea just how big this thing might be?"

"I'd say probably six feet," a girl with bright red hair said. She was wearing a pink bikini top and jean shorts that could only be described as Daisy Dukes.

A guy next to her laughed. "Oh, come on, Misty. I'm five-foot-ten, and that thing was not near as tall as me."

"It wasn't tall at all, Todd. But with that tail, it had to be close to six feet long."

"I'd say maybe three feet at the most," Todd said to Luke, then nodded toward the red-haired girl and rolled his eyes.

"Okay," Luke said. "Anyone else have any ideas?"

"I'd say three feet is probably close," another girl said. She was a bleach blonde and was also wearing short shorts and a blue tank top that exposed a colorful array of tattoos on her chest and arms. She was standing next to Ox, so Luke assumed she was his girlfriend's daughter.

"This is Beth," Ox said. "She's the one who called me."

Luke was just getting ready to ask the group another question when Misty pointed and said, "Here comes the TV station. I called them and told them about the alligator."

"Great," Luke said.

As soon as Luke saw the reporter climbing out of the small car with the TV station call letters on the side, he recognized him.

"Hey, Officer McCain," Simon Erickson said. "Didn't know you would be here."

"Hi, Simon. I got the call about the same time you did."

Erickson was carrying a portable camera, and as he walked toward the group, he said, "Did you see da alligator?"

Simon Erickson was a hard-working reporter for the local ABC station who had a minor speech impediment. Luke believed that

English was a second language for the young man, and for some reason, when he said any word with a "th" in it, he pronounced it as a "d". For someone who made his living talking on television, you'd think the impediment might have been too big a hurdle to jump, but Luke had to give it to Simon, he plowed right through and seemed to not worry about it a bit.

"I haven't seen the alligator yet, but some of these folks did," Luke said. "We were just figuring out how big it might be, so I know what steps to take next."

"Wow," Erickson said. "Anyone know how da gator got in da lake?"

"I'm guessing someone bought the thing as a baby, and as it grew, they figured it was too big to care for and set it free in the lake," Luke explained.

"Can I get you to say dat for me on camera?"

"Sure, but let me go take a look around first if you don't mind. I want to make sure this thing isn't going to be an issue for the residents here until we can figure out what to do with it."

"Are you going to shoot 'em?" Todd asked with a big smile. "Like the dude does on that TV show Swamp People down in Arkansas or wherever it is."

"Louisiana," Beth said.

"That's not going to be an option," Luke said. "I think we can probably catch it. Then we can see if one of the zoos around the area might want it."

"Great stuff," Erickson said from behind his camera. "Can we do dat again, wid a mic on you?"

Luke took a stroll down around the edge of the lake, watching for anything that might be the eyes and nose of an alligator resting just out of the surface of the water. A group of six people trailed behind him, including Ox, Todd, Misty, Beth, and a couple others. Erickson trailed the group, shooting video for his story.

When Luke was done surveying the area, he agreed to do a short interview. Erickson put his camera on a tripod, affixed the mic to Luke's shirt lapel, and, with the lake in the background, he started asking questions.

"So, Officer McCain, dare is a report of an alligator here at Lake Aspen. Do you believe da people actually saw one?"

"The report seems credible. We're treating it like it is true."

"How would an alligator get in a lake here in Washington?"

"Someone probably obtained a baby alligator, illegally I might add, and when it outgrew its aquarium, they let it go in the lake, is my guess. It happens all the time."

"Wid alligators?"

"No, not specifically alligators, but with other animals. Turtles, snakes, rabbits, lizards, all kinds of fish."

"So, what are you going to do wid da alligator?"

"We have to catch it first. Then, we'll see if there's a zoo or wild animal park that might want it."

"Would it be able to survive if you didn't catch it?"

"Wild animals have a way of surviving. I'm sure it would, but the last thing we need is an alligator living here, growing bigger and bigger. Pretty soon it would be a menace to pets and eventually, even people."

"How big is it now?"

"The most credible report is it is about three feet long. Even that small, they have incredibly sharp teeth. We are asking people around here that if they see it, stay away and please call the authorities."

"Tank you, Officer McCain."

Erickson quickly moved around to the front of the camera and said, "Dare you have it. An alligator has been seen here in a lake in Yakima. For da six o'clock news, I'm Simon Erickson."

As soon as he was done, he grabbed the camera and headed over to get interviews with some of the folks in the crowd. He seemed to be most interested in talking to Misty and Beth who seemed more than happy to get their fifteen seconds of fame.

Luke continued to look around the lake, and in a minute or so, Ox wandered over.

"How you gonna catch that big lizard?" he asked.

"I think we have a couple live traps at the office that might work," Luke said. "We'll throw some raw chicken pieces in there, and we should have it in a day or two. Not very smart of someone, letting something like that go around here."

"I'd be glad to keep an eye on the trap fer ya," Ox said. "And I could keep the looky-loos away. That would maybe speed up the capture, you think?"

"You know what, Ox. That would be great. Normally, I would do it myself, but I'm trying to make some headway on this elk poaching deal. I'll go get the traps and bring them back down here. If you could run and get some raw chicken pieces, I'll reimburse you, and we can have the traps set right away."

"That's a deal," Ox said. "This will be one to tell the grandkids about."

When Luke got to the office, he told the alligator story to the captain and a couple other enforcement officers who were there, including Hargraves.

"You really think it was an alligator?" Hargraves asked.

"Yeah, I do. I'm going to take two of those big live coyote traps down there and throw some raw chicken in them. I'm guessing we'll have the thing caught in twenty-four hours."

He told them about Ox Smythe keeping an eye on the traps and about his interview with Simon Erickson.

"Hope you catch it quickly," Captain Davis said. "When this hits the news, you're going to have all kinds of alligator hunters down there."

"Yeah, I'm a little worried about that, but I'm counting on Ox. He's a pretty imposing man. I think he'll keep folks at bay."

Before he took the traps to the lake, Luke pulled the elk meat, still in foil, out of a lunch cooler where he had placed it on ice that morning. He put the meat in an evidence bag, marked it by name and date, and then put it in an express package to be delivered to the lab in Ashland the next day.

He had his doubts that the DNA from the meat Austin had given him would match any of the DNA from the illegally killed elk, but it was worth a try. He needed a break on this investigation. He was grasping at straws, but every now and again, you got one of those suckers.

CHAPTER 18

They caught the alligator a mere eight hours after Luke and Ox set two traps in some brush and long grass on the shore of the lake, not far from where it was last seen.

Luke's phone rang, and seeing who it was on the caller ID, he answered right away.

Ox didn't even let Luke say hello.

"Gottum," he said. "Whatcha want me to do with it?"

"Just stay right there," Luke said. "I'll be there in fifteen minutes."

"Did you catch the alligator?" Sara asked as Luke was grabbing the keys to his truck.

"Yep. I'm going down there to get it."

"And then what are you going to do with it?"

"I'll figure that out when I get there."

"Don't bring it back here."

"Love you too," Luke said as he was headed out the door.

On the way to the lake, Luke called Simon Erickson.

"We caught the alligator. If you want to come get some footage of it, we have it at the lake."

"I'll be dare as quick as I can," Erickson said.

When Luke arrived at the lake, another small crowd had gathered. Misty was there, still in her summer attire, and so were Todd and Beth. They were standing with a few others in a big half-circle down by the lakeshore. In the middle of the semi-circle was Ox Smythe, sitting on a lawn chair, holding a big stick, smile on his face, with the live trap cage sitting next to him.

Sure enough, in the trap was a small alligator. The reptile seemed no worse for wear and was calmly chomping on some chicken parts.

"It got to that chicken fair and square," Ox said. "So, I let him keep it."

"Fine by me," Luke said. He had no idea how to tell the sex of an alligator, but Ox was calling it "him," so he went along with it. "He looks to be in good shape."

"How long is it?" Todd asked from the crowd.

"I'd say about three foot," Ox said.

Todd turned to Misty and said, "See, I told you."

About then, Simon Erickson came around the apartment building, camera and tripod in tow.

"I tink dis may make da national news," Erickson said. "I sent my story from the six o'clock show to our Spokane station, and dey said da network wants it for dare nightly news."

Misty and Beth got all excited when they heard that.

"You mean, we might be on the national news?" Misty asked.

"Maybe. For sure, Officer McCain will," Erickson said.

"Great," Luke said. The last time he was on the national news, a deranged woman with a large knife in her boot came to town looking for him. "So, we're going to pick up the trap, haul it to my pickup, and then I'll take it someplace safe."

"Okay," Simon said. "Let me get da camera set up."

When Simon was set, Ox and Luke picked the trap up at each end and carried it up the small grass hill, along a sidewalk, and out to the parking lot where Luke's truck was parked. The crowd followed along like the alligator was the Pied Piper. Of course, it didn't hurt that they might get in the video that Simon was sending to the national news.

"Where are you going to take it?" Simon asked.

"Don't tell my wife, but I am going to take it to my house tonight. Then we'll figure out what to do with it tomorrow."

Luke was glad that Erickson didn't want another interview. The young man seemed to be in a hurry to get the footage to wherever it was going. There was not much more he could tell him anyway.

"Don't tell me we have to keep the thing in the bathtub," Sara said after Luke told her he had brought the alligator home.

"No, it will be fine in the cage overnight. I can put it in the storage shed. They like water, but they don't need it, especially at night."

"Make sure that cage is locked, and the storage shed is too."

When Luke was unloading the cage, Jack wandered out to see what was going on. He looked at the alligator, and the alligator looked back. Jack gave the cage a couple good sniffs, turned, and wandered back into the house, like he saw alligators all the time. The gator just lay there, like nothing to see here.

*

The next morning, Sara turned the TV to ABC News. About fifteen minutes in, there was the story about the alligator capture in Washington State. She saw Luke and some other man carrying the alligator in a big cage to Luke's truck, and then they cut to Luke talking about how the alligator might have survived in the wild, and if it did, could become more than a nuisance. Pets and people could be in danger.

"Well, they won't have to worry about it now, I guess," said the anchorman with a perfectly coifed head of dark brown hair, dimpled cheeks, and blindingly white teeth.

"Thanks goodness," said an anchorwoman sitting next to

him with matching dimples and teeth. "My grandma lives in Washington. I'd hate to have to worry about Nana living up there with a wild gator running around."

They both laughed and then sent it over to some gal named Ginger for the weather.

"You looked pretty good on TV there, mister," Sara said to Luke as he was coming out of the bedroom. He'd gotten up early, worked out, showered, and now was ready for work. "I hope some incredibly hot chick doesn't come looking for you."

"Like lightning is going to strike twice in the same place," Luke said. "I'm off to go figure out what to do with an alligator."

Finding a home for the alligator was actually easier than Luke had anticipated. He asked one of the office assistants to call around to some of the zoos in the Northwest, and the first place she called said they'd be happy to give it a home.

"The person at the Portland Zoo had seen the story on TV this morning, and she was getting ready to call us to offer the alligator a home. They are even going to come pick it up."

"Great," said Luke. "I'll leave it here next to your desk."

"Not on your life, buddy. The biologists said they'll deal with it until the people from the zoo get here."

With the alligator safely secured, and soon to be on its way to Oregon, Luke decided he would run back up and check on Buzz Seifert and his giant of a friend, Tiny. He had given Seifert a week to get the registration transferred and some insurance purchased for the LeSabre. It had only been three days, but Luke figured that was close enough.

Like Seifert's ex-wife had said, the man was most likely up to no good. Based on the response Luke had gotten to his question about knowing anyone who might be selling elk meat, he believed Seifert knew more than he'd let on.

When he arrived at the driveway for the Wilburn cabin, Luke stopped the truck, rolled down the windows, and just listened for a bit. The cabin was mostly obscured by small trees and brush, so it was difficult to see much of anything. Soon a noise came from the direction of the cabin that sounded like a table saw or a band saw. The high-pitched whine would go for three seconds, and then it would stop. Over and over again, he heard the sound of the saw.

When he didn't hear the whine of the saw again, Luke started the truck and drove up the driveway. As he got through the trees, he saw the silver Buick and the yellow Scout sitting pretty much where they were three days before.

A second later, Tiny Wilburn, wearing the same humungous pair of bib overalls, came lumbering around the corner of the cabin. The big man labored as he walked, as if he was carrying a grand piano on his back. He was also wearing rubber gloves, the kind that would cover a normal person's arms to the elbow. On Wilburn, however, the gloves went about four inches above his wrist where it looked like they had exploded due to some massive inner pressure put on them by his forearms. The rubber was ripped and tattered around the opening of the gloves.

"Shit," Luke muttered to himself. The man truly was a giant.

When Wilburn finally noticed Luke's truck sitting there, he turned a hundred and eighty degrees with surprising agility and walked back around the cabin toward the outbuilding. Luke climbed out of the truck and started walking that way but only made it a few steps before Tiny and Buzz Seifert came walking back around the cabin.

Seifert, who was wearing safety goggles and a black cloth apron, was wiping his hands on an old dirty towel. Luke noticed the rubber gloves that Tiny had been wearing had magically disappeared.

"Wha-choo want?" Seifert asked. "You told me I had a week to get that paperwork done. It ain't been a week. I know. I been counting."

"I was just driving by and thought I'd stop in to say hi," Luke lied. "I'm guessing you haven't changed the registration yet then?"

"No. But I will. I still have a few days."

"So, what have you boys been up to?" Luke asked. "Looks like you're working on a home improvement project." He took two steps toward the men. "Can I see?"

Tiny took a giant step forward, bumping Seifert and about knocking him down.

"No, you can't," he said as he folded his giant arms across his chest.

Luke noticed specks of something dark on the big man's arms, just above where the rubber gloves had ended.

"In fact," Tiny said. "You can just leave."

"No problem," Luke said and turned to his truck. "I'll be back before the week is out. Get that registration changed, and don't forget the insurance."

Neither Tiny nor Seifert moved.

Backing down the driveway, Luke took one more look at the cabin. The men were still standing there like a couple of statues.

"What are you boys up to?" Luke said to himself.

He knew he would need a search warrant to get into the cabin or the shop in the back. The specks on Tiny's arms looked like blood, but Luke couldn't tell for sure. They could also be paint or stain or even transmission fluid if the men had been working on a car.

Going out to the main road and sneaking back in to see what he could see was an option, but legally, he couldn't use anything he saw against the men, if they were doing something against the law. Plus, there was always the chance the men might spot him, and if they did and called it in to the sheriff's office, Luke could be in some hot water. Worse yet, the men could shoot him. Stranger things had happened.

No, he'd wait it out, but he was going to keep an eye on these two. They were definitely up to something.

Chapter 19

I t was going to be a beautiful early September day, Luke thought
to himself as he walked out to his truck to head to work.

The weather girl, part of the Storm Chaser team on the
local NBC station, said it was going to be another cloud-free,
eighty-degree day, and as Luke looked at the sky to the west over
the Cascade Mountains, he knew the weather girl was going to be
right on.

At the same time, however, there was just the tiniest of a chill
in the early morning air. It happened every year about this time,
the first sign that summer was starting to turn into autumn. In the
next few days, he might actually have to wear a jacket first thing in
the morning.

Luke thought about the local weather people who called
themselves "storm chasers." They always made him think about the
movie *Twister* with Helen Hunt and Bill Paxton, whose characters
chased tornadoes in Kansas or wherever it was. It was rare to see a
tornado in Washington, but they did occur. The National Weather

Service showed there were an average of two a year in Washington, and they were extremely mild on the destruction scale. Most were just glorified dust devils, and none had obliterated even one mobile home park.

The last rain Eastern Washington had seen was back in late June. So, the storm chaser team had pretty much nothing to do for the last two months. A good gig if you could get it, Luke thought.

As nice as the day was, it got even better when he arrived at the office and saw there was an email from the Wildlife Lab in Ashland, Oregon. He clicked on the email and punched up the report. He couldn't believe his eyes. The meat from the elk that Austin Meyers had given him was a perfect DNA match to the fourth elk that Luke had investigated as poached a couple weeks earlier.

He immediately printed out the report and took it to Captain Davis.

"So, what's the plan?" Davis asked.

"Well . . ." Luke said, and then thought about it a minute. "I think I'll go have a chat with Charlie Tucker to see where he got the elk meat."

"Didn't you say he ran an import-export business?" Davis asked.

"Yes, he does. I think he sells apples and maybe some other fruit. But I don't know what else. Hope it's not fresh elk meat."

"I hope not too. Let me know what you find out. And if you need any help, holler."

"Will do," Luke said and headed out the door.

As he drove, Luke thought about Charlie. The man was a conundrum. He came and went, often gone for weeks on end. Austin and his mom seemed to really like Charlie, and from what Luke could tell, he treated them both very well. He'd helped Austin buy his truck and had given him work. Still, he had somehow got his hands on poached elk meat, either knowingly or not. Luke intended to get to the bottom of it.

When he got to his house, Luke looked across the street. The

Mercedes SUV that Charlie drove was not there. Neither was Austin's pickup. But Jessie's Nissan SUV was there, so Luke walked across the street and knocked on the door.

"Hey, Luke," Jessie said when she opened the door. "Austin's at school right now."

"Actually, I'm looking for Charlie. Is he around?"

Jessie gave him an inquisitive look like, why would you want to talk to him?

"No, he's at work. Do you want me to call him?"

"Do you expect him home tonight?"

"Yes, I think so. He's not told me otherwise."

"Okay, I'll just talk to him then."

"Is there something I should know?" Jessie asked.

"No, I just have a few questions about exporting. I know that's his business and I figured he'd be a good one to ask."

Luke thanked her and headed back to his place. He was now worried that Jessie would call Charlie and tell him Luke was looking for him. That might be good, or it might be bad. If Charlie received the elk meat innocently, he wouldn't be concerned about Luke wanting to chat with him. But if he knew the meat was from a poached elk, or worse yet, was selling or exporting the venison, he'd surely want to avoid a meeting.

Am-Ex Trading Company was located in the industrial part of town, down in what was referred to as "fruit row." The small office building was tucked between two huge concrete fruit storage warehouses. The location of the business would suggest that Am-Ex worked with growers and packers to help export their fruit out of the country. Luke and Sara both had casually asked Austin and Jessie about Charlie's business, and neither could really describe it. Their responses were always very vague.

"He sells fruit to businesses in other countries," Jessie had told Sara after she started dating Charlie.

Luke decided to take the bull by the horns and drove to Charlie's office. When he pulled up to the small office building, Luke saw that Charlie's black Mercedes GLC 300 was parked out front. So, he got out of his truck, walked up the steps, and in the front door. A slightly overweight, middle-aged woman dressed in blue jeans and a purple sweater sat at a desk just on the other side of a counter. The woman's dark hair was cut short, and she wore little to no makeup.

"Can I help you?" she asked in a voice that had to have been altered by about twenty-five years of cigarette smoke. The woman was looking at Luke over the top of glasses perched on her nose. A small nameplate on her desk read, "Debbie Jamison." A sign next to the nameplate read, WARNING: FREQUENT F-BOMBS DROPPED IN THIS AREA. Luke believed it.

"Yes, I'm here to see Mr. Tucker."

"Does he know you're coming?" Jamison asked. Luke could almost see smoke oozing out of her nose as she talked.

"He might."

Luke was pretty sure Jessie Meyers had called Charlie after his visit with her.

"Can I tell him who is here?"

"Tell him it's his next-door neighbor."

"You got a name, neighbor?"

Tough lady, Luke thought. "Yep. Luke McCain."

"Like the TV show guy on *The Rifleman*?"

"Yes, ma'am."

"Loved that show," she said and then went into a coughing jag that sounded as if one lung might have just come detached. "Sorry," she said. "Got a bit of a cold."

"Stuff's going around," Luke said, although he knew a smoker's cough when he heard one.

Jamison walked over to a closed office door, knocked lightly, opened the door, and said, "Hey, boss. The long arm of the law is here looking for you. Sez, he's your neighbor."

"Luke! Come on in!" a voice boomed from inside the office.

Luke walked through a small swinging door and past Jamison, who was still standing at her boss's door. He immediately smelled a combination of cigarette smoke and some kind of cheap perfume coming off her clothes.

Charlie stood behind a big walnut desk littered with stacks of papers. He walked around the desk with his right hand extended. Charlie was fairly tall, maybe two inches shorter than Luke, and he was fit. Wearing tan chino slacks and a white polo shirt, Charlie looked like he just stepped off the eighteenth green. His dark brown hair was short, with some gray appearing at the temples.

"Nice to see you, Luke. Sit down, please."

Luke shook Charlie's hand and said, "Thanks for seeing me without an appointment. I appreciate it."

"No problem. What can I do for you?"

"I'll just get right to it. I'm working on a pretty serious poaching case. Several elk have been killed in the mountains west of town in the past three weeks. During my investigation, I've been able to collect meat from five of the illegally killed elk. The meat was sent to a wildlife crime lab for DNA analysis. After talking to Austin the other day, he mentioned that you had brought some elk meat home for dinner. Just on a whim, I asked Austin to grab a small piece of the leftover meat and sent it in for analysis as well. It turns out the elk meat you had came from one of the poached elk."

Luke had been watching Charlie's eyes closely as he explained everything. When Luke finished the last sentence, he let it sink in.

After thinking about it, Charlie said, "I had no idea. Gosh, I got the steaks from a guy who said he had a source for commercial game meat."

"Well, the science shows that to not be true," Luke said. "So, can you give me the name of this guy?"

Again, there was a slight hesitation.

"I didn't get his whole name, but his first name was Butch or Buzz. Something like that."

Bingo. Luke wouldn't need the full name. He believed he knew right where to find the man with the steaks.

"Listen, Charlie. I have no idea what all you export here, but the elk thing is a serious situation. If you are selling and shipping illegally gotten game meat, you are in some very hot water."

"No, no, I wouldn't ever do anything like that. You can check our books and computers, whatever you want. We strictly export fruit, and we import some items from out of the country like bananas, guavas, kumquats, and other fruits from Central and South America."

As he was talking, Luke saw movement outside the office window. Debbie Jamison was standing in front of the parked cars smoking a cigarette and talking on her phone. He wondered if she had heard the conversation and was now talking to Buzz Seifert.

"Does your secretary know this Buzz guy?"

"I don't think so. Why?"

"Just wondered. So, if you can hang here for just a couple minutes, I am going to go out to my truck and get a photo and have you look at it. Do you mind?"

"No. Anything you want, Luke. I swear to God, I didn't know anything about the elk meat being poached."

From the fear in his eyes, and the shaking in his voice, Luke was starting to believe Charlie.

As soon as Luke walked out the door, he heard Jamison say into the phone, "Oh, I gotta go." Then she stamped out the last of her cigarette and marched back into the office.

It didn't take too long for the DMV photo of Buzz Seifert to come up on the computer. Luke had no way of printing the photo, so he grabbed the laptop off the special console is his truck and walked back into the office.

Jamison was in Charlie's office, and they were talking very quietly when Luke came in. The secretary backed away from Charlie but stayed in the office as Luke brought the laptop around to show him the photo.

Charlie looked at the photo of Buzz Seifert for about a half second and said, "Yep, that's the guy."

"Okay. Here's what we are going to do," Luke said. "Ms. Jamison, you can stay here as a witness if you have time."

"Sure," she said in a husky voice and then started into another lung-rattling coughing fit.

"Maybe you should have that cold looked at," Luke suggested.

Luke saw Charlie open his mouth to say something, like that his secretary had had that cough for years and it has nothing to do with a cold, but he thought better of it.

"I want you to tell me the whole story," Luke said to Charlie. "Tell me how you know Buzz Seifert and how you ended up with the poached elk meat."

And Charlie did. He said he had never met Seifert before the day he'd showed up at the office and said Seifert claimed to have a source for game farm buffalo and venison. Seifert was hoping that Charlie could find a market in Europe or South America for the meat.

"Of course, I told him if we were even going to consider looking at exporting game meat, he would need all the appropriate paperwork from the state and the US Ag Department," Charlie said.

"Of course," Luke agreed.

"Before he left, he gave me a package of steaks. He said, 'Take this home and try it. You'll see we have some excellent product.' He was supposed to get me the paperwork this week."

"Any idea how he got your name as a potential exporter?" Luke asked. As he asked the question, he looked at Jamison who would not return his gaze.

"No idea," Charlie said. "He just showed up one day with a lunch cooler full of elk steaks and a story."

"How 'bout you, Ms. Jamison?" Luke asked. "Do you know Mr. Seifert or know how he came to arrive on this doorstep?"

The secretary was looking at her feet.

"Yeah, I know him," she said finally. "I dated him for a while after he got his divorce. He knew where I worked, and I guess he thought I might help him get a foot in the door here. But I never knew the meat was from poached animals. The story he told me on the phone was he worked for some company in Montana that was raising buffalo, elk, red deer, and other game animals for meat to sell."

"Who were you talking to on the phone in the parking lot a few minutes ago?"

"Not him, if that's what you're worried about. I shoulda known he wasn't on the up-and-up. When we were dating, he was always chasing one get-rich-quick scheme after another."

Then she turned to Charlie and said, "Sorry, boss. I really didn't know."

"That's okay," Charlie said. "I'm just glad we found out what he's up to."

Luke took Jamison's contact information and told her and Charlie that he was headed to get a search warrant for where Seifert was living, and there was chance a judge would call them to confirm what they had told him.

"No problem. Glad to help," Charlie said.

"I just shoulda known," Jamison said. Her hands were shaking. She definitely needed a cigarette.

Luke left the office and headed west out of town. He wasn't sure who Debbie Jamison had called, but if it was someone who could tip Seifert off to what was coming at him, he wanted to get to the cabin as quickly as possible, before Seifert and Tiny Wilburn could hide whatever it was they were doing there.

On the way, Luke called Captain Davis who said he'd get the search warrant going and send it up with Stan Hargraves. Luke gave him the contact information for Charlie and Jamison and the address for Wilburn's cabin.

"I'll have Stan call you when he's on his way," Davis said. "Good work, Luke."

"We don't have 'em yet," Luke said. "But we're getting closer."

CHAPTER 20

It took Luke thirty-five minutes to reach the road where the Wilburn cabin was located. Instead of driving all the way to the cabin, Luke used the same little pullout he'd used when he pulled Seifert and Tiny Wilburn over a few days earlier. He thought that might be the best plan, watching in case the men left while waiting for Hargraves and the search warrant.

The phone call from Hargraves came after Luke had been sitting in the pullout for almost an hour. During that time, two vehicles had passed, but neither was a silver Buick LeSabre or a yellow International Scout.

"I'm on my way," Hargraves said. "They had to find the judge at lunch, which evidently includes a short nap. He wasn't overly happy to be awakened."

"I'm guessing he'll get over it," Luke said. "I'm in a pullout about a half mile from the driveway into the cabin."

"Ten-four," Hargraves said. "I'll meet you there."

While he waited for Hargraves and watched the road, Luke

thought about the different dead elk he had seen over the past few weeks. If there were five that they knew about, there could be another five or more out there that no one had seen or reported. If Seifert and Wilburn were selling the meat, who might be buying it? And the bigger question was, who was doing the actual killing?

He was still of the belief that it was two people shooting the elk just by the fact that there were two different guns being used. Elk wouldn't stand around to wait while a lone shooter switched rifles.

It could be that Seifert and Wilburn were doing the killing too, but Luke just couldn't see Tiny up there stalking around in the hills quietly, climbing steep trails. Seifert maybe, but if there were two shooters, who was the other person?

He thought about that more and couldn't come up with anything. He was pretty sure Seifert's old partner, Eddy Cruz, had cleaned up his act and wasn't involved. Most likely it was someone else.

Unless Seifert gave up the shooter's names, it was going to be tough to catch them. Maybe, instead of rushing right in there and doing a search of the property, they should just watch the cabin and see who else might join the party.

Luke called the captain back and ran that idea by him.

"I guess we could," Davis said. "But bird in the hand and all that."

"I know," Luke said. "I'd sure like to get the poachers though. If Seifert goes to jail, they most likely will fold up the operation, at least for now."

"Do you think we can make a deal with Seifert or Wilburn? Would they give up the shooter for reduced or no jail time?"

"I don't know. I don't have a real feel for Seifert yet. He's a slippery one. On the other hand, Tiny might not be made for doing jail time. He could be the weak link in this deal."

"I'll go with whatever you think. Talk it over with Stan and see if he has any thoughts."

"Will do. Thanks, Cap. We'll let you know what we come up with."

Hargraves arrived twenty minutes later and parked next to Luke. He got out of his brown, state-issued, Chevy 1500 pickup and walked over to Luke's open window.

"Hop in. Let's talk about this for a minute," Luke said.

"So, you're having reservations about just going in there and taking them down?"

"I'm afraid that we're going to lose the shooter if we do. I'm thinking that Seifert and Wilburn are just the middlemen. They're buying the bulk meat, cutting it, and then selling it wherever they can for a profit. I heard a saw running when I was up here last time. Very well could've been a band saw used to cut meat."

"Or they could be building Adirondack chairs," Hargraves said.

"True," Luke agreed. "The big man had dark specks of something on his arms. Could've been blood, but also could've been paint or a dark stain."

"I guess we'll never know until we go look," Hargraves said.

"It's probably the right move," Luke said. "We could be sitting on these guys for a month before the shooters come in with more meat. Now that archery season is open, there's a bunch more people in the woods. The elk are going to be more skittish, and gun fire would definitely draw some attention."

"So, let's go," Hargraves said.

They decided they'd go in in Luke's truck. As they drove up the road, Luke tried to describe Tiny Wilburn to Hargraves.

"My daddy always said, the bigger they are, the harder they fall," Hargraves said.

"Jolene Seifert said, just don't let him get hold of ya, or he might pinch your head off."

"Noted," Hargraves said. "Think pepper spray would subdue him?"

"I think it would just piss him off. Seriously, let's be careful with him."

Before they went up the driveway, they stopped and listened for a few minutes. All they heard were some camp robbers chattering away in the trees somewhere near the cabin. Gray jays—commonly called camp robbers—were known to hang out wherever there was food around. And they had a particular fondness for meat.

"They might be scrounging some elk scraps," Hargraves said when he heard the birds.

"Like you said, I guess we'll never know until we go look."

As they went up the driveway, Luke noticed that the LeSabre was gone. The yellow Scout sat right where it had been the previous two times Luke had been there.

"Well, that's not good," Luke said.

"What?"

"Seifert's car is gone. And something just doesn't feel right. It looks—"

"Dead?"

"I was going to say abandoned, but okay, we can go with dead."

The men got out of the truck. Luke walked toward the front of the cabin, and Hargraves went around to the back.

"I think the sawing the other day was coming from the shop back there," Luke whispered.

"Got it," Hargraves whispered back. He had his right hand on his pistol with the safety strap removed, just in case he needed to get to it quickly.

Luke looked inside the Scout as he walked by. A twenty-two-caliber rifle sat behind the front seat. Luke opened the truck's door, reached in, grabbed the rifle, and quickly unloaded it. The last thing he needed was a loaded weapon where someone could get to it.

The front window was covered in curtains, but Luke could see through a small crack in the middle. Nothing in the front room looked out of place except for a mountain of a man lying face down, blood coming out of his very large head.

Luke pulled his pistol, grabbed the radio mic attached to his left shoulder, and said, "Wildlife 148 requesting an ambulance and back up."

He gave the address to the dispatch person and told her there was a man down, injuries unknown.

"Roger, 148. YSO and ambulance on the way."

Hargraves came walking hurriedly around the corner of the cabin. He had heard the call for assistance.

"Tiny is face down in the living room. Blood coming out of his head. I can't tell if he's breathing or not."

"No one in the shop," Hargraves said. "I'll go to the back door and come in that way."

Luke proceeded to the front door and tried the doorknob. It was unlocked, so he turned the knob, and slowly pushed the door open.

"State police!" Luke yelled. "Anyone in here?"

With pistol at the ready, Luke moved forward to have a better look at Tiny. There was so much blood pooled around the big man's head, there was no way of telling what was making it bleed.

"Coming in," Hargraves said. "I'll clear the kitchen."

Luke had moved to the one bedroom in the small cabin. He checked out a closet and then looked in the bathroom.

A second later, he heard Stan say, "Holy Christ!"

Luke turned around, and in the hallway stood Tiny Wilburn. Blood was running through his blood-matted hair and down over his face. The man's massive body filled the hallway, blocking Luke's view to the main room.

"Mr. Wilburn, down on your knees," Hargraves said from somewhere behind the man.

All Luke could see of Tiny's face were two white eyeballs staring at him through the blood.

"Raise your hands and get down on your knees," Luke said.

"I can't," Tiny said.

"What?"

"I can't."

But the giant raised his hands until they rubbed against the ceiling.

"I ain't gonna hurt you," Tiny said. "I just need some help to stop this bleeding."

"Okay," Luke said. "Can you back down the hallway slowly? We have an ambulance on the way."

Tiny started backing toward the main room, hands still raised as high as the cabin ceiling would allow. Hargraves grabbed a kitchen chair, pulled it into the main room, and then went and grabbed two dish towels out of a drawer next to the sink. When he got back to the main room, Tiny was sitting in the chair, looking like an adult sitting in a kindergartner's school chair. Luke stood in front of him, pistol at his side.

"You promise you aren't going to try something?" Luke said. He put his pistol back in the holster but pulled the Taser out. "If you do, I'm going to hit you with fifty thousand watts, and you'll be flopping around here like a fish outta water."

"I promise," Tiny said.

Hargraves handed him one of the towels, and once Tiny wiped some of the blood away, they could see the wound. His scalp was laid back as if someone had purposely taken a knife to it.

"Jesus," Hargraves said. "Who did this to you?"

"I don't know. Last I knew, Buzz was here. He got a call from someone who said you was a comin', so he got all bent outta joint and started yelling at me that we gotta get outta here."

Tiny kept wiping his head and looked around. "The next thing I know, I'm waking up with a burning head and you was in here."

"You think Buzz would have done this to you?" Luke asked.

"No, I don't. But I don't know who else could have done it."

"Tiny, do you know who was selling Buzz the elk meat you were cutting up?"

The big man froze. "You know about that?"

"Yes, we talked to some people today who Buzz tried to sell meat to. We know it was from some elk that was killed illegally up this way."

"Ah man. Buzz said we wouldn't get caught."

"So, who was killing the elk and bringing the meat to you?"

"Well . . ." There was a long pause. "Buzz was shooting the elk.

He had his cousin help sometimes. His last name is Fitzsimmons. Everyone calls him Fitz. Kinda like they call me Tiny. I guess I don't know what his real first name is."

In the distance, the whine of sirens was getting closer.

"Do you think Fitz could have done this to you?" Hargraves asked.

"Naw, he's no bigger than a pint of piss. I think he mighta been a jockey or something."

"Is that twenty-two rifle out in the Scout yours?" Luke asked

"Yeah, but those guys used it sometimes when they went out huntin' for elk."

"Where does Fitz live?" Luke asked.

"Down in Sunnyside, I think, or maybe Grandview."

"Do you know what kind of car he drives?"

"It's not a car. It's a Ford pickup. He helped Buzz haul some of the meat outta the mountains."

"Any clue where Buzz might go?"

Tiny sat and thought about it a minute. "Not unless he went to Jolene's place or her mama's house."

The sirens were close now. Hargraves looked out the window as red and blue lights flashed up the driveway.

"Ambulance and the sheriff's deputy are here. I'll go give them a sitrep."

A minute later, two EMTs came in with backpacks in hand. They immediately went to work on Tiny. They had brought a gurney with them, but as soon as they saw Tiny, they pushed it aside. After they had him cleaned up and stemmed the bleeding, one of the technicians asked Tiny if he could walk. He said he could, and with an EMT at each elbow, they helped him out to the back of the ambulance.

One of the technicians came back in to collect their bags and the gurney. "He should be fine," she said. "Head wounds bleed a lot. He'll need some stitches, but I think he'll be okay."

"Any idea what caused the scalp to separate like that?" Hargraves asked.

"Not for sure. Could have been from a fall, and he hit his head on something. Or someone hit him in the head. Wasn't caused by a knife, I don't think."

They thanked the medic and then went out and talked to the deputy.

"Well, if it isn't the rifleman," Bill Williams said. He was a longtime deputy in the Yakima County Sheriff's Office and liked badgering Luke about his name.

Luke ignored him. "We need to keep ahold of Mr. Wilburn there after he is released from the hospital. Can you give us a hand with that?"

"Sure, we can hold him overnight. But then we'd need to charge him with something."

"Right now, just hold him on suspicion of selling game animals without proper authority. We might throw some poaching charges in as well. That should be enough for the time being."

"That'll do," Williams said.

The two wildlife officers thanked Williams and sent him on his way back to Yakima.

"We need to locate this Fitzsimmons guy. Can you see what you can find?" Luke asked Hargraves.

"Little guy with that name. Can't be too many of them in the area."

"I know where Seifert's ex-wife and his ex-mother-in-law live, so I'm going to go try to run him down there."

Luke dropped Hargraves off at his truck, and they both headed east, back into town.

CHAPTER 21

Nobody was home at Jolene Seifert's place. Or at least no one answered the door. There was no sign of Seifert's Buick either, so Luke headed to the mother-in-law's house. As soon as he turned down the street, he spotted the silver LeSabre parked in front of the old lady's house. Luke pulled up and parked in front of the car. He walked past the dead rose bush, up the step, and knocked on the old door with cracks in the paint.

As soon as he knocked, Tinker started barking, and he heard the old woman yell, "Shut up, Tinker!" It didn't help. Luke heard footsteps slowly walking to the door, mixed with the yipping of the dog.

When the old woman, who was wearing the same pink and purple house coat as the last time, opened the door, she looked at Luke and said, "He ain't here."

"Do you know where he is?"

"No. His cousin picked him up. Little guy, named Fitz something."

"White Ford pickup?"

"I wouldn't know a Ford from a frying pan," she said with a scowl on her face. The little brown dog was still yapping in the background, and she shouted, "Tinker! Shut up!" Then, to Luke, "Is that all?"

"If Buzz comes back, would you give me a call?"

"No," the old lady said and closed the door.

Luke stood on the doorstep for a minute. Then he walked back to his truck and radioed the sheriff's office.

"Wildlife 148, needing a wrecker to impound a vehicle."

"Go ahead, Wildlife 148."

Luke gave a description of the silver Buick with the license plate number to the dispatcher. Then he gave her the address.

"Roger, Wildlife 148. We'll get a wrecker on the way."

Next, Luke called Hargraves.

"Any luck on finding Fitzsimmons?"

"Working on it," Hargraves said. "There are three Fitzsimmons in the DMV records with addresses in the lower valley. Only one, a James Fitzsimmons, might qualify as a jockey. His stats show he is five-foot-four, weighing one hundred thirty-seven pounds. Age, twenty-nine."

"That's gotta be our guy."

"His last known address was in Outlook. I'm going to head that way."

"Ten-four. It looks like Buzz Seifert is with him. I located his car at his ex-mother-in-law's house, and she said Fitzsimmons came by and picked Seifert up. I'm having the car impounded right now. As soon as I get this car on a wrecker, I'll come your way. Text me the address."

"Sounds good," Hargraves said and ended the call.

While he waited for the tow truck, Luke called Davis and told him what had transpired up at the cabin and what he and Hargraves were doing now.

"Sounds like you've got the right guys," Davis said. "It'd be nice to get this one closed."

"I agree," Luke said. "We'll let you know when we have 'em."

Ten minutes later, a large red flatbed truck with Acme Towing painted on the side pulled up alongside the silver LeSabre. The driver climbed out and walked over to Luke's truck.

"Hey, Luke," the man said. He was wearing black work boots, tan shorts, and one of those green uniform-style shirts with a patch on the chest that read, "Chuck."

"Hey, Chuck. Thanks for coming so quickly."

Luke had bowled in a league one year when he first moved back to Yakima, and Chuck had been on the team.

"So, how's Marcy and the kids?"

"Doing well," Chuck said. "The oldest girl is a sophomore at WSU."

"That's hard to believe. Seems like she was just this tall," Luke said, holding his hand about waist-high.

Luke moved his truck, and Chuck backed the wrecker up to the front of the Buick, hooked it up, and started winching it up the inclined flatbed.

The front door of the house opened, and the woman came out on the concrete step.

"You can't do that!" she yelled. "That's my car!"

Luke walked over to her and said, "This is Buzz Seifert's car, and we believe it has been used as part of a crime."

"I bought it back from Buzz, just this morning."

"Doesn't matter," Luke said. "It is being impounded as evidence. You should get your money back from Buzz as quickly as you can."

"I'm calling my attorney! You can't do this."

"That's your right, ma'am. Have him give me a call."

"It's a she, and she's gonna sue your ass to hell and back."

"Well . . ." Luke started to reply, but the woman turned and walked back into the house, slamming the door.

When Chuck had the Buick securely strapped to the flatbed, he said, "I assume this is going to the sheriff's office impoundment lot?"

"Yessir. Thanks, Chuck."

The words hadn't left his mouth when down the road came a white pickup. Luke took a quick look and saw two men in the cab of the truck. In the passenger seat sat Buzz Seifert.

Luke pulled his pistol, stepped out into the road in front of the white truck, held up a hand, and yelled, "Stop!"

Rather than slow down, the white truck sped up. Right at Luke.

He wanted to shoot the driver so badly, but he restrained himself. He had three seconds to move out of the way of the truck, so he spun and ducked just before the extended mirror on the passenger door of the truck took his head off.

"What the hell?" Chuck said from the cab of his truck. "Are you alright, Luke?"

"Yeah," Luke said as he ran to his truck, climbed in, and took off after the white pickup.

Luke radioed that he was in pursuit of a white Ford pickup. He gave his location and told the dispatcher that the owner of the truck was James Fitzsimmons and the passenger was Buzz Seifert.

"They are both wanted on multiple counts of poaching and illegally selling game meat. They may be armed."

The rules of engagement and pursuit in Washington State had changed in recent years. Luke knew that he could try to pull the truck over, but if they didn't want to stop, he couldn't push it, especially in the city where it might risk the safety of others. High-speed chases frequently ended badly.

Union Gap police and the Yakima County Sheriff's Office both responded and said they were on the way. Luke followed the white pickup as it sped down the main street and then onto the on-ramp to Interstate 82 where they headed south, picking up even more speed.

Luke stayed with them the best he could, radioing in his location as he went. He watched as the pickup exited at the next off-ramp. The rig then turned onto a two-track dirt road that paralleled the Yakima River and tore down the road, creating a big dust cloud. Luke was too far back to see exactly where the truck had gone because it turned into a big stand of cottonwood trees and wild roses.

The dust was still settling when he pulled up to where he had last seen the truck. Luke looked into the trees and spotted the pickup sitting behind some rose bushes. Both doors were wide open, and from what he could see, the cab was empty. Luke really wished he had Jack with him. He heard sirens in the distance and radioed in his location.

"Wildlife 163, I'm two minutes out," Hargraves' voice crackled over the radio. "I heard your call and turned right around."

"Ten-four. I'll wait for you," Luke said into the radio. "Looks like we could use a K9 unit if one's available."

"Roger, Wildlife 148," the dispatcher said.

Luke kept an eye on the brush around the truck and waited for Hargraves to arrive. He wondered why the men would drive down into this area. They could still be on the freeway headed for Oregon if they wanted to be.

Two minutes later, Hargraves' truck came bouncing down the road in a cloud of dust. He slammed to a stop and climbed out of the truck, shotgun in hand.

"I have no idea which way they went," Luke said.

"Where's Jack when we need him?"

"At home, unfortunately. Let's go check out the truck."

The two officers walked carefully up to the truck and took a look inside. Empty. Luke started looking for boot prints. He assumed the men had gone upriver, so he looked that way.

"Here's a print," Hargraves said. "Small shoe size. Must be Fitzsimmons."

The men slowly and cautiously tracked through thick brush and trees angling toward the river. Luke pulled his pistol and kept it ready. If they didn't see a print in the soft dirt, they'd find where a branch was freshly broken. As they went, they kept an eye out ahead of them. If Seifert or Fitzsimmons had a weapon, this was the type of cover that could make an ambush deadly to the officers.

"Big tracks go this way," Hargraves said softly, pointing his shotgun upriver. "Little tracks go that way."

Luke looked downriver.

"I'll follow the big tracks. You take the little ones," Hargraves whispered.

Luke nodded, found the smaller tracks, and started slowly that way. He'd only gone about thirty yards when he heard a scream and a shot from behind him. He turned just in time to see Seifert crash through the brush and hit Hargraves like a middle linebacker tackling Russell Wilson. Hargraves' shotgun went flying as both men smashed into the dirt.

Instinct took over as Luke ran toward the men rolling around on the ground. He was only ten yards from them when he saw Seifert roll away from Hargraves. The man had Hargraves' pistol and was raising it toward Hargraves.

"Freeze!" Luke yelled, aiming his pistol at Seifert.

Seifert froze for a second. He looked at Luke and then just past him. A half second later, Luke heard footsteps coming hard from behind. He wanted to turn and deal with whoever it was coming at him, but that would give Seifert the advantage. Just as Seifert was about to fire at Hargraves, Luke shot Seifert, grazing his shoulder and causing Seifert to fire Hargraves' pistol into the ground. Almost simultaneously, Fitzsimmons slammed into Luke sideways like something you might see in professional wrestling. Even though Luke had the guy by a foot and close to a hundred pounds, the hit was just enough to spin Luke around. Fitzsimmons hit the ground, then scrambled to his feet and ran back through the brush toward the river. Rather than pursue the jockey, Luke opted to protect Hargraves who, as it turned out, didn't need any protection. As Seifert was distracted by his shoulder wound, Hargraves pulled his Taser and lit Seifert up with 50,000 volts. An instant later, Seifert was in the dirt, flopping around like a goldfish on a hardwood floor.

"Drop it," Hargraves was yelling at the man writhing on the ground. But the electrical current running through Seifert was preventing him from releasing the pistol, which in turn gave Hargraves good cause to send another jolt of electricity into the suspect.

That might have continued for several more minutes if Luke hadn't stepped in.

"I got it, Stan. You can turn off the juice," Luke said as he held his pistol on Seifert and moved in. He didn't want to grab the weapon out of the man's hand until Hargraves stopped sending thousands of kilowatts into the guy.

"Are you okay?" Luke asked.

"No, I'm not okay. That son-of-a-bitch came this close to killing me," Hargraves said. "If you hadn't shot him when you did, I'da been toast."

Hargraves hit Seifert with another burst from the Taser.

"Okay, okay," Luke said. "I gotta go after Fitzsimmons. Do I need to take the Taser from you?"

"No, I got this. Go."

Luke headed toward the river. He wasn't positive, but he thought he heard a slight buzz of electricity and Seifert start flopping in the dirt again.

As Luke neared the river, he heard someone screaming in the distance downstream.

"Help, help!"

Luke moved toward the screams, and when he got to the edge of the river, he saw Fitzsimmons hanging onto the trunk of a downed tree jutting out into the river. The water was rushing fast against the tree, holding Fitzsimmons hard against it.

Luke ran over to the tree and, as quickly as he could, walked like he was on a balance beam down to Fitzsimmons. Just as the water was about to pull Fitzsimmons underwater, Luke grabbed the man by the back of his shirt collar and jerked him up on the tree trunk.

"Thanks," Fitzsimmons muttered. "I woulda been underwater in another two seconds."

Luke kept his grip at the scruff of his neck and slowly walked back up the trunk toward the bank, dragging a sopping wet Fitzsimmons along as he went.

When they got back on dry land, the little man fell to the ground and just lay there. Even though it was a warm day, Fitzsimmons was shivering uncontrollably.

"What were you thinking?" Luke finally asked.

"We use-ta swim down here when we was kids," Fitzsimmons said. "I thought I could get across the river and get lost on the reservation."

It looked like Fitzsimmons was starting to cry. Then he asked, "Did you shoot him? Seifert, I mean. Did you kill him?"

"No, I didn't kill him, but I did shoot him. And he took a pretty good hit from the Taser. But he's going to be fine."

Fitzsimmons said no more. He just lay there and shivered.

Luke could hear sirens getting close. A second later, he heard Hargraves call on the radio, telling dispatch that they had one of the perps in custody. Luke radioed in that he had the other one and called off the cavalry.

It took another ten minutes for Fitzsimmons to stop shivering. Luke figured the man was shaking more out of fear from almost losing his life than from the effects of the cool waters of the Yakima River.

Hargraves had Seifert in handcuffs when Luke and Fitzsimmons returned to where the men had jumped them. Hargraves had ripped Seifert's shirt to check out the gunshot wound to the shoulder. The bullet had just grazed him, slashing a small cut in the flesh.

Luke and Hargraves walked the two handcuffed men back to their trucks. As they walked, Luke asked them some questions.

"So, what happened up at the cabin? When we arrived, Tiny was face down on the floor with blood all around his head. He looked like he'd been scalped."

"Was he dead?" Seifert asked. "Because he wasn't dead when I left."

"No, he wasn't dead. What happened?"

166

"I got the call from Debbie," Seifert said.

"Debbie Jamison at Am-Ex?" Luke asked.

"Yeah, she said her boss had told you about me."

Luke said something under his breath and shook his head.

"What?" Hargraves asked.

"I saw her out in the parking lot talking to someone on the phone. When I asked who she was talking to, she specifically said, 'Not Buzz Seifert.' I believe I'm going to have a little chat with Ms. Jamison when I get a chance."

"What happened next?" Hargraves asked Seifert.

"So, I decided we needed to get outta there right away. Tiny got all flustered and started to run to the bedroom to get a bag of clothes. He tripped over his own big feet and fell right into the fireplace hearth. There was no way I was going to get him outta there on my own. I know because I tried. I drug him about three feet into the middle of the room, and that's where he was when I left."

"Nice guy," Hargraves said. "You could have called an ambulance."

Seifert just dropped his head.

"How many elk have you guys killed?"

"Eleven," Fitzsimmons said proudly.

"Shut up!" said Seifert. But it was too late.

They separated the two men at the trucks. Hargraves put Seifert in the back seat of his truck, and Luke put Fitzsimmons in the back seat of his. When they had the men securely loaded, Luke and Hargraves chatted outside the trucks.

"Sounds like Fitz here might be willing to talk," Luke said. "I'll see what I can get out of him, and you do the same with Seifert."

During the ride to the county lockup, Fitzsimmons talked and talked and talked. He told Luke that they would drive the Forest Service roads and look for elk at dawn or dusk. Sometimes they were able to shoot an elk near the road, but other times they had to follow them up into the woods. If the elk were too far to shoot with the .22, which Fitzsimmons always carried, then Seifert would shoot them with the .300. Luke asked him who they were selling the meat to, and Fitzsimmons said they would go to some of the taverns around town and sell some, but most people weren't interested. He said they had a bunch of steaks wrapped and frozen in a freezer in the shop by the cabin.

"Then Buzz got this idea about selling the meat to some foreign places that like to eat game meat at restaurants," Fitzsimmons said. "He'd dated that chick who works for the guy who sells fruit to London and other countries, and she thought he might be able to sell our elk meat."

While they were chatting, Luke had opened his voice recording app on his phone and got the whole story. Once Luke got Seifert's rifle and could match the bullets and possibly the brass, the prosecutor would have plenty to charge these guys with—and hopefully could put them away for a while.

After they got Seifert and Fitzsimmons booked, Luke headed to the office to let the captain know what had happened and fill out his report. He was glad to have this thing wrapped up. Just in time too. His trip with Cale was coming up fast, and he needed to get a few more things ready to go.

CHAPTER 22

The drive from Bellevue to Chelan was uneventful. Skyler Sloan and Tory Green arrived in the little town at the lower end of Lake Chelan at 5:15 the afternoon before they were to meet Skip Harvey. When they got to town, they checked into the motel where Sloan's dad had picked up the tab for his son and his friend.

After checking in, Sloan said, "Let's go grab a burger and check this place out."

They found a little mom-and-pop drive-in right on the lake and ordered cheeseburgers, fries, and milkshakes.

"This is going to be so cool," Green said. "I've really been looking forward to this."

"Me too," said Sloan as he looked out at the lake where a few boats were moving slowly. "The people in those boats must be fishing."

"I wonder what they're fishing for."

"I heard there are some big lake trout in this lake."

"We'll have to come some time and fish," Green said.

The boys finished their burgers and fries, then took their shakes and walked down to the boat launch at the city park.

"This is where we're supposed to meet Skip," Sloan said.

They sat on a bench and watched the seagulls scrounging for food. A boat came in from the lake, motored up to the dock, and tied off. An older man climbed out, and as he walked by the boys toward the parking lot, Sloan asked if he had caught any fish.

"A couple lakers," the man said. "It was pretty slow."

Two minutes later, a black GMC Sierra pickup swung in above the boat launch pulling a big aluminum boat. Two men got out of the truck and started transferring gear from the back of the pickup to the boat. Sloan and Green watched as they put sleeping bags, backpacks, long guns in soft cases, and some other items into the boat. Once loaded, one of the men climbed into the boat, the other got into the pickup and backed the boat down the launch a short way into the water. The man in the boat came to the front of the boat, disconnected it from the trailer, went back, and started the big outboard motor. The man in the truck backed the boat a bit farther into the water, and the boat slid off the trailer and into the water. Finally, the driver pulled the trailer back up the ramp and looped around into a giant parking lot. The driver got out, let a big yellow dog out of the back seat of the truck, and they headed back down to the dock.

The dog immediately ran over to Sloan and Green. They petted the dog as he wagged his tail and rubbed against them.

"C'mon, Jack. Leave those guys alone," Luke said as he walked over to the boys.

"Are you going hunting?" Green asked.

"Yes, we are. My buddy has a deer tag."

"Cool," Sloan said as he patted Jack's sides. "Can you take dogs deer hunting?"

"Well, no. Jack and I will be doing some grouse hunting while my friend is deer hunting."

"I've never seen a grouse," Green said.

"What are you guys up to?" Luke asked.

"We're going out on a week's stay in the wilderness," Green said.

"By yourselves?"

"Naw, we're going with a guy who has a wilderness survival school," Sloan said. "It should be pretty cool."

"I bet it will be," Luke said. "You'll probably see some grouse out there. And maybe some other animals too."

"Yeah, the guy who's taking us said we might even see some bears."

"You might," Luke said. "Well, you guys have fun and be careful out there."

"We will," Sloan said. "Good luck on your hunt."

"Thanks," Luke said. "C'mon, Jack. Let's go."

He and the yellow dog walked down onto the dock where Cale had the boat waiting for them.

"That would be cool too," Green said.

"Yeah, I wish my dad was into hunting."

"Maybe with what we learn this week, we'll be able to do some hunting sometime."

The boys watched as Luke and Jack jumped into the boat and slowly headed into the lake. When the boat cleared a line of buoys, the big outboard motor revved, and soon the boat was moving up the lake at a high speed, slapping the small waves as it went.

"I wonder if that's the kind of boat we're going on in the morning," Green said.

"I don't know. Skip said it's a jet boat, so maybe. C'mon, let's go do some more looking around."

*

Lake Chelan, situated in northcentral Washington State, is one of the largest natural lakes in the state. Fifty-five miles long with a maximum depth of one thousand four hundred and eighty-six feet, it is the third deepest freshwater lake in the United States. Fed by glaciers in the Cascade Mountains, the lake flows into the Columbia River via the Chelan River. The lake is extremely popular for water sports in the summer. Over the past twenty years, hundreds of high-dollar homes had been built on and near the lake's shorelines.

"It'll take us about an hour and a half to get up to Lucerne," Cale said as he and Luke headed up the lake. "We should still have a little daylight to get unloaded and up the road."

The men had made arrangements with one of the few full-time residents of the small community of Holden Village to pick them up at the boat dock at Lucerne. They'd go with the man to his house, where they would spend the night before heading up into the backcountry.

"Sounds good," Luke said. He was already decompressing. Spending some time in the mountains and not having to worry about anything was what he really needed.

A moment later, he asked, "Have you ever heard of a wilderness survival school?"

"Yeah, there are a couple of them over around Puget Sound, I think. They take folks up into the mountains and teach them different outdoor skills. It's getting pretty popular. Why?"

"Oh, those two kids I was talking with at the dock, they said they're going up into the mountains somewhere around here, part of a wilderness survival school."

"I would have loved that as a kid," Cale said. "But we kind of did our own survival school, learning by the seat of our pants."

"That's the truth. We did survive, though sometimes I don't know how."

The men talked about old times and then about the upcoming hunt as Cale steered the boat up the lake.

*

In Moses Lake, Bakshi, Patel and Singh were making their final plans for meeting Rod Fredricks and Bart Rogers in Chelan. They would get up early and drive to the small town on the lower end of the big lake.

"Have you decided on what we will ask for a ransom?" Singh asked as they loaded some clothes into the Ford Explorer.

"I have," Bakshi said. "From the information that Darsh has obtained, it looks like the father of this Skyler Sloan makes seven hundred and fifty thousand dollars a year before bonuses. With the stock he owns in Starbucks, he has a net worth of over twenty million dollars."

"It might be more than that," Patel said. "Depending on what the stock market does."

"So, we will demand five million dollars for the safe return of his son," Bakshi said. "With our expenses deducted, that should leave each of us over a million apiece."

Patel and Singh smiled.

"But," Bakshi warned. "We are coming up to the most critical part. If Fredricks and Rogers foul up, we will have nothing."

"I surely would not want them to get caught," Singh said. "But if they do, they will not be able to put this on us. They don't even know our real names."

"We will not worry about that now," Bakshi said. "We will be ready to go in the morning."

With the tracking device they had affixed to Fredricks' Suburban, Patel had followed the men on his laptop over the past week. They stayed in and around Ephrata and showed no signs of skipping town with the money that Bakshi had advanced them. It looked like, based on the many places they'd been, including a few taverns, they were spending the money here and there, but rabbiting didn't seem to be in their plans.

Bakshi called Fredricks on the burner phone that night and confirmed they were all set to follow the boat and then the boy.

"Me and Bart borrowed, or should I say, rented the boat. We tested it out on Banks Lake, and it runs good."

"Alright. Good to hear. We will meet you in the park near the boat launch. Our information shows that the boy will meet the instructor at the boat launch next to the park at ten in the morning."

"We'll be there," Fredricks said. "And don't forget our money for when we deliver the boy to you."

✻

Fredricks and Rogers had spent the week after their last meeting discussing the plan that the men from India, or wherever they were from, had laid out for them. At one point, Rogers brought up the possibility that their part of the operation might have nothing to do with rescuing a young man from his mother, but in fact, could be a true kidnapping.

"It could be," Fredricks said. "And in that case, Dinesh and the boys might be asking for a whole bunch of ransom money. When we get the kid, we'll have a little chat with him about his mom and pops. That'll give us a better idea what's going on."

"I'd be in for some more money if that's the case," Rogers said. "We're the ones with our balls hanging out on this deal."

"That's why we need to play it smart. We'll go with the plan, until we don't."

Rogers smiled and said, "Just remember, I ain't into killing no one . . . but if I had to shoot a raghead or two, well, I guess I might be able to."

"Let's hope things don't come to that," Fredricks said. "Our main focus tomorrow is to get the tracking device in the kid's pack."

The men spent the next two hours drinking Keystones and talking about the day to come.

"We're headed for a big payday," Fredricks said. "Finally. I can just feel it."

The next morning at eight o'clock sharp, the men met at the west end of town. Their plan was to take two cars to Chelan for, well, they weren't sure, but it seemed like a good idea. Fredricks pulled the boat borrowed from Ernie Borsman with his Suburban. Rogers followed in a blue 2002 Ford Ranger.

The boat, a twenty-foot aluminum boat made by Hewescraft in Colville, Washington, had a canvas top, vinyl windows, and backdrop. The motor was a two hundred Mercury. It was set up as a fishing boat, but today the boat would be used for tailing. The boat's forty-gallon gas tank was filled with fuel, and the men hoped that would be enough to get to the end of the lake and back.

The men had discussed possible issues with leaving the boat at Stehekin when they followed the kid into the mountains. They weren't wild about the idea, but it seemed the only option. They'd just have to leave the boat at the dock there, Fredricks had said, and, when they got back to Chelan, they would catch The Lady of the Lake back to Stehekin. The Lady of the Lake was a ferry service that featured three different boats beginning at Chelan, hitting several stops along the lake, and ending at Stehekin before turning around and heading back to Chelan.

As they drove to Chelan, the two men chatted with each other on the phones provided to them by Bakshi.

"I hope we don't have to walk too far after the kid today," Rogers said. "I'm kinda hungover. Didn't need those last few beers, for sure."

"Not much you can do about it now," Fredricks said. "I think tomorrow will be the hard day. We're going to have to really huff it to get to the campground by four o'clock."

A while later, after they had passed through Wenatchee, Rogers called and said he needed to stop to pee.

"Okay, we'll stop at one of the mini-marts ahead. We can grab some food and something to drink."

They pulled off the highway at a gas station with a mini-mart attached. When they got out of their trucks, Fredricks asked Rogers how he was doing.

"I've been better," Rogers said. "But I'll be fine. Get a little caffeine and some food into my system, and I'll be good as new."

The men went in, used the restroom, and both filled large Styrofoam cups with coffee. Fredricks grabbed a box of old-fashioned donuts, and Rogers decided he'd go for two beef and bean burritos.

"Can you handle those gut-bombs the way you're feeling?"

"Oh yeah. It's what I eat. Breakfast of champions and all that."

"Okay," Fredricks said. "It's your asshole."

When they came up over the hill and started to drop down into Chelan, the men got a good look at the lake.

"There it is," Fredricks said to Rogers on the phone. "Almost game time."

When they hit Chelan, Fredricks paid particular attention to the speed limit. The last thing he needed was to be stopped right here, right now. They wound their way into Chelan and caught the road that headed out of town toward Manson. The city park and the boat launch were just ahead.

Fredricks was surprised how many rigs pulling boats were in line to launch. He got in line and watched as Rogers drove over to an adjoining parking lot. He saw Rogers pay to park, put a ticket stub in his windshield, and start walking his way.

As Rogers walked to Fredricks' truck, he was watching for the guys from India. And for the kid. One of the guys from India had printed out a photo of the boy and had given it to Fredricks. He then made a color copy and gave it to Rogers, so they both had one.

"We're a little early," Fredricks said when Rogers climbed into the passenger seat. "The boy isn't supposed to meet the wilderness guy until ten. Let's get the boat in the water and then we can hang for a bit."

"I saw Dinesh sitting at a picnic table over in the park, but I didn't see the other two guys," Rogers said. He would have used the other men's names, but frankly he had forgotten who was who. Not that it really mattered. Dinesh was the money man. They knew his name.

"Okay, we'll get the boat in, tie off, I'll pull up and park, and then we'll go touch base with him. Keep an eye out for the kid."

They had no issues launching, other than the fact that the guy who launched just ahead of them had his wife or girlfriend hold the rope to the boat as he backed in to float it off the trailer. Either he hadn't specifically told the woman to walk the boat down the dock to give room for the next boat and trailer to back in, or she was too stupid to look at the situation and see there wasn't enough space for another boat. Either way, it didn't happen. So, they sat and waited. Finally, Rogers climbed out of the truck, walked down to the gal, and explained that because she was standing there holding her boat where it was, no one else could launch.

"My boyfriend told me to just stand here and not say a thing," the twenty-something blonde said. She wore two-hundred-dollar sunglasses and a big floppy straw hat.

"All you have to do is pull the boat down the dock about thirty feet," Rogers explained.

She didn't move. Two minutes later, the boyfriend stomped down the dock and asked, "We got a problem here?"

"The only problem is, with your boat right here in the launch zone, there's no room for anyone else to put their boat in."

"You had to wait, what, four minutes? What's your hurry?" the guy bristled.

"Just trying to keep the line moving," Rogers said and turned back to the truck. Any other day he'd have walked right into that guy and most likely put him in the lake with a broken nose. But he didn't have time for that right now. As he walked away, he heard the guy say, "Asshole."

Rogers stopped. He wanted to go teach the punk a lesson so badly. But again, he thought better of it and kept moving back to the truck.

Once the idiot couple had their boat out of the way, Fredricks backed the trailer with the Hewescraft down into the clear waters of Lake Chelan. Rogers walked it down the dock and tied it up, away from the launch area. He then went up to the park where he had last seen Bakshi sitting.

*

Bakshi watched the two men launch their boat. He saw the taller man, Rogers, talk to a young blonde woman in a big hat at the dock. Then a man showed up. It looked like a confrontation of some kind was developing, but Rogers walked away.

Seven minutes later, Rogers and Fredricks were at the picnic table.

"Are we all set?" Bakshi asked.

"Yep, ready to go. All we need to do now is identify the kid, get the tracking device in his backpack, and we'll be ready to rock."

"Have you located the boat that will take them to the other end of the lake?"

Fredricks looked around at the two dozen boats sitting in slips and tied to the docks. Some had people in them, others did not. He almost made a smart remark about the stupid question but bit his tongue.

"Not yet. But as soon as we see the kid climb on board one of these boats, we will know."

"Okay. We will plan on meeting you at the campground that is marked on your GPS."

"Oh, shit," Fredricks said. "We forgot the GPS."

"You what? How will you find us? I can't believe—"

"Just kidding there, Dinesh buddy. We got it."

For a second, Bakshi wondered who Dinesh was. Then he remembered it was the fake name he had given himself when he first met the men.

"That is not funny," Bakshi said. "This is serious business. You don't show up at the right place at the right time, and you will see how serious we are."

"Take a chill pill, dude," Fredricks said. "We want the payday just as bad as you guys. We'll be there. Now, we gotta find the kid."

Bakshi just stared at Fredricks. His whole plan rested on the ability of these two to snatch the kid in the wilderness and get him back to the campground on time, in one piece. He was beginning to worry. Finally, he said "go" like he was dismissing the two. But they had already turned their backs and were walking back to the boat at the docks.

CHAPTER 23

They'd been motoring up-lake for a little over an hour when Cale leaned over to Luke and said, "There it is."

Luke looked and saw a small landing with maybe a half dozen boats. He had enjoyed the ride up-lake, but Luke was ready to get his feet on terra firma and start walking. Jack lay asleep at his feet.

As they got closer to the landing at Lucerne, the men could see a lone man standing next to a '70s vintage Chevy pickup. The man waved to them.

"There's Earl," Cale said. "He's our ride up the hill."

They pulled up to the dock, tied the boat off, and started offloading their gear on the dock. Jack jumped out of the boat, ran up the dock to the man walking down, sniffed him for a millisecond, and then ran over to a tree to relieve himself.

"Hello, gentlemen," Earl said. "You must be Cale and Luke?"

"We are," Cale said. They climbed out onto the dock and shook the man's hand.

Earl was what might be described as slight. He was maybe five foot, ten inches tall, and Luke guessed his weight at around one-fifty. Probably in his late 60s, Earl was wearing a red hat with a yellow Winchester logo on it, the hair sticking out from under it white as snow. He wore green Carhartt pants and a green and black checkered shirt with a tan Carhartt vest over the top.

"Glad to be of service," Earl said. "Now, let's get that gear loaded and up to the house. Joyce has some stew simmering on the stove."

"Sounds great," Cale said, and the men packed all their stuff up and threw it in the bed of the truck.

"Hope you don't mind my hound coming along with us," Luke said. "He's pretty well mannered, and frankly, he'll probably just find a place to curl up and go to sleep."

"Cale said you'd have a dog. No problem with us. We love dogs. We had a St. Bernard that passed just a couple months ago, so it will be nice to have a four-legged critter in the house again."

"C'mon, Jack," Luke called. "Load up."

Jack came on the run and jumped into the bed of the truck.

The plan was for Cale and Luke to shack up at Earl's place in Holden Village, and then Earl would take them as far as he could on the primitive road up near Glacier Peak Wilderness the next morning.

The men got to the house, where Earl and Joyce treated them like long-lost relatives. Joyce was also slight of build. Four inches shorter than her husband, she might have weighed a hundred and five after a big meal. Also in her late 60s, Joyce's hair was a reddish shade of gray, and she wore it in a bob cut. Under a knee-length apron, she wore blue denim britches and a white blouse with blue flowers splashed around on it.

"I'd be careful of that," Luke said when he saw Joyce put some stew meat in Jack's dog dish. "He might just decide to stay, and then you'll have a hundred-pound mooch on your hands."

"Oh, we'd love that," Joyce said as she rubbed Jack's ears. "We've really been missing Arthur, our big old lovable St. Bernard."

"I assume you want to get an early start in the morning," Earl said.

"Yes, if we could," Cale said. "How long will it take to get to the end of the road?"

"Only about a half hour. Daylight is right around six, so if we leave here at five-thirty, that should be about right."

"I'll have breakfast ready at five," Joyce said.

"Oh, no need to do that," Cale said. "We've imposed too much already."

"I won't take no for an answer."

Luke looked at Earl, who was giving a look like everyone would be smart to just go along with the lady of the house.

After breakfast the next morning, which included sausage, farm-fresh eggs, and hotcakes with huckleberries and homemade huckleberry syrup, the men climbed into the old Chevy and, with Jack in the bed, slowly drove up the road.

"We have no idea how long we'll be up here," Cale said as they drove. "But Luke has a satellite phone, so if you're around when we get back down to the road, maybe we could call for a lift to the boat?"

"Oh, sure," Earl said. "We'll be here for another week, then we need to go to Chelan for some groceries and a few other items. We're starting to get ready for winter."

It was just getting light enough to make out some trees in the distance when Luke and Cale climbed out of the truck, grabbed their backpacks from the truck's bed, thanked Earl again for all the hospitality, and headed up a fairly obvious trail. Because it was opening day of deer season, and they might stumble into a nice buck at any time, Luke kept Jack at heel.

The men hiked at a robust pace, and Luke was glad he'd been working out all summer to get his lung capacity to where he could keep up with Cale. The man was a beast when it came to climbing around in the mountains.

"I'd like to get to that peak by noon," Cale said, pointing to a mountain off in the distance after they'd hiked for two hours. "We can set up camp there, and it will give us a great spot to glass from in the morning."

Luke looked at the peak. He figured it had to be four miles away. He wasn't totally sure they could make it by late afternoon, but he was willing to give it a try.

"Let's keep our eyes open for grouse," Luke said. "Fried grouse for dinner would be better than freeze-dried meals."

The men were trying to walk as quietly as they could, but they were pushing along at a pretty good pace. They'd occasionally stop for a breather, and when they did, they would glass the surrounding slopes.

It was on one of their stops that Luke spotted a group of four mule deer bucks about a mile away. From that distance, it was too hard to count points on their antlers, but one of the bucks stood out because its antlers were definitely wider than its ears.

"There's some deer. Looks like all bucks," Luke said. "And one looks pretty nice."

"How far?" Cale asked.

"A mile or more. See that dead snag just below that rounded rock bluff?"

Cale looked where Luke was telling him, and finally found the bucks in his binoculars. Then he pulled out his spotting scope to get a closer look. No sense walking a mile or more, if the bucks weren't legal to pursue.

"That one is definitely a shooter," Cale finally said.

The two men talked about where the deer were located. They checked the wind and decided they would need to go down the hill, drop into a side canyon, and try to get as close as they could from there. The wind would be crossing, and Cale hoped that would get him within four hundred yards of the biggest of the bucks.

Luke knew that should be plenty close for Cale with his sniper training. Cale never talked about it, but Luke knew his friend had killed men in Afghanistan. And many of those had been taken from long range, most likely out to a thousand yards. Four hundred yards was not a simple shot, but it would definitely be doable for a skilled marksman like Cale.

"I'm going to let you go from here," Luke said. "I'll stay here with Jack. By law, I can't let him be any part of this."

"Sounds good," Cale said. "You can keep an eye on the deer and let me know if they move."

They worked out some signals. If the deer stayed where they were, Luke would take his hat off and wave it when Cale checked in with him. If the deer had moved, he would cross his arms over his head. Then he'd point in the direction the deer had moved.

Cale took off down the hill, dropping into the next canyon. Luke knew it would take him a while to get within decent rifle range, and while he couldn't see his friend, he was able to watch the bucks.

After twenty-five minutes, Luke finally saw Cale slowly make his way up the side of the draw, in line with the deer. His friend had pulled his rifle from his pack and now had it in his hands, ready to set up and shoot. Luke watched as Cale turned and looked back at him with his binoculars. Luke took his hat off and waved it. He saw Cale hold one arm up, giving a thumbs up, then he turned and kept moving toward the deer. About that time, Luke felt a slight breeze hit the back of his neck. He hoped the same breeze didn't hit where Cale was because it would be blowing his scent right at the deer.

Luke observed through his binoculars as Cale inched slowly up the hill and then saw him drop to his belly. Luke checked the deer. The bucks suddenly raised their heads in unison, ears forward, and were looking right back at Cale. Then they took off, bounding up the hill in a line, the biggest of the four bringing up the rear. One by one, the bucks crested a small ridge and then disappeared from sight. For some reason, the last buck stopped for just a second to look back before going over the ridge. It was a fatal mistake. The buck's legs folded underneath him, and he started rolling back down the hill. A second later, Luke heard the crack of Cale's rifle.

"Nice shot!" Luke hollered, although from that distance he wasn't sure Cale could hear him.

Luke watched as the deer kept rolling down the hill until it was stopped by a big rock. He then looked back at Cale, who was now on his feet, aiming the rifle in the deer's direction. His friend was ready if the buck were to get up and start going again, although Luke knew by the way the deer had gone down that it wasn't getting up again.

After five minutes, Luke watched Cale put on his pack and start walking to the downed deer. Luke kept an eye on the deer until his friend made it to the animal.

"Let's go, Jack," Luke said, and they headed to meet Cale at the deer.

"That's a beautiful buck, Cale," Luke said when he and Jack finally got to the mule deer. "You'll not find a much better one in Washington State."

Just by eyeballing it, Luke figured the outside spread of the buck's antlers was pushing twenty-six inches. It was a typical four-by-four with eye guards, and there was a sticker point coming off one of the antlers on the right side. The antlers were heavy, and the forks on both sides were deep. There were still some tiny patches of the fuzzy velvet near the base of each antler.

"It got pretty intense there from where I was watching," Luke said. "I didn't know if he would stop, or if you were even in range."

"I figured he was a little over five hundred yards," Cale said. "I had ranged the group just before they took off, and they were three hundred and ninety-six yards. Then I felt the wind change."

Cale was shooting a Savage Model 111 in .260 Remington. He'd practiced with the rifle in the month leading up to the hunt at ranges out to seven hundred and fifty yards. The practice—and using one of the most accurate long-range rifles and calibers—made the one-shot kill quick and clean.

"Well, from where I was, it looked like a heckuva shot. Let's get some photos."

Cale cut the notches on his deer tag with his knife and wrapped electrical tape around the license, affixing it to the buck's antlers. They took several photos and then went to work breaking the deer down. The men were going to have to pack it more than three miles back to the road over some rough country, so they decided they would remove all the meat off the bone to make the load as light as possible.

It took a little over an hour to get the deer cut up and into game bags. Luke tied the bags in the shade of some spruce trees to allow the mountain air to circulate and cool the meat. The bags kept the meat clean from debris and pesky flies.

"Why don't we set up camp down there?" Cale said, pointing to a flat spot four hundred yards downhill, surrounded by some spruce trees. "We could call Earl and try to get down to the road before dark, but I like the idea of staying up here, at least one night."

"Sure," Luke said. "I like that idea. The meat will cool nicely tonight. We can even cut some steaks off the backstrap and have those for dinner."

"Now you're talking," Cale said as he washed his hands with water from the camel bladder inside his pack.

By the time the men had an area cleared of branches, pine cones and a few rocks, and had their one-man tents set up, the sun was dropping behind the mountain. They set their pads and sleeping bags in their tents, and while Cale rounded up a few rocks to build a fire ring, Luke and Jack went in search of firewood.

Luke felt bad for Jack because basically the whole day he'd had the dog stay at heel, or very close by. Now, he let Jack run, and the dog took advantage of it. Jack swung back and forth, searching here and there, as if they were actually hunting grouse.

They were walking uphill in the direction of where they had left the entrails and the bones of the dead mule deer when Luke spotted something dark moving toward the carcass.

"Jack! Come!" Luke hissed. The dog came right to him. "Sit, boy." Jack sat.

Luke still had his binoculars on his chest, and he took a better look at what he had glimpsed uphill. Luke had assumed it was a bear coming to scavenge the remains of the buck, but a closer look showed it was a wolverine. And not just one wolverine but two of the ferocious animals.

The largest members of the weasel family, wolverines are fierce predators known to take on coyotes, wolves, cougars, and even bears when protecting a kill. They have incredibly strong jaws, very sharp teeth and claws, and can do serious damage to a man or dog.

Not wanting to get too close, Luke just watched with Jack sitting at his side as the two wolverines ran quickly to the carcass and started eating the entrails. Within five minutes, they were done with what they wanted. Then, with much more ease than Luke could have imagined, the biggest of the two wolverines picked up the rib cage and carried it like a dog with a bone back the way they had come, disappearing into the trees.

It was then Luke thought about his cellphone. Why hadn't he taken some video of the wolverines? Oh well, it was an incredible encounter, and one he knew he'd never forget.

When he got to their little camp with the firewood, Luke told Cale about the wolverines. They built a fire, and once the wood was burned down into some hot coals, they cut some steaks, poked them on some green aspen branches, and let the meat cook.

"Better throw one on there for Jack," Cale said. "He's at least as hungry as we are."

The men and Jack ate their venison steaks and enjoyed every bite of them.

"That has to be the best deer I've ever eaten," Cale said.

Luke agreed that it was good. Of course, the men were hungry, and just about everything tastes better when eaten by a fire in some remote place.

The two old friends talked and talked until the last piece of wood in the fire was reduced to embers.

As they crawled into their tents, Cale said, "Thanks for being here, Luke. It's been a great day, and I can't think of anyone else I would have wanted to spend it with."

"My sentiments exactly."

Luke was as physically tired as he had been in a while. With Jack by his side, Luke fell asleep in about a minute. His last thoughts were of the two wolverines working on the deer carcass.

Sometime in the middle of the night, he was awakened by Jack's low growl.

"What is it boy?" Luke whispered.

Jack growled again. Luke listened, but he heard nothing. He had his shotgun lying next to him, not so much for protection but because he wanted to keep it dry. Now he was glad he'd put it in the tent with him and hadn't leaned it up against a tree next to his pack.

They had hung the deer meat in the game bags fifteen feet off ground on a limb of a spruce tree about a hundred yards from the tent. Luke was pretty sure it was safe from bears and the resident wolverines.

Jack's ears perked, and he growled again. This time louder.

The dog could certainly be smelling something, and his hearing was way better than Luke's, but there was no way of knowing what might be out there. He figured if a bear was getting too close to the tents, Jack would go berserk. Luke decided to just wait and see what might happen.

Finally, after ten minutes or so, Jack relaxed, put his head down, and went back to sleep. Luke did the same, but it took him a little longer to fall asleep this time around.

After what seemed like only another twenty minutes, Luke heard movement around outside and then realized it was light. He checked his watch. It was a little after six.

"Morning in there," Cale said. "Thought you might want to sleep in a bit."

"Yeah, it felt good," Luke said as he let Jack out of the tent, then pulled on some pants and climbed out.

Cale had his backpacking stove fired up and was boiling water for some coffee.

"You want to take the time to cook some breakfast?" Cale asked.

"Naw, I'm good with a granola bar. We should probably get going if we're going to meet Earl at the road by nine o'clock."

After they had set their camp up the night before, Luke had called Earl from his satellite phone and arranged to have the man pick them up in the morning.

"Sounds good. Coffee will be ready momentarily," Cale said.

Luke started to pack up his pad and sleeping bag and pull down his tent.

"Did you hear anything weird in the middle of the night?" Luke asked.

"No, did you?"

"I didn't, but Jack did. Could've been the wolverines running around up the hill or who knows."

Both men looked at where they'd put the bags of venison in the tree. They were still hanging from the branch of the spruce, right where they had tied them the night before.

"The meat's safe," Cale said. "Could've been anything, coyotes or maybe a cougar."

They drank their coffee and ate a quick granola bar, then went and retrieved the meat. Luke placed one bag in his pack, Cale the other in his. They looked around their little campsite, making sure they were leaving nothing behind, and started down the hill. As they walked, Luke let Jack run ahead, now not having to worry about him spooking deer.

It took a little over three hours of hiking to get to the road, and when they arrived, Earl was there waiting in his truck.

"Sure appreciate you doing this," Cale said. "We thought about staying another night or two up there, but as warm as it is, we wanted to get the meat back to our boat and on ice."

"Glad you had some success," Earl said. "Joyce is working on some fresh blueberry muffins. We'd love to have you stop and have one with us if you have the time."

Luke looked at Cale. It was his decision.

"I think we can do that," Cale said.

"Great," Earl said. "She really wanted to see Jack again, so this will make her happy."

They were just about to Earl's house when Luke heard his satellite phone ringing in his pack in the back of the truck.

"No one should be calling now," Luke said. "You mind stopping for a second so I can answer it?"

Earl stopped the truck, and Luke pulled his backpack to the tailgate of the truck, sat on it, dug out the ringing phone, and said, "This is Luke."

Cale saw Luke's face go from happy to very serious in an instant.

CHAPTER 24

Skip Harvey met the boys at the city park at 9:30, a half an hour before they were to board the boat for the ride up to Stehekin. He wanted to size the two boys up and figure out how much each of them could carry once they left the boat. His packing assessment was akin to loading packhorses. They could only carry so much, and someone had to figure out just how much that was.

Both boys were typical sixteen-year-olds. They were long and lean. The blonde-haired Sloan stood just over six feet tall. Green, who wore his black hair short on the sides and longer on top, looked to be two inches shorter than his friend. They both looked to be in pretty good physical shape.

In talking to Sloan's father before they met, Harvey knew the boy had played basketball on the high school team and played AAU ball most of the summer. And Green was part of an elite soccer club that played throughout the spring, summer, and fall. Those activities would help, for sure, but Harvey knew even at that, they'd have a few sore muscles after climbing some of these mountain trails.

He had seen them pull into the parking lot and now watched as they unloaded their backpacks and pulled them onto their shoulders. They walked toward the park, and when he caught their eye, he waved them over.

"Hi, guys," Harvey said. "I'm Skip."

"Hey, Skip," Sloan said. "I'm Skyler, and this is Tory."

Harvey shook hands with the boys and said, "Good to meet you guys. Are you ready for a new adventure?"

"Boy, are we," Green said. "We've been looking forward to this for some time."

"It doesn't hurt that you're missing a week of school, huh?"

"No kidding," Sloan said. "This will be so much better."

Harvey noticed a dark-haired man with a jet-black beard sitting at a picnic table watching them closely but just figured the guy was jealous of the young men getting ready for a backpacking trip into the wilderness. He didn't see the man wave to two men sitting in a boat down at the docks.

After chatting with the boys for a few minutes, Harvey walked with them back to the parking lot where his truck was parked. Their week's supply of food, as well as a few other necessary items, were waiting to be divided up and packed into backpacks.

By the time the boys had everything loaded, their packs were right at fifty pounds. Harvey's pack was pushing seventy.

Sloan and Green groaned when they picked their packs up, and both had some trouble getting into the shoulder straps.

"You'll get used to it," Harvey said. "And each day, they will get lighter."

He helped Sloan and Green make adjustments to their packs so the load was riding on their hips, taking most of the weight off their shoulders. They worked on the packs until both boys felt good in them.

"OK," Harvey said. "Let's go find our ride."

*

Rod Fredricks saw the man they knew as Dinesh waving at them from a picnic table. He then discretely pointed to two young men walking with a guy in hiker's shorts and boots to the parking lot.

"There's our target," Fredricks said.

"I see two boys," Rogers said. "Which one is the target?"

"Not sure. Where's the photo I gave you?"

"I didn't bring it. I thought you'd have yours."

"I thought you would have yours."

"We'll figure it out."

"The hiker dude looks to be in pretty good shape. Hope we don't have to tangle with him."

"We won't if we do it right. Now, we need to figure out how to get the tracking device in the kid's pack."

"Maybe when they come down to the docks, one of us could help them set their gear into their boat."

"Or," Fredricks said, "we can maybe bump into him or brush up against him and place it then."

"I've been thinking about this," Rogers said. "We don't have to place the thing in his pack here. We could do it up where we're going to get out to start hiking. In fact, since we know where they're going, we could take off now and be waiting for them when they get there. That way they don't think we're following them."

Fredricks thought about that for a minute.

"You know, that's a pretty good idea. We're loaded, just sitting here. Let's do it."

Rogers got out, untied the dock lines, and jumped back into the boat as Fredricks started the motor and backed out.

*

As soon as Bakshi realized the men in the boat were leaving without placing the tracking unit on the boy, he pulled out his phone to call Fredricks. This was not part of the plan.

"Hey, Dinesh," Fredricks said.

"What are you doing? What about placing the tracking device in the boy's pack?"

"We got a different plan for doing that. Don't worry. We'll do it up at the other end of the lake."

"I hope you don't lose them because of this. It is imperative that you know where they are camping tonight."

"Understood. We got it." Then Fredricks pushed the button to end the call.

*

Harvey had seen a photo of the boat that was going to shuttle them to the end of Lake Chelan. It was a large North River aluminum boat with a blue top and twin hundred-and-fifty-horsepower motors in the back. He watched as a Duckworth boat with two men in it headed out of the marina and motored up-lake. Then he spotted the bigger North River slowly motoring from some slips in another area over to where the Duckworth had been.

"There's our ride," Harvey said. "Let's go."

With heavy packs on their backs, the three marched down the ramp to the docks and out to where the boat captain was wrapping the bow rope to a cleat.

"Hi, fellas," the captain said. "I'm Jim Werenski."

Harvey, Sloan, and Green introduced themselves.

Werenski jumped into the back of the boat and said, "Hand me your gear. I'll get it stowed, and we can be on our way."

Once the gear was in and securely stowed, the captain went through a quick safety chat, telling them where the life jackets and fire extinguisher were stored.

"It's about two hours to Stehekin. Keep an eye on the hills along the lake. There's a good chance we'll see some wildlife."

The boys asked what kind of wildlife they might see, and Werenski told them they might see deer, bears, turkeys, Bighorn sheep, and maybe even some mountain goats.

"Any wolves around here?" Sloan asked.

"They're around, but I've only seen wolves once. They're pretty shy."

"How about cougars?" Green asked.

"Chances of seeing one are slim. I spotted a female and two young ones last spring. So, you never know."

"That'd be cool," Green said.

As they motored up the lake, Harvey talked to the boys about what they could expect from the week.

"Once we get to Stehekin, we'll need to get going right away," Harvey said. "I've located our first camping spot on the GPS map. It's not too far, but I want to get there with some daylight left, so you can see how the tent goes up and what we need to do to make camp each night. You'll each have tasks that will be your responsibility every day."

He explained that there was a chance for some rain and possible snow later in the week. Knowing who was doing what, and how to get the tent up quickly and correctly, could mean the difference between spending the night in a dry sleeping bag or puddles of water.

The boat ride was smooth, and it seemed like they were going faster than they really were. About halfway up the lake, Werenski shut the motors down.

"Look up on that rocky ridge," he said. "There are some sheep up there."

They all looked, and finally each of them located the small herd of sheep containing two mature rams. About that time, the rams faced off, stood up on their back legs, and then smashed into each other, head-to-head. The head crash was so violent, it sounded like someone had shot a rifle.

"Wow, did you see that?" Sloan asked.

Werenski explained that this was the breeding season for the bighorns, and the rams would be butting heads with one another for days, fighting for the right to breed the ewes when they came into heat. They watched the sheep for a few minutes, then Werenski fired the motors up, and they continued their run up the lake.

Sloan spotted some deer, and Harvey spotted a black bear as they traveled up-lake. They stopped to get a better look at the bear. Neither Sloan nor Green had ever seen a bear in the wild.

"I hope we don't see one up close and personal when we're camping," Green said.

"They're more afraid of you than you are of them," Werenski said. "Just keep any food up outta their reach, and you'll be fine."

It was a beautiful ride up the lake, and at certain spots Werenski would give a little history on the lake or the wildlife. When they arrived at Stehekin, two guys in a Hewescraft were sitting at the docks. They had offloaded backpacks onto the docks but now seemed to be just sitting there. Werenski pulled up right behind them. Harvey jumped out onto the dock, grabbed the rope at the bow of the boat, and held it until Werenski could get out and tie it up.

"You have enough room?" the shorter of the two guys from the Hewescraft asked Werenski.

"Plenty, thanks," Werenski said as he finished securing the bow rope to the dock.

"Let's get your gear out," Harvey said. "We're burning daylight."

Werenski helped set the packs on the dock, and the boys and Harvey picked them up.

"Thanks so much, Jim. We'll see you right here on Sunday."

"Yessir," Werenski said. "You guys have fun and be safe."

Harvey untied the ropes and pushed the big North River off. Werenski waved his thanks, and he turned the boat out into the lake for the run back to Chelan.

The men from the other boat were standing around their packs, blocking the path, so Harvey said, "Excuse us," and he and the boys walked around them, Green bringing up the rear.

About that time, the shorter man stood and said, "You got something hanging out of your pack." He then tucked something into the side pocket of Green's pack.

"Thanks," Green said. And they kept moving.

*

They had to wait twenty-five minutes at the dock before they finally saw the big North River boat motoring up the lake.

"You have that device ready?" Rogers asked.

"Yeah, let's just hope we get a chance to get it in the kid's pack," Fredricks said.

They got lucky when the boat the boys were in pulled in just behind them at the docks.

"Let's set our stuff on the dock," Fredricks said quietly. "If we keep it there, they'll have to walk around it, and maybe we can place the tracker."

After Fredricks slipped the tracker in a small pocket in the pack of one of the boys, Rogers said, "That worked out well."

"Let's keep an eye on it and make sure it's working. If it isn't, we'll need to hurry it up and try to stay within eyesight of them."

After turning the tracking GPS unit on, Fredricks dialed it in and soon found a red dot moving along a line, indicating a road up the hill.

"It's working," Fredricks said. "So, we don't have to hurry. We'll know right where they stop for the night and move in then."

The men put their backpacks back onto the boat and then moved the boat around to one of the available slips in the public marina. After throwing out some bumpers and tying off, Fredricks looked around. A sign on the lodge said the café inside was open.

"How's your stomach?" he asked Rogers.

"Better. Why?"

"Let's go up there and get something to eat. Then we'll come back, get our packs, and be on our way."

While the men waited for their lunch to arrive, Fredricks watched the GPS. The boys and the wilderness coach had walked up the hill and were now on a trail identified as the Purple Creek Trail on the screen.

"They're on the trail," Fredricks said. "They'll most likely stay on it today."

"You know what we shoulda bought?" Rogers asked.

Fredricks stared at the GPS and just shook his head.

"Some night vision goggles."

"Too expensive. I thought about them, but we got headlamps. That'll be good enough."

The men ate their hamburgers and fries and watched some of the tourists come and go. After sitting in the café for an hour, they wandered back down to their boat, pulled their backpacks out, and put them on.

Fredricks looked at the GPS tracking unit again.

"They're still moving" he said. "Probably a mile ahead of us. That should be perfect."

"This is gonna be a piece of cake," Rogers said.

CHAPTER 25

Skip Harvey led the way as he and Sloan and Green walked around a small building with a sign that read visitor's center and headed up the gravel road.

"Can we stop for a minute?" Green asked. "I promised my mom I would text her and let her know we're here. If I don't, she'll totally freak."

"There's not much phone service here," Harvey said.

"She got me one of these SpotX satellite messengers," Green said. "As long as there's not a bunch of trees overhead, I can send and receive text messages. I practiced with it last week."

Harvey was familiar with the device. He had a satellite phone in his pack, but it was there for emergencies only. He didn't like letting the participants in his weekly outings know he had a phone, or they'd all be wanting to call someone.

"Sure," Harvey said.

Green took his pack off and started digging in a pocket for the small device. If he had reached just a little farther into the pocket, he would have found the tracking device.

"You know, that was kind of weird that guy on the dock zipping a pocket on my pack," Green said as he texted a short message to his mom. "I'm pretty sure I had them all closed."

"Yeah, you'd think they woulda moved their stuff outta the way on the dock," Sloan said. "It looked like they were gonna be up here someplace too."

After Green pushed send on his text, he put the little GPS texter back in his pack, and the three continued their hike.

Where the road ended, there was a sign that read Purple Creek Trail. They hit the trail and kept walking. Along the way Harvey would occasionally point out plants that would be edible if they were stranded in this area.

"This is chicory," Harvey said, plucking a long-stemmed purple flower out of the grass next to the trail. He pulled a couple leaves off the plant and stuck them in his mouth. "The leaves of the young plants are the most edible. And you can eat the flowers and roots too."

Sloan and Green each pulled one of the plants out of the ground and ate a leaf.

"Not great tasting," Sloan said. "But I guess if I was hungry enough."

After an hour of hiking, gaining elevation as they went, they stopped for a much-needed breather.

"Get a good drink from your bottles," Harvey said. "We'll be passing a spring ahead, and we can refill them there."

As they rested, the boys ate some GORP trail mix that Green's mom had prepared and sent with them. The GORP was a mixture of raisins, nuts, sunflower seeds, dried cranberries, and M&M's.

"This is way better than chicory," Sloan said as he munched on a handful of the mix.

As they sat eating and drinking, Harvey pulled out his GPS unit and fired it up. Once the unit had acquired the appropriate number of satellites, he demonstrated for the boys some of the things the GPS unit could do, showing where they were and checking the longitude and latitude and elevation.

"Zoom out a bit and look at the trail we're on," Harvey instructed as he pointed to the GPS screen. "We're right here now, and this is where we will camp tonight."

"So, it's about two miles away," Sloan said.

"That's right," Harvey said. "So, we better keep moving."

They had gained about fifteen hundred feet of elevation from where they'd hit the trail at the boat docks, and soon they hit Sawtooth Ridge. At that point, there were three trails they could take. They followed the trail that ran due north along the ridge.

When they reached a flat spot just off the trail that was protected from the wind, Harvey said, "This is the spot. We'll make camp here for the night."

The boys were tired, but they were also excited.

Harvey asked Sloan to go find some good, dry firewood. "Get some small diameter pieces, and also some bigger pieces for when the fire gets going." Then he asked Green to round up some rocks for a fire ring. "About the size of a volleyball will be good."

The boys went to work gathering the essentials for a fire. Harvey had brought two backpacking stoves, but teaching the boys how to make a fire was one of the first lessons. On the list of items that he had the boys bring was a waterproof container that held some stick matches. He would show the boys how to start a fire without matches later. Right now, he just wanted them to learn how to build the fire with the good, flammable materials available in the vicinity.

Sloan was still out gathering wood, but because there were about five million rocks on the ridge, Green had rounded up plenty, and Harvey showed him how to make a good fire ring.

"If you have something to dig a bit of a hole or impression in the ground, start with that," he instructed. "If you don't have a shovel, a small frying pan or even a sturdy piece of wood will work."

The two worked on the hard ground for a bit and made a slight dent in the dirt. They then placed the rocks around the area they had dug out.

"The rocks work in a number of ways," Harvey said. "They block the wind, they help retain the heat, and they can be used to help with the cooking."

Sloan returned with another armload of dry branches. Harvey then sent both boys for some longer, thicker branches. When they returned, he showed the boys how, by placing the branches between two trees or rocks, they could bend and break them down into burnable size.

"Now, go find some pine cones and check down in that thick grove of evergreens," Harvey said. "Grab as much dried moss and lichen as you can get from them."

The boys returned with big armfuls of both. Harvey showed them how to start with the dried moss, then add tiny twigs to build a tent around the moss. He lit the moss, and it was burning with high flames in an instant. The twigs caught fire too, and Harvey added the pinecones. Once the fire was burning good, he put a couple larger branches on the fire, and in a minute, there was a nice fire in the pit.

"We'll keep adding bigger pieces, and soon we'll have some good coals for cooking," Harvey said. "You think you can build a fire like that?"

Both boys nodded and said they could.

"Good, because from now on, that's one of your jobs. Now, let's get the tent set up."

Harvey explained to them that normally he would put the tent up first, especially if there was the possibility of rain for bad weather approaching, but today he wanted them to learn how to build a fire.

The two young men followed instructions well, and in a few minutes, they had the tent erected. Harvey showed them how to anchor the tent and the rain fly in case of wind by using rocks tied with cord to the tent.

When the tent was up, Harvey pulled his sleeping pad and bag out of his pack and put them inside. Sloan and Green did the same.

With that done, Harvey sent the boys out for more firewood because, he told them, "You can never have too much." And then, when they had a pile of wood that a white-tailed deer couldn't jump over, he sent them into a nearby aspen grove and had them cut several stout branches with a small hatchet he magically pulled out of his backpack.

As they were walking to the aspen grove, Green said, "I wonder what else he has in that pack?"

"For sure, he has a pistol," Sloan said. "Remember, he told my dad he would have one with him for protection from bears."

"That's right. I forgot about that. He said we might get to shoot it sometime this week."

"I don't know how he carries that pack. It must weigh twice as much as ours."

When they got back with the branches, Harvey showed them how to use their knives to peel the leaves and small twigs off them. When they'd finished that, he lay them on the rocks over the fire. Crisscrossed at ninety-degree angles, they made a neat grill.

"The green branches will burn at some point," Harvey explained. "But they'll resist long enough to cook a fish or a burger."

"Do we have burgers?" Green asked.

"No, we do not. But now you know how to do it if we did."

"We should've tried to catch a fish out of the lake on the way up here," Sloan said.

"It wouldn't have been fit to eat after our hike up here," Harvey said. "No, we'll do freeze-dried stroganoff tonight."

He pulled a small pot out of his pack, poured water into it from his camel bladder, and placed it on the aspen branch grill.

"The camp stoves will boil water much faster, but no sense burning the fuel when we have a nice fire burning."

The boys dug into their packs and found a pack of freeze-dried beef stroganoff. When the water was at a rumbling boil, they opened the food pouches, and Harvey poured the hot water into them. All three then used their sporks to stir the ingredients of their pouches until they were good and mixed together.

"Hey, this isn't too bad," Green said. "It really does taste like stroganoff."

"It's definitely not like the beef stroganoff my mom makes," Sloan said. "But it'll eat."

Harvey smiled. Just this summer he'd eaten about a thousand of the meals. He was definitely getting tired of them.

When they were done with the main course, Harvey had them dig out a packet of freeze-dried banana pudding. The boys tore into that and finished it in a minute.

After they finished dinner, Harvey had the boys take out a few of the items they had been asked to bring with them. Harvey grabbed the small, bright orange bag that Sloan had pulled from his backpack. Bold print on the bag read, "Life Bivy." He opened the little bag and pulled out a very lightweight, bright orange sleeping bag and a whistle on a parachute cord. Green had an identical bag in his pack.

"These can be lifesavers," Harvey said. "The sleeping bag is good to fourteen degrees."

Then he blew the whistle. The noise it emitted as Harvey blew on it almost hurt the boys' ears.

"Geez, that's loud," Green said.

"Yep, it can be heard from a mile away," Harvey said. "And the paracord can be used for all kind of things when you need it."

"But we have good sleeping bags with us," Sloan said. "Why would we need this?"

"This a wilderness survival school," Harvey said. "I'm trying to get you prepared for anything. And believe me, just about anything can happen up here."

He went on to talk about how they might be taking a side-hike farther up onto the mountain, away from the trail, leaving the tent and their sleeping bags at the campsite.

"What if one of you get separated from us, or someone were to get injured and had to stay up here overnight until help arrived? This stuff would be nice to have. It could be a lifesaver."

The boys both thought about that for a few seconds and then agreed. They put the bivies back into their packs.

Next, Harvey picked up a small orange thing that looked like an oversized thumb drive. He pulled the thing apart, exposing a flint surface on one side and a striker on the other. Next, he grabbed some of the moss the boys had gathered, balled it up, and started striking sparks onto it. After three sparks, the moss started smoking. Harvey blew on it gently, and a small flame erupted.

"See how easy that was," he said as he stamped out the little fire. "Now you try it."

Both of the young men had no trouble starting a fire.

"These will work when it's wet too. They make sparks three times hotter than a match."

"Do we really need this compass?" Green asked as he picked up the small watch-like device. "Wouldn't a GPS tell us where we want to go?"

"What if you lose your GPS, or the batteries go dead?" Harvey asked. "Everyone needs to know how to use a compass."

"I kinda learned in Cub Scouts," Sloan said. "But I'm not sure I could use one now with any real confidence."

"We'll go over that tomorrow when we're moving," Harvey said. "For now, let's repack our packs and start thinking about bed."

As the sun sank behind the hill, the temperatures began to drop as well. Harvey put on a jacket and placed the small pan back on the fire. He poured some water into it, and when it was good and warm, poured some on a washcloth and started washing his face and neck.

"You guys want some hot water to wash up with?"

"Actually, that sounds pretty good," Sloan said.

He found the washcloth he had packed and copied Harvey. Green did the same.

A bit later, after darkness had set in, the three sat around the fire and chatted. The boys told Harvey about their school, their sports teams, and the girls they liked. Harvey told them about his guiding jobs around the Northwest, fishing different rivers, climbing several of the big mountains in Washington and Oregon.

As the fire was dying, Sloan looked up into the night sky for a minute and said, "I never knew there were so many stars."

"They're there all the time," Harvey said. "You just need to get away from the city lights to see them."

"There's Uranus," Green said with a smile.

It was a juvenile joke, but within seconds, all three of them were laughing.

When they were done laughing like a bunch of seventh graders, Harvey pointed to the southeast and said, "Actually, you can see Uranus with binoculars. It's a blue planet. Looks like just another star, but you can see it if you know where to look."

The boys grabbed their binoculars and looked, but neither could figure out which of the tiny light specks was Uranus. They could see Mars though, and Harvey pointed out several constellations.

"How do you know all this stuff?" Green asked.

"When you spend as much time outdoors, staring at the night sky as I have, you just learn it. I think it is really interesting."

They looked and talked about the stars and the moon phases for another half hour.

"Okay, guys, let's hit the rack," Harvey said. "We've got some miles to walk tomorrow."

CHAPTER 26

They had watched the school instructor and the two boys sitting around the fire. The two men were cloaked in darkness and knew they couldn't be seen. Even so, they stayed way up on the ridge where they wouldn't be noticed.

"Looks like they're going to bed," Fredricks said. "Let's wait until midnight, and we'll move in. They'll be good and asleep then."

"Maybe we should catch a cat nap while we can," Rogers said. "They ain't going anywhere."

"Good idea. Once we grab the kid, we're in for a long day."

As they had hiked up the trail, following the boy with the GPS tracker, they'd talked about how they were going to take him.

"What do we do with the other two?" Rogers had asked.

"We'll just tie them up," Fredricks said. "Some hiker will be along at some point, and they can yell for help."

Rogers thought about that and, even though he didn't like it, he couldn't think of another way. He didn't want the instructor with them. He looked fit and was probably as tough as a piece of steel. And the other kid would just be an added nuisance.

"I hope so," he said to Fredricks.

"In fact, when we get some kind of cell service, we can call nine-one-one and tell the cops where they are."

That made Rogers feel better, although he figured Fredricks would never call.

The men pulled their sleeping bags out of their packs, unzipped them, and wrapped themselves in them. Fredricks put his GPS unit next to him and lay down. He didn't notice when the unit slid down into the leaves under the dead log he had leaned against.

In a few minutes, both men were asleep.

*

"Hey, hey," Rogers whispered to Fredricks. "It's two o'clock."

"What? Shit! We need to get going."

The men got up, quickly crammed their sleeping bags into stuff sacks, and put them into their packs.

When they had their packs secure and on their backs, Fredricks said, "Let's go, but we need to take our time and step carefully."

They walked very carefully down the hill. Twice, they stepped on small branches, sending a noisy crack out into the darkness, but they watched the tent and saw no lights come on. As they got to within twenty yards of the tent, they moved even slower. They placed every foot down slowly, lightly, feeling for anything that might make a noise. Fredricks pulled his pistol from the holster on his hip. Rogers did the same. They were close enough to hear the slow, steady breathing of the people in the tent.

They had worked this part out up on the hill. Rogers would get to the zipper on the tent door, and when Fredricks gave him the signal, he'd unzip it quickly, and Fredricks would turn on his powerful headlamp and go through the door, gun first.

When he felt Fredricks tap him on the shoulder, Rogers pulled the zipper up, opening the flap in the door. Fredricks switched on his light, stepping past Rogers into the tent.

"Nobody move!" he yelled.

But it was too late. Harvey was rolling to the right, reaching for his backpack. Fredricks jumped on Harvey and smacked him in the head with the pistol. It didn't knock him out, but it dazed him. Harvey put his hands to his head and didn't move.

"Do exactly what we tell ya to do," Fredricks said with great authority. "And there will be no more need for violence."

Sloan and Green had sat up at the noise, but now they didn't move, not knowing what to do.

In the hurried chaos, Fredricks couldn't tell which kid was the one they were supposed to take, so he made a snap decision. They would take both boys and let Dinesh sort it out.

"Get up and get dressed," Fredricks ordered. "Now!"

"What's going on, Skip?" Green asked.

"I'm not sure," Harvey mumbled. "But for right now, let's just do as we're told."

The lights continued to shine on the three campers, and as of yet they had not seen the person barking the orders.

"We have guns pointed at the three of you," Fredricks said from behind the lights. "Don't make any sudden moves, or we will shoot."

The campers pulled on their pants, shirts, socks, and boots in the brightness of the lights.

"You two boys, grab your backpacks," Fredricks ordered. "Leave the sleeping bags. You won't need them no more."

"Is this part of the class?" Sloan whispered to Harvey.

"Unfortunately, no it isn't," he whispered back. "I'm not sure what it is."

"Come on you two," Fredricks said, shining his light on the boys. "Outside."

"Get your packs on, guys," Harvey said, handing his pack to Sloan. Sloan noticed it wasn't the right pack, but Harvey looked at him, telling him with his eyes to take it. "We'll get this straightened out soon."

Harvey's GPS wasn't in the pack. It was lying next to his

sleeping bag. He hoped the boys wouldn't need it. The satellite phone was in the pack, but the boys didn't have the passcode to open it. He wished he had the phone, and the boys had the GPS, but it was what it was.

While he was putting items into his pack, Green grabbed the small GPS texting device his mother had sent along. He stuffed it into his pocket. When they figured out what was going on, he would use the device to ask his mom to send help.

"Isn't Skip going with us?" Green asked.

The man with the headlight didn't answer. A different man went into the tent with Harvey.

"Hey! What are you going to do?" Sloan asked.

Again, no answer.

There was some rustling in the tent, and two minutes later, Rogers came out of the tent.

"It's done."

"What's done?" Sloan asked. "Is he okay?"

"I'm fine, guys," Harvey said from inside the tent. "Just do as you're told, and everything should be just fine."

"Let's go," Fredricks said as he headed north along the Sawtooth Ridge, away from the trail they needed to hike to the rendezvous with the men from India, or wherever they were from.

In his hurry to get away from the wilderness instructor, Fredricks continued to push the boys along the trail to the north. He would check his GPS and the location of the campground later, but right now they just needed to keep moving.

"Where are you taking us?" Sloan asked.

"Never mind. Just keep walking," Fredricks said.

"What's going to happen with Skip?" Green asked.

"He'll be fine. Walk."

And they did. For an hour they walked steadily in the dark, staying on the well-worn trail. Finally, Green said, "I gotta pee. Can we stop for a second?"

"Yeah, I have to pee too," Sloan said to Fredricks.

"Okay, but I still have my pistol on you two, just so you know."

Green stepped off the trail a short way and turned his back. As he did, he pulled the GPS texting device out of his pocket and held it down at his pants zipper. He thumbed a short message into the device.

WE'VE BEEN TAKEN. SEND HELP! NOT A JOKE.

Harvey had showed the boys how to use his GPS at the camp. Green remembered the longitude and latitude coordinates from that spot, so he punched those into the message and pressed send.

"What the hell!" Fredricks said.

It made Green jump, and he almost peed himself. He just knew the man had seen him texting.

"Where'd my GPS go?" Fredricks said as he looked into his backpack. "Did you grab it, Bart?"

"No. Why would I do that?"

"Shit! We need that thing to get to the campground."

Fredricks looked through his pack again, pulling his sleeping bag and a few other items out of the pack. He stood and looked down the trail, like the GPS unit would just magically appear. Then Fredricks looked all around, into the darkness.

"In must have fallen out of my pocket," Fredricks said.

"We won't be able to find it while it's still dark," Rogers said. "It won't be light for another two hours. And if we have to backtrack to look for it, we're going to be really late. Dinesh will shit a brick."

"We could sit here for two hours," Fredricks said. "And then we'll have a better idea where we're going. Or we can press on this way. I think I remember the trail heading this direction when I last looked at the GPS."

Sloan and Green just stood there and listened. Sloan didn't know for sure because he hadn't seen it, but he was pretty sure he had Skip's pistol in his pack, and that's why he wanted Sloan to take it. He thought the pack also held Skip's GPS units, but he wasn't going to offer that up to these two morons. Not until they asked anyway.

"Let's keep going this direction," Fredricks said. "At least until it gets light."

*

The text didn't land in Jennifer Green's phone until five that morning. But when it did, her whole world started falling apart. It was her worst fear. Her husband had died two years earlier from a brain tumor, and now her only son was in trouble out in the wilderness somewhere.

She immediately called the police.

When the 911 operator answered, Jennifer Green was talking so fast the operator couldn't understand what she was saying.

"Please, ma'am. Slow down. First give me your name and where you are calling from."

"My name is Jennifer Green. I'm calling from Bellevue. I just received a text from my son's satellite texting device that said that he and his friend have been taken."

"Where is your son now, ma'am?"

"That's just it. I don't know. He was going on a wilderness retreat with a survival school. He and his friend. His message says, 'Send help. No joke.' What am I going to do?"

"What's your son's name and how old is he?"

"Tory . . . Tory Green, and he's sixteen."

"Do you have any idea what part of the state they were going to?"

"The boys stayed in Chelan the night before last. So somewhere around there."

The operator asked her the name of her son's friend, the name of the survival school, and took down some other details.

"Was there anything else in the message?"

"Yes, two numbers. But I have no idea what they mean."

She read the numbers off to the operator.

"I believe those are longitude and latitude numbers," the operator said. "That will help, for sure, if that is where they are. I'm going to contact the Chelan County Sheriff's Office now and let them know that you've called. Expect a call from them shortly."

She disconnected and immediately called Steve Sloan, Skyler's dad. He didn't pick up, so she left a quick message to call her just as soon as he could, that there might be an issue with the boys.

Then, she texted Tory back. Two words: HELPS COMING. And pushed send.

CHAPTER 27

It was almost 9:30 when Luke received the call on his satellite phone as he rode down the hill in Earl's truck. It had come to him in a convoluted way. Evidently, the Chelan County sheriff had called John McCarthy, director of the Region 2 office of the Department of Fish and Wildlife, asking if he had any enforcement officers up near Stehekin.

McCarthy did not, but he remembered talking to Region 3 enforcement captain Bob Davis who'd mentioned that one of his men would be up in that area. McCarthy called Davis to confirm.

"Yeah, Luke McCain is up there somewhere," Davis said.

"Cell service up that way is spotty at best. Any way of getting in touch with him?"

"Let me check with his wife. She's an FBI agent here in Yakima. She might know."

"Chelan County is sending two deputies, but it's going to take them a while to get there."

Captain Davis had called Sara, and Sara had called Luke on

his satellite phone. That was the call he'd received as they were driving down to Earl's place.

"There's a longitude and latitude included with the text from the kid," Sara said. "I looked it up. It looks to be about three miles northeast of Stehekin."

Luke wrote down the coordinates and told Sara to call Davis back and let him know they were headed there now. "We should be to Stehekin . . . hold on. Hey, Earl. What's it take to get to Stehekin from here?"

Sara heard him say, "About twenty, thirty minutes."

"We'll be to Stehekin in thirty minutes. Tell them that and have him let the sheriff know. You might also mention there'll be a WSP special agent along with me."

"Will do. Good luck. Let me know what's happening."

"What's up?" Cale asked after Luke clicked off.

After Luke told the men what he knew, he asked Earl if he could drive them directly to their boat at Lucerne.

"No problem," Earl said, and he pushed the old Chevy a little harder down the road.

*

At the dock, the men quickly unloaded their gear and put it in the boat.

"I have a pretty big freezer if you'd like me to store your venison," Earl said as the men were starting to put it into a hundred-gallon ice chest.

Cale thought about it for a few seconds and said, "You know what, that would be great. We can swing in here on the way back down to Chelan and pick it up. And help yourself to some, please."

"Joyce and I might cut a roast out and put it in the crock pot," Earl said. "Thanks."

After putting the two game bags with the sixty pounds of meat back into Earl's truck, Cale jumped into the boat and fired up the big motor. Luke had Jack get in, untied the dock ropes, and hopped in. In two minutes, they were running up-lake as fast as the big Yamaha outboard could push them.

As they ran up-lake, Luke pulled out his GPS and started looking at the area to the northeast of Stehekin. He brought up the screen that showed longitude and latitude and put a pin on the spot that matched the coordinates where the boys were last known to be.

"Why would someone take two teenaged boys?" Cale asked as he drove the boat.

"Good question. I'm calling the mother now to see what I can find out."

Luke dialed the number that Sara had given him and waited a minute for it to ring.

"Hello," a stressed woman's voice said.

"Ms. Green, my name is Luke McCain. I am an officer with the Department of Fish and Wildlife. I am just a few minutes from Stehekin. I have a State Patrol special agent with me. We will be heading to the coordinates you were given by your son as soon as we hit land."

"Thank you, thank you," Jennifer Green said. "Do you know anything else about what is going on?"

"No, I was just going to ask you the same thing. Do you know why someone would want to take your son and his friend?"

"Not really. I've talked to Steve Sloan, the father of Tory's friend Skyler. He doesn't know why anyone would do this either."

"Well, if you can think of anything, or if you hear from Tory again via text, please call me as soon as you can on this number."

Luke gave her the number and then asked for the phone number for Steve Sloan.

"I sent a text to Tory and told him help was on the way, but I've not heard back from him. I'm scared, Officer McCain. I'm really scared."

"I understand. Just know we're going to do everything we can to get your son home, safe and sound."

"Thank you," she said and hung up.

Next, Luke dialed Steve Sloan. Again, it took a bit for the

connection, but it hadn't finished ringing one time when a man answered. Luke told Sloan who he was and that they were on their way to start searching for his son.

"Why would someone take those boys? And what happened to Skip Harvey?"

"Who is Skip Harvey?"

"He's the owner of the wilderness school. He told me he would be carrying a satellite phone for safety. Why hasn't he called?"

"Maybe he's incapacitated, or they took his phone," Luke said. "Do you have the number for the phone?"

"Just a minute. Let me grab it."

Sloan gave him the number, then Luke turned the question around and asked Sloan if he could think of any reason why someone might want to take the boys.

"I don't know. Do they kidnap kids for ransom anymore? My wife and I have done pretty well for ourselves. That's the only thing I can think. But we certainly aren't the richest people in Seattle. We're like paupers compared to Bill Gates or Jeff Bezos. Wouldn't they go after their kids?"

"When you say you've done pretty well, what does that mean in numbers?" Luke asked.

"We're worth just over twenty million."

"That might do it," Luke said. "But it could be something else. Maybe the boys saw something they weren't supposed to see or who knows."

"Well, if there is a ransom, I'll pay whatever they want. We just want Skyler home." Suddenly, Sloan broke down. He sobbed for a minute and then composed himself and said, "Sorry, officer. Thank you so much. Please let me know if you find out anything."

"Will do. And you can call me at this number if you hear anything or think of anything else."

"Some pretty upset parents there," Luke said to Cale after the phone conversation ended.

"I bet. What was the discussion about ransom?"

"That was a thought the father of the Sloan kid had. He's

worth twenty million bucks. Someone might think kidnapping is worth it to get some of those millions."

"When did they grab the kids?" Cale asked.

"The text came in about five this morning, but sometimes it takes a while for those satellite texts to get to where they are going. I've done some research on them. The texts get through, but sometimes hours later."

"They must have grabbed them sometime in the middle of the night. If it was a ransom, how the hell did they know where to find the kids?"

Luke thought about that for a minute and then said, "They must have followed them. Or they could be tied in with the wilderness instructor. Maybe he was part of it."

"Or he might have been abducted too. Didn't you say Sara said the message said, 'We've been taken'?"

"Could be. But if the Sloan boy was the target, why drag two other people along? It's definitely a weird one. And if someone did want to take the kid, why not grab him at the mall or at the gym or someplace? It would be a helluva lot easier than going out into the wilderness to do it."

"We don't know he's the target. Maybe the instructor was the target, and they took the kids along to make sure the guy did what he was told."

"We need to get up the mountain to those coordinates as quick as we can," Luke said.

*

They pulled up to the docks at Stehekin at ten forty. Cale put the boat into one of the public slips, and Luke jumped onto the dock and tied the boat off. As they were getting their backpacks out, a man came running down the hill from the lodge.

"Are you Officer McCain?" the man asked.

"Yessir."

"I got a call from the sheriff a bit ago. He said you were headed here. He has two men on the way, but they won't be here for another hour. He asked that you wait for them."

"In an hour, we can be a lot closer to finding those boys," Luke said. "Give them this number and tell them we couldn't wait."

Luke gave the man his satellite phone number, then he looked at the other boats sitting in the slips.

"Do you know who owns these boats?" Luke asked.

"I know a couple of them, but not all."

"Tell the deputies to check on the boats that you don't know to see if there is any registration information, or anything else that would tell us who owns them. They should be able to get it from the numbers on the side of the boat."

"Will do, officer."

Cale stashed Luke's shotgun in a rod locker, grabbed his deer rifle, and climbed out of the boat. Jack had run up the dock and was peeing on a tree.

The two men shouldered their packs. Luke pulled his service pistol out of the pack and put it on his belt. Then he looked at his GPS and started walking up the hill, past the visitor center, headed for a trail that was labeled Purple Creek. He figured if they could keep up a steady pace, they could be at the GPS coordinates in two hours. That would put them roughly ten hours behind the boys.

"That's some pretty good time to make up," Cale said after Luke had given him his calculations. "And how will we know which way they went?"

"The GPS map shows there are three trails that come together close to those coordinates. Hopefully, we can figure out which one they're on."

"Can Jack track them?"

"Yes, but he has nothing to go on. If we had something with one of the kid's scent on it, he probably could. But where are we going to find that?"

"Maybe we'll get lucky."

"Hope so."

Then they put their heads down and kept walking.

CHAPTER 28

Skip Harvey had been lying on his side for two hours. His hands were tied behind his back with parachute cord. His feet were bound together, and they were tied by a four-foot length of cord to his hands. Basically, he was hog tied.

He had tried to loosen the cord around his wrists until he'd rubbed away about six layers of epidermis. His wrists burned, and his arm muscles ached. He tried to get to his feet without success. But even if he had, and then been able to hop over to the door of the tent, he didn't know how he was going to work the zipper to open it.

When he rested, he listened. His only hope was for someone to come along the trail who he could yell at for help. But nobody came.

*

The two men, with the two boys in front of them, walked through the darkness. They didn't know it, but they were headed due north on the trail. Every step was taking them farther from the campground where they were to meet the man they knew as Dinesh.

At the first hint of daylight, they stopped to take a break. The boys pulled their water bottles out and drank. The men talked quietly.

"Do you remember which direction the campground was from their tent?" Rogers asked Fredricks.

"I think it was east."

"This trail is heading north," Rogers said. Then he turned and pointed to the right. "The sun comes up in the east. It will be coming up over there in a half hour or so."

Fredricks didn't say anything. He just looked at the sliver of gray light coming over the farthest horizon to the east.

"How many miles you think we've walked since we grabbed the kids?"

Rogers thought about it for a half minute and said, "I'd say four, maybe a little more."

"We shoulda stayed put," Fredricks said. "I just wanted to get away from that dude in the tent."

"I tied him up pretty good. I bet he's still tied up. We could go back that way. Your GPS has to be around there someplace. Maybe we could find it."

"We're already going to be late. I don't know what that Dinesh guy is capable of, but he kind of insinuated that if we didn't get the kid to him on time, our necks might be on the line."

"We could just turn the kids loose, head back to the boat, and forget we ever got involved in this deal."

"What about the money? The money we were supposed to get, and the money they already paid us? They're gonna want that back."

"If they can find us. They don't know where we live."

"Yeah, but my boss does, and that's who turned them on to us. They'd talk to him and hunt us down pretty quick."

"I was looking forward to the cash."

"Me too. So, let's think about this for a minute. If we head due east from here, there's gotta be a trail that way that will get us to the campground."

"I don't know. There's some pretty rough country up here. I hunted deer once on the other side of the lake, and it about killed me. Deep canyons, blowdowns, thick brush. It was miserable."

"That was the other side of the lake. I say we give it a go."

"Okay, but I sure wish we had that GPS."

"Wishes in one hand, shit in the other," Fredricks said. "No one said this was going to be easy."

He turned to the boys and said, "Ok, fellas. Tighten up your boot laces—we're going to bushwhack for a while."

They worked their way down to a side-ridge and kept following it down. It was slow going because there were huge rock bluffs about every hundred yards blocking the way. When they got to the point of the ridge, they were stuck. It dove straight off into some of the thickest trees either man had ever seen.

"We ain't going through there," Rogers said.

"Nope. And we're not going back up over those rock bluffs." Fredricks pointed left and right and said, "So, we have to go this way or that."

From where they stood, north looked to be easier going, so they headed that way until they came upon a nearly vertical canyon.

"Now whatta we do?" Rogers asked.

The boys were getting tired.

"Can we stop and eat something?" Green said. "I'm starving. We need fuel to keep going."

"I don't see no McDonald's anywhere round here. What are you going to eat?" Fredricks asked.

"We have some freeze-dried meals," Sloan said. "And a stove in our packs to heat water."

Rogers perked up. "Don't sound too bad to me."

"It's going to slow us down," Fredricks said.

"If we get to the point where we just can't go anymore, you're never going to get us to wherever it is we're going," Green said. "We need to eat."

"Okay, okay," Fredricks said. "But let's make it quick."

The boys pulled the packs off their backs. Sloan reached into the pack Harvey had handed him and dug around for the stove. His hands ran across the pistol. He stopped his search and thought about grabbing the gun.

The men had put their pistols in their holsters as they walked and had left them there when they stopped. Sloan knew he could probably shoot one, but he didn't know about both. He was afraid if they saw him pull the pistol, they would rush him. So, he decided against it for now.

"What's the hold up?" Fredricks asked.

Sloan pulled the stove and the little fuel canister out of Harvey's pack and put them together. Then he fished out a small pot, poured water into it from his camel bladder, struck a wooden match, and fired up the stove. Green did the same with the cooking supplies in his pack.

It only took a couple of minutes for the water to boil in the small pots.

Sloan reached into the pack for his eating utensil and thought about pulling the pistol again. After he had touched the gun in the pack, he started thinking. From the pistol training he'd been doing, he definitely knew how to handle the weapon. And he was confident he could hit what he was aiming at. But he was struggling with the idea of shooting another person.

"Whatcha got in there?" Rogers asked.

Sloan froze for a second and then realized the tall man was asking about the food pouches.

"Spaghetti or macaroni and cheese," Green said.

"I'll do the spaghetti," Fredricks said.

"That's what I wanted," Rogers said.

"We have three spaghettis," Green said. He opened a pack, handed it to the short man, and poured the hot water in it.

Rogers dug around in his own pack and came up with a couple of plastic forks. He gave one to Fredricks and held on to the other.

The boys got Rogers his spaghetti and fixed two packs of mac and cheese for themselves. With their sporks, they shoveled the food from the pouches to their mouths.

It took the four of them about two minutes to devore the meals from the pouches.

"Get that stuff put away, and let's get going," Fredricks ordered.

When Sloan put the small stove and pot back in the pack, he again saw the pistol. This wasn't the right time, but he'd keep thinking about it. If he thought that his life or Tory's was in danger, the pistol was a definite option.

*

They'd been bushwhacking another two hours when Rogers broke his ankle. Or Fredricks believed his friend's ankle to be broken.

After eating, they'd hiked in an easterly direction. They were ultimately heading downhill, but in the mountains you often must go up before you can go down. And, as the men were finding out firsthand, Mother Nature will throw a few obstacles in the way. Downed trees, cliffs, steep ravines, and one obstinate bear altered their path over and over again.

They had run into the bear feeding in a wild blueberry patch, and even after yelling and waving their arms, the bear was not of a mind to move. The big bruin just sat up and looked at them like they were nothing more than some pesky magpies.

"I'd just as soon not end up as a bear turd," Rogers said. "Let's just go around him."

Which is what they did.

Sloan and Green thought it was cool seeing the bear, but they were of the same mind as the taller man. Seeing the bear was one thing—staying clear of it was another. Again, Sloan thought of the pistol in his pack. He could definitely shoot a bear if it was coming at them, but he had no idea if the pistol was powerful enough to actually kill the thing.

So, they backtracked and worked their way down a steep sidehill. Rogers never saw the badger hole. His foot went into it, twisting as it did, and the length of his body and the weight of his pack got sucked up in the gravitational pull of the steep grade and over he went.

"Ahhhh!" Rogers screamed as he went down. He would have rolled down the hill, but the badger hole held his foot.

"You okay?" Fredricks asked.

"Hell no, I'm not okay. I think I broke my leg," Rogers said as he was gingerly trying to work the appendage out of the hole.

Fredricks climbed back up to Rogers and helped him get his leg free.

"Careful," Rogers barked. "It really hurts."

When his foot was free from the hole, Rogers lay back on the hillside and covered his eyes with his forearm. He felt like crying, his ankle hurt so bad, but he didn't want Fredricks and the kids to see him do so, so he fought it.

"Do you think you can walk?" Fredricks asked after a couple of minutes.

"I don't know. I guess I'm gonna have to, or I really will end up as bear shit."

Fredricks went around to Rogers' shoulders and tried to help him up. The steep hillside and the pain in his ankle kept Rogers from moving.

"Maybe if I had a crutch," Rogers said. "I don't think I can put any weight on it."

"Well, let me go look. Be careful, though. One slip, and you'll roll all the way to the bottom."

Both men looked down the hill. There was a pile of rocks and brush that would make for a less than soft landing.

"You boys come with me," Fredricks said. "We need to find a sturdy branch that'll work as a crutch."

They hiked back up the hill and searched. Green found an aspen branch that seemed pretty sturdy and about the right length.

"That should work," Fredricks said as he grabbed it and headed back down to where his friend lay.

The boys followed, but as they did, Sloan whispered to Green.

"This might be our chance to get away."

"I was thinking the same thing. That guy's not going to leave his buddy. We could probably turn and run right now."

"Let's wait until the time is right. I have Skip's pistol. I think I can pull it, and we can just back away."

"Hey! Come on. Get down here," Fredricks ordered.

Sloan and Green worked back down the hill, careful to not step in any other holes, and then just stood out of the way and watched as Fredricks helped Rogers up on his one good leg and placed the branch under his arm. There was a crook at the top of the branch, making it somewhat usable as a crutch.

Green stuck his hands in his pocket and felt the texting device. He needed to text his mom, but there just hadn't been an opportunity. Maybe with all of this going on, he'd be able to.

When Rogers was finally off the sidehill, he began hopping on one foot with the aid of the makeshift crutch and Fredricks helping him at times. Rogers had to sit often and his face was beginning to look gray.

"I think I'm going to puke," Rogers said. And then he puked. Twice. Freeze-dried spaghetti.

While he was waiting for Rogers to recover from the little barfing episode, Fredricks started thinking. They'd never get to the campground by dark, let alone by four o'clock when Dinesh was expecting them. The only chance to get the kid there today was to leave Rogers behind and take the kid himself.

If he left the kid that Dinesh didn't want with Rogers and only took the kid Dinesh did want, he could make the drop, collect their cash, and then come back for his buddy. He would have time to do that, Fredricks reasoned, because nobody should know the kids were not with the wilderness coach. If he could find the campground, trade the kid for the dough, and get back here, Rogers would only have to be alone with the kid for maybe eight hours before Fredricks could get back to him. The next challenge would be convincing Rogers that the plan was worth a try, that it might be the only way they would get a payday out of this deal.

After another fifty-yard slog, they all sat again.

"This is no good," Rogers said. "My ankle is throbbing and hurting so much. Maybe I should take my boot off."

"I don't know about that," Fredricks said. "I think it's probably holding the swelling down by being in the boot."

"I wish we had some pain pills," Rogers said.

"I have some Tylenol in my pack," Green said.

"Oh man. Can I have some?"

Green dug through his pack, found a small first aid kit, grabbed the pain pills, and gave him two.

"I'm going to need more than two," Rogers said.

Green gave him two more.

"Thanks, kid," Rogers said as he swallowed the tablets without water. "I appreciate it."

"So, I've been thinking," Fredricks said. Then he proceeded to lay out his idea on splitting up the boys and making the trek to the campground sans Rogers.

CHAPTER 29

It had taken Skip Harvey and the two boys two hours to hike from Stehekin to where they'd camped. Luke and Cale made it in just over an hour.

"There's a tent," Cale said.

Luke looked at his GPS. The latitude and longitude were right.

"That's gotta be theirs," Luke said.

The men walked that way, and when they were two hundred yards from the tent, they heard a man yelling.

"Hey, help me!" the voice came from inside the tent.

Luke and Cale ran down the hill and opened the tent door.

"Man am I glad to see you," Harvey said as Cale cut the cords on his wrists and legs.

"You're Skip Harvey, I presume?" Luke asked.

"Yeah. Those guys took Skyler and Tory. I have no idea why."

Luke introduced himself and Cale, telling him they were law enforcement officers and had been contacted through the Chelan County Sheriff's Office.

"How did they know what's going on?"

"The Green boy has a satellite texting device. He texted his mom that he'd been taken. The text said it was no joke."

"Oh, that's right. He used it to text her when we left the boat in Stehekin."

"He was smart enough to include the longitude and latitude for the campsite. You must've showed him how to figure that out."

"We did do some work on my GPS before we went to bed. He must have remembered the coordinates."

"It's good he did because we might not have found you as quickly as we did."

"Do you have any idea what direction they went?" Cale asked.

"I could hear them walking up the trail to the north."

About that time, Jack stuck his head in the tent.

"That's my dog, Jack," said Luke. "He's a decent tracker. Any chance the boys left something with their scent on it?"

"These are their sleeping bags. When the men took them, one of them said they wouldn't need the bags. I thought about that, and I'm guessing they were planning to get them out of the mountains before the day was over."

"When did they leave here?" Luke asked.

"They jumped into the tent about two this morning," Harvey said. "The one guy whacked me with his pistol, and then another guy tied me up. He knew what he was doing. I've been working on those ropes off and on ever since."

"Anything else you can think of?"

"Didn't get a real good look at them. Their lights were shining in my eyes. Both are white guys. One was shorter, and he seemed to be calling the shots. The taller guy is who tied me up. They had pistols, or at least the guy who clubbed me did. And they seemed to be in a hurry."

They climbed out of the tent, and Harvey said, "I don't know what I'm gonna tell their parents. They were trusting me to keep those boys safe."

"Not your fault," Cale said. "Could've happened to any one of us. We'll run them down."

"You want me to come with you?" Harvey asked. "I'm pretty good getting around out here."

Luke thought about that for a minute. He liked the idea of having a survival expert with them, but he thought that maybe someone should stay there at the campsite.

"Why don't you stay here," Luke said. "Unless you think you need medical attention. There's a chance one or both of the boys could get away from those guys, and they might come back here. Plus, there are two Chelan County sheriff's deputies on their way up here. Someone should be here to tell them what's going on."

"I'm fine. Just got a bump on the noggin and some rope burns on my wrists. I've had worse. I just feel like I need to be helping."

"Staying here for right now will be helping."

They talked for a couple more minutes about what kind of supplies the boys had in their packs. Harvey told them he had handed his pack to the Sloan boy, who he believed knew there was a loaded pistol in the pack.

"The kid wanted to bring a pistol on the trip," Harvey said. "He's been taking shooting lessons and thought it would be good protection. Our policy is no firearms for the students. But since he'd had gun safety and shooting lessons, I told him I'd bring my pistol, and one day we would do some shooting. I wouldn't have given him the pack if he didn't know how to handle a gun."

"Let's hope he doesn't have to use it," Cale said.

"Can you describe the two boys?" Luke asked.

Harvey gave them a good description of the boys and said it was Skyler Sloan's father who had arranged and paid for the week.

"I talked to him on the sat phone as we were coming up here," Luke said. "Sounds like the family is pretty well-to-do, and the men might have taken his son for a ransom."

"If they wanted Skyler, then why would they take Tory too?"

"Maybe they didn't know there were going to be two kids here," Cale said. "Or they possibly didn't have a description of the Sloan boy."

"How would they even know he was up here with me?"

"Who knows. The kid probably plastered it all over social media," Cale said. "It doesn't take much of a hacker these days to find out that kind of stuff."

"Let's get going," Luke said. "Thanks, Skip. We'll find them."

Luke pulled one of the boys' sleeping bags out of the tent and had Jack smell it. It had been a hot, dry summer in Eastern Washington, and the morning dew that might have held some scent from the nighttime had already evaporated. It was going to be tough for the dog to get on a scent trail. But they had to try.

"Come on, boy," Luke said as he and Cale headed back to the trail to try to get on the boys' tracks.

When they hit the trail, they found several different fresh boot tracks in the dry dirt.

Luke turned around and hollered at Harvey. "What kind of shoes were the boys wearing?"

"Hiking boots," Harvey said. "Don't know the brand, but one of the boys' tracks was the old waffle stomper sole. I remember seeing them after we hiked down to the camping spot."

Luke looked around him at the trail. Mixed in with the different tracks was one with four four-leaf clovers centered in the heel and main foot. The pattern of a waffle stomper.

"Great. Thanks, Skip."

Jack sniffed around the tracks and then moved up the trail to the north.

"I don't know if Jack has anything," Luke said. "But at least he's headed in the right direction."

"My guess is they'll stay on the trail until they get where they're going," Luke said.

"Most likely," Cale said. "If they know where they're going."

They headed up the trail to the north at a quick pace—much quicker than Luke would normally have gone when tracking. Luckily, the waffle stomper pattern was easy to follow, and Jack didn't seem to want to deviate from the trail. The boot print wasn't showing all the time, but it would appear every fifty or hundred yards when the trail was more dirt than rock.

They stayed on the trail for just over four miles when the waffle stomper pattern disappeared. They walked down the trail another half mile, trying to pick it up again, but it never reappeared.

"Let's go back to where we saw the last track," Luke said. "And we'll spread out on each side and see if we can pick it up leading off the trail."

They went back to the last waffle stomper print, and Luke took the left side of the trail, and Cale worked the right side.

A few minutes later, Cale said, "Something here."

Luke headed that way, with Jack, and took a look.

"There's boot tracks heading down the hill this way," Cale said. "I don't see the waffle stomper print, but these are definitely fresh."

Jack started sniffing around the tracks with more interest and then headed down the hill.

"I hope he's on them," Cale said.

"Me too. Let's keep an eye out for the waffle stomper track."

They found one about seventy-five yards down the hill. A perfect track in the soft, brown dirt of a fresh gopher mound. It was slower going downhill. They had to traverse some huge metamorphic rock bluffs and the occasional fallen trees. But Jack kept them on the trail, verified occasionally by a boot track.

"Where are these guys going?" Cale asked, almost rhetorically.

"I don't think this was part of their original plan," Luke said. "It doesn't look like they really know where they're going."

Luke was watching Jack try to decipher the trail twenty yards downhill when his sat phone started jangling.

Luke answered and said, "This is McCain."

"Yeah, this is Deputy Hanson with Chelan County. We followed up on the boats in the slips at Stehekin. One of them is owned by an Ernest Borsman of Ephrata. We called him, and he said he loaned the boat to a guy by the name of Rod Fredricks. We ran his priors. He's done a little time in the Grant County Jail, mostly for drunk and disorderly and a couple of bar fights."

Luke asked for a physical description of Fredricks.

The deputy gave him the information and said, "We're still checking around Stehekin. We've not seen Fredricks, and no one here seems to know who he is. Borsman said that Fredricks and a buddy were going to use the boat for fishing, but there's no fishing gear in the boat. He must be up in the mountains somewhere."

Luke thanked the deputy and hung up.

"We may know the name of one of the men," Luke said. "It could possibly be the short guy who whacked Skip Harvey on the head."

"Jack's pretty interested down there," Cale said. "Maybe we're getting closer."

"I hope so," Luke said. "It's going to be dark before too long."

Chapter 30

It took some convincing, but finally Rogers agreed with Fredricks' plan to separate, with the boy Dinesh didn't want staying with Rogers.

Fredricks pulled his pistol and aimed it in the boys' direction. "You guys go over there and sit by that downed log. And don't try to get away. I'm watching you."

The boys moved to the log, and Fredricks asked Rogers what he thought.

"I think we forget this whole thing and try to figure out how to get me to the hospital. My leg feels like it's going to fall off."

"I'm going to take the blond kid. He's the one that Dinesh wants based on the photo he showed us. I'll leave the other one with you. He has the Tylenol and can help you until I return."

"What do we do with him after that?" Rogers asked.

"We'll cross that bridge when we get to it," Fredricks said.

"If we get to it," Rogers mumbled. "Go then, but get back as quickly as you can. I'm hurting bad."

*

While the two men were talking, Sloan and Green also discussed their situation.

"We need to do something," Green said. "It's going to be dark in an hour, and I really hate the idea of being out here at night."

"We could run," Sloan said. "I really don't think that guy would shoot us. They need us for some reason. And even if he did shoot, I don't think he could hit us from that distance with a pistol."

"Are you willing to take that chance?"

"No, I guess not," Sloan said. Then he paused to think and said, "With that guy having the broken leg, I could pull Skip's pistol and shoot the other guy."

"Do you really think you could kill someone?"

"I couldn't have twelve hours ago, but I'm seriously believing I could do it now."

"I say we wait and see what happens here. The guy with the bad ankle isn't going anywhere. He's not going to hurt us. But I am a little worried about the other guy. He looks like he could be mean."

"Hey, you should text your mom," Sloan said. "Tell her we're still with two men, and we've been hiking north and east of the last coordinates."

Sloan watched the two men while Green pulled out the texting device, waited for it to hook up with the satellite, and typed a message.

TAKEN BY TWO MEN. ONE NOW INJURED. HEADING NORTH EAST OF LAST COORDINATES. WE ARE OK.

He pushed send just before the men called back over to them.

*

"Hey, you guys. Get back over here," Fredricks barked. He'd seen them fiddling with something.

When the boys got back to the men, Fredricks asked, "What were you doing over there?"

"We were hungry," Sloan said. "We were just sharing a granola bar."

Fredricks looked at Sloan and then at Green.

"Plans have changed. Tory, you are going to stay here with Rogers. Skyler, you are going with me."

"Where are we going?" Skyler asked.

"All you need to know is you are coming with me and you'll do as I say."

"I think I'll stay here with Tory because you obviously have no idea where you are going."

Fredricks slapped Sloan hard across the face. It knocked him down.

"You'll do as I say," Fredricks yelled. "Now, come with me."

Sloan wiped blood from his mouth with the back of his wrist and followed the man. If his pack hadn't been on his back where he couldn't reach into it, he would have pulled the pistol and shot Fredricks right in the face.

Then he walked down the hill, ahead of the man, mouth burning, and seething with anger.

*

Green watched his best friend get knocked to the ground, and it really made him mad. But there was nothing he could do. Skyler had done a good job of thinking quickly when Fredricks had asked what they were doing when he was sending the text to his mom. If he could have reached the pistol in Skip's pack, he would have pulled it and shot that guy. Or he would have tried. He'd never shot a pistol before.

He hoped his message would reach his mother, although he wasn't sure what good it would do other than to let her know he was still alive somewhere in the wilderness near Lake Chelan.

Green watched as Sloan and Fredricks hiked down the hill and out of site. Now he was stuck with the man with the broken ankle.

He kind of felt sorry for the guy because he was definitely in pain, but hey, what could he do?

Actually, as he thought about it, there might be something he could do. Last year in PE, the teacher did a unit on first aid, and one of the things they taught was how to immobilize an appendage. He could put a temporary splint on the man's ankle to keep it from flopping around as he tried to move on the crutch.

Once he had his leg immobilized, he would figure out a way to get away. As the boys had hiked down the mountains, they both had paid attention to landmarks, and he was positive he could make his way back up to the trail and follow it back to where Skip was at the tent. The only issue was that the hike uphill would take a few hours. And night was coming. He wasn't sure he wanted to be wandering around in the dark with no protection from whatever critters did their hunting at night.

"I think I can help with your leg," he said to Rogers. "I learned how to create a splint in first aid class."

Rogers was lying in the grass, half asleep. The pain was obvious in his face. "You think it would help?"

"I do. It will probably hurt some as I'm applying the splint, but it should keep it from moving around."

"That'd be good. It hurts every time I move."

"I'm going to have to go look around for the right pieces of wood. But, I promise, I won't run."

"Okay. Go ahead."

Green walked over to some trees. He would need two stout branches about a foot long. After Skip had showed him how to do it, he knew he could break a bigger piece of wood down to the right size, and that's what he did.

When he had the two lengths of wood, he brought them back and pulled some parachute cord out of his pack.

"I need to put these on the inside and the outside of your foot and tie them at the ankle and a little farther up your leg."

"Okay. I'm ready."

As quickly as he could, he placed the wood pieces and tied the cord around them. Rogers let out a muffled scream as Green tied the cord good and tight.

Once everything was in place, Rogers said, "It feels better already. Thanks."

Green got into his pack and gave the man four more Tylenol tablets and a water bottle. "I only have eight more pain pills, so it's up to you when you want them."

"Thanks a lot."

"I'm still hungry, so I'm going to fix another freeze-dried meal. What about you? You think you can keep something down?"

"Yeah, that'd be good. Whatever you got would be fine."

He fixed Rogers a macaroni and cheese dinner, fished the plastic fork out of Rogers' pack, and let the man eat. Then he fixed the last spaghetti dinner he had in his pack for himself. The two ate quietly. As he ate, Green thought about their situation.

"You know, I think we should find a decent place to build a fire and prepare to spend the night," Green said.

"Well, I ain't going anywhere very far or very fast. That's a pretty good idea."

After he looked around for a bit, Green found a relatively flat spot protected by some trees on one side and some big boulders on the other. He walked back and helped Rogers to his one good foot and got his crutch under his arm.

"It's not too far. Take your time."

"You know what?" Rogers said. "That splint is really helping. My ankle doesn't hurt near as bad as it did."

After he got Rogers settled against a tree, Green went and found some rocks to build a fire ring. When he had enough rocks, he went and got an armful of dry branches. Then, with one of the bigger branches, he worked at digging out a pit to put the rocks around.

"Looks like you know what you're doing there," Rogers said.

"Yeah, we learned how to do this last night."

Green thought about what he had just said. Was it really just last night? It seemed like it had been days ago.

When he had the rocks placed, he went to some trees and found some dried moss. Then he built a teepee of small branches over the moss in the fire ring and struck a wooden match on the rock. He lit the moss, and in a few seconds he had a small fire going. He placed some bigger branches on the fire and went to get more. Three trips later, he had a large pile of wood. Some would need to be broken down, but there should be enough to last for at least a few hours.

It wasn't cold yet, but it would start getting chilly as soon as the sun dropped behind the mountains. In September, it would almost always get down below freezing at night in this part of the world. The fire would help fight the cold when darkness hit.

"That fire feels good," Rogers said as he closed his eyes and fell asleep.

✳

Fredricks and Sloan were moving quickly down the mountain. Sloan's mouth still hurt where Fredricks had hit him, and he occasionally would touch his cracked, fat lip with the back of his hand.

"Oh, buck up," Fredricks said when he saw the boy touching his face. "I didn't hit you that hard."

Sloan didn't say anything. In fact, he hadn't said a word since the man slapped him. He just kept thinking about the pistol in his pack, and the many ways he might be able to use it on his captor.

Fredricks had been carrying his pistol much of the time since they left Green and Rogers. Sloan figured the man must be worried that he was going to make a run for it. He stayed close to Sloan, which made bolting a tougher proposition.

Patience, Sloan kept thinking. The time would come. But there were other considerations. Night was coming on quickly, and even though he had been keeping an eye on landmarks and believed he could get back to his friend, he didn't think he could do it at night. He had Skip's pistol, so he wasn't terribly concerned about the animals he might encounter at night. He was more worried that he wouldn't be able to see the landmarks he'd memorized, like the dead snag and the craggy peak in the distance.

Hunger had come on about an hour earlier. It had been several hours since they ate the freeze-dried macaroni and cheese. Those calories had burned off several miles ago. But Sloan wasn't going to say anything.

When Fredricks stopped to take a drink of water, Sloan would take a drink of water too. But the stops weren't much of a rest. As soon as they'd had their drink, they were off again. The man was on a mission. It made Sloan wonder again what this was all about. Why had he and Green been taken and where were they going? It made no sense.

He had seen Skip's satellite phone in the pack, but he hadn't tried to turn it on. Did they work like a cellphone or Tory's satellite text device? He didn't know. And there never seemed to be an opportunity to use it.

When Sloan had been getting the food pouches and stoves out of the packs, he had looked at Skip's pistol closely. He couldn't tell who the gunmaker was, but the pistol's design was very similar to the Glock .45 caliber he had been shooting the past year at the shooting school. He noticed that the magazine was in the butt handle of the pistol. If there wasn't a cartridge in the chamber, one quick pull of the slide behind the barrel and a cartridge would slide in. Flip the safety, and it would be ready to shoot. He wasn't positive that all pistols worked the same, but he assumed they would be close.

"You're a real Chatty Cathy there, ain't ya?" Fredricks said after they had paused for another drink.

Sloan didn't say anything.

"Suit yourself," Fredricks said. "If you got a headlamp in that pack, now would be a good time to dig it out and put it on."

Sloan pulled the pack off his shoulders and opened up the main compartment. He thought about pulling the pistol, but again, he'd be in the dark, literally, about where to go from here. He had Skip's emergency survival bag. He could make a fire. He had food and some water. He had the satellite phone if he could work it. But it still didn't feel like the right time.

With the headlamp on and the backpack on his shoulders, Sloan was ready to keep moving.

"Let's go," Fredricks said, pointing down the hill with his pistol in his right hand. "We gotta be getting near a trail soon."

CHAPTER 31

The three men from India had arrived at the campground where they were to meet the men from Ephrata at just after three o'clock in the afternoon. They were early, but they had nothing better to do. They certainly didn't want to be late.

They sat in the Ford Explorer and talked. There were two tents set up in the campground, although they never saw another person out walking around. Occasionally, another vehicle would drive by.

"Who would want to come out here and live in the trees and the dirt?" Patel asked. "It seems like a very unusual recreation."

"People from the big cities come here," Singh said. "It is a way to get away from all the people and the traffic they live in every day."

"We live amongst one billion people in our country. I would never want to go out to sleep in the dirt, with the bugs and wild animals wandering about."

At four o'clock, Bakshi checked his watch and looked up the road, as if willing the men with the boy to come walking in.

They sat for another half hour.

"Do you think something might have happened to them?" Patel asked.

"I would not know," Bakshi said. "They are traveling through some difficult terrain, so it is most likely that they are just behind schedule."

"You do not think they took the boy elsewhere and have made their own deal for a ransom?" Singh said.

"Again, I would not know. But how would they know who to contact, or even if the father was wealthy?"

Bakshi had tried to call the men on the cellphone he had purchased for them. But every time the calls went straight to an automated message.

"The cell service up here is virtually non-existent," Singh said after Bakshi tried again to call Fredricks.

After two hours of sitting and watching and waiting, Patel said, "It is not looking good. How long should we wait?"

"We will wait as long as it takes," Bakshi said.

"What if the men have been caught by the authorities," Singh said. "They might send the police here to arrest us too."

Bakshi hadn't considered that. They probably should go someplace else, but where?

About that time, some hikers came down the road. At first, the men thought it was Fredricks and Rogers with the boy, but it was only a young man and a woman. They walked right by the men sitting in the Explorer and went over to one of the tents.

As the couple took off their packs and started stirring around the campground, they would occasionally look at the men in the Explorer.

"This is not good," Singh said. "We should move."

Bakshi turned on the SUV, spun around, and headed back down the Forest Service road until they found a spot where they could pull off and be somewhat out of sight.

"This is better than the campground," Singh said. "There are no people around."

"We will drive by the campground every half hour to see if they have arrived," Bakshi said.

By the time the darkness of night had settled, they had driven by the campground five times. The men and the boy were not there. Bakshi was starting to get very concerned. The millions of dollars he had planned for were seemingly slipping through his fingers.

*

They had been walking for almost two hours in the dark, following Jack in their headlights. Luke would check the occasional footprint, and he was convinced Jack was still on the trail of the boys.

Suddenly, Jack stopped with his ears forward, staring down the hill into the dark.

"What's he doing?" Cale asked.

"He hears or smells something," Luke said.

They both looked down the hill in the direction Jack was looking.

"I think I just saw the flicker of a campfire," Cale said.

"I did too," Luke said. "Let's take it slowly the rest of the way down the hill. I'll keep Jack at heel. Turn off your headlight."

Cale was a step ahead of him and had just turned his light off. He pulled his rifle out of the scabbard on his pack and said, "Ready."

They moved quietly down the hill until they could clearly see the fire flickering in the dark. Two people were lying near it.

"Two people," Luke whispered to Cale. "I don't know if it's our guys. There's supposed to be four of them."

"There's only one way to find out," Cale said. "I'll go around to the right. You go to the left."

They worked slowly into position. Luke gave Cale plenty of time to get where he was going and then yelled, "State police! Nobody move!"

Luke had his service pistol drawn and moved in. Cale stayed back in the darkness covering Luke.

One of the people stood with his hands up and said, "My name is Tory Green. This guy came with another man and forced me and my buddy to go with them. Then he broke his leg, so the other man took my buddy, and they are still hiking down the hill and—"

"Whoa, whoa, slow down," Luke said, keeping his pistol on the man lying near the fire. "I'm Officer McCain." Then to the man on the ground, "What's your name?"

"Bart Rogers."

Luke looked at the makeshift splint on his left leg.

"Mr. Rogers, it looks like it's been a rough day in your neighborhood."

"It hurts like hell, but the kid here fixed me up with this brace deal."

Luke then saw the pistol in the holster on Rogers' belt.

"We got a gun! Come on in Cale while I cover him."

Rogers didn't move. Cale came into the light of the fire, and with his rifle in his right hand, he moved in and pulled the pistol out of the holster at Rogers' side.

"This is Officer Harris," Luke said. "We're going to get you to safety, Tory, and you some medical attention, Mr. Rogers. Tory, I've talked to your mother. She's quite worried about you."

"Can I text my mom and let her know I'm okay?"

"Actually, if you'll wait a minute or two, I'll do you one better. We can call her from my satellite phone. But when you talk to her, don't mention anything about Skyler. We need to go find him next."

"They left us about two hours ago," Green said.

"So, I take it you can't walk?" Luke said to Rogers.

"Not very well."

"Okay, for right now you are under arrest for kidnapping. We'll read you your rights, and then we'll figure out how to get you out of here."

Rogers dropped his head then said, "This day just keeps getting better. I knew I shouldn't have gone along on this crazy deal."

"You could be dead," Cale said.

"Yeah, well, there is that," Rogers said.

While Luke called the Chelan County sheriff, Cale read Rogers his rights and asked the man with the broken ankle what had happened. Rogers told him about his friend Fredricks, and how Fredricks' boss at the mini-mart in Ephrata had hooked him up with some dudes from India who said they were working for a man who hadn't seen his kid in a few years. The Indian guys had been hired to grab the kid for the father because the mom was a crazy bitch.

"Somehow, they knew the kid was going to be up here at a wilderness school, so they offered Fredricks and me ten grand each to come up here and grab him."

"Where were you supposed to take them?"

"Some campground a few miles away. It was marked on a GPS unit they gave us, but Rod lost it somewhere along the line, so he's trying to find it with the other kid."

"Why'd you take both boys?"

"We didn't know there'd be two kids with the instructor," Rogers said. "And in the dark we couldn't see the one we needed, so we grabbed them both. We didn't know we were kidnapping the kid. That's God's honest truth."

Rogers moved a little bit and then winced in pain. "Can I get some more of those pain pills?" Rogers asked Green.

Green dug into his pack, pulled the last four tablets out of the small bottle, and gave them to Rogers. Then he handed him a bottle of water out of Rogers' pack.

"Seems like this young man has been taking pretty good care of you," Cale said. "If it would have been me, I'd have kicked you in your broken leg and run away."

"I thought about doing that," Green said. "The running away part, not the kicking him. I figured I'd be better off with him here next to the fire tonight rather than running around up there, not being able to see where I was going."

"You did a great job of getting the fire set up," Cale said.

"That's a great looking Lab," Green said. "Did he help you track us?"

"He sure did. His name is Jack. He'll be your best friend if you pet him a little."

Green walked over to Jack and started to scratch his ears.

As Luke continued to speak with the sheriff, he pulled out his GPS and gave him their current coordinates. "I don't know how we're going to get this Rogers guy out of here," Luke said. "It doesn't appear that he can put any weight on that leg, so walking is out of the question."

Luke listened for a minute or so and said, "Yes, I think he could ride a horse if you could get him up on one. I don't think you can get a helicopter in here based on the trees and terrain." He listened again for a few seconds and said, "Ten-four. Thanks, Sheriff."

Luke then turned to Rogers and said, "Well, the sheriff is rounding up some search and rescue folks to come get you, Mr. Rogers. Sounds like they'll be coming with horses. It's going to take them a while, but you should be fine."

Luke and Cale chatted for a minute. Cale told him what Rogers had said about how they got involved in this and that some men from India were going to pay for one of the boys.

"They were told they were rescuing the kid from a mother who was keeping him away from his father."

"Well, we know that's not the truth," Luke said. "So, it most likely is a kidnapping for ransom situation. And the man still out there has the right kid."

Luke turned to Rogers and asked, "Do you know what kind of vehicle the men from India were driving?"

"The times we met with them, they were driving a late-model Ford Explorer. All white. Kinda looks like all the State Patrol rigs. Definitely a rental."

"Had they paid you something to do this?"

"They were giving us ten grand each. We got a third up front.

They were going to give us the rest when we delivered the kid."

"What about the names of the men?"

Rogers moved and winced again. "The one guy who seemed to be calling the shots was named Dinesh. They told us the names of the other two guys, but I forgot them."

"No last names?"

"Not that I ever heard."

Luke asked for a description of the three men, and Rogers gave it to him the best he could. He told Luke and Cale that the three men looked pretty much the same. Black hair, about five foot ten, although he thought Dinesh might be a bit taller, and he had a black beard.

"We need to call the sheriff and have them keep an eye out for that white Explorer," Cale said. "And they need to let Okanogan County know too. I think we're now in their jurisdiction."

Luke dialed up the Chelan County Sheriff's Office and gave them the description of the three men and the vehicle they were last seen driving. The deputy who answered the phone said they would inform Okanogan County and that they had two men headed down the mountain to the last coordinates they had been given.

"One of our deputies hunts up that way most every year and knows the country well," the deputy said. "He thinks he'll be there in the next half hour."

That created a dilemma for Luke. He wanted to keep moving as quickly as he could after Fredricks and the Sloan boy. He wanted Cale with him, but he really didn't want to leave Green and Rogers alone. Rogers was technically in their custody. And Green had been through a long, rough day.

Luke and Cale talked it over and decided they'd better stay right there and hope the Chelan deputies got there soon.

✳

247

At about the same time that Luke was trying to figure out whether to stay or go, Fredricks and Sloan finally stumbled onto a well-worn trail. Fredricks was now facing a dilemma of his own. He had no idea if the trail would take them to the campground where he was supposed to meet the men from India. He knew he had to go east from the ridge trail they had left several hours before, but the trail on which they now stood ran north and south.

He thought about it for a minute. Fredricks believed that going south would lead him to a lower elevation and should get him to a road. But which road? He tried to remember the map he'd been looking at on the GPS that had the campground marked on it. He knew the campground was on a road, but he just couldn't picture where it might be in relation to where he and the kid were at this moment. Of course, walking for hours in the black of night hadn't helped.

While Fredricks stood and contemplated their next move, Sloan removed his backpack.

"I'm getting a drink," he said.

Fredricks barely gave him a look.

Sloan opened the main compartment of his pack, reached in, grabbed the pistol, felt for the safety, slid it down, pulled the gun from the pack, and pointed it at Fredricks.

"South would be easier walking," Fredricks said as he turned to Sloan. He couldn't believe his eyes. The kid had magically made a pistol appear like a rabbit out of a hat.

"Whatcha got there, kid?" Fredricks asked with a sly smile on his face. "Guns are for adults. You don't want to be playing with that. Someone might get hurt."

"Like you?" Sloan asked.

Fredricks had put his pistol in the holster on his hip and was slowly moving his hand toward it.

Sloan shot the ground, hitting an inch from Fredricks' foot, making the man jump.

"I wouldn't do that," Sloan said.

"Okay. Okay. Take it easy, kid. You're still not mad about that little slap in the face are ya?"

Sloan didn't answer. He was weighing his options. One way or the other, he was going to get away from this jerk. If he had to shoot him, so be it.

"Carefully, with two fingers, take your pistol out and throw it over here," Sloan said.

Sloan had seen TV shows where the good guys told the bad guys, or vice versa, to do that. He had no idea if it would work the way it did on TV, but it was worth a try. If the asshole Fredricks did it the right way, he'd walk the man down the trail to the road, and hope to get someone's attention so they could call the sheriff. If he didn't, well, Sloan would just shoot him.

Fredricks didn't do it the right way.

CHAPTER 32

They heard the shots way off in the distance.

"You think that's them?" Green asked.

"I don't know," Luke said. "Could be, I guess. But what would they be shooting at?"

"Skyler has a pistol in his backpack," Green said. "It was Skip's. He knows how to shoot. Do you think he could've shot that guy?"

"I hope not," Cale said.

They talked a bit more, then Green asked about calling his mom on Luke's satellite phone.

"You know what, on second thought, maybe you should just text her," Luke said. "That way you can let her know you're fine, and we can stay away from questions about Skyler until we know he's safe."

While Green was texting his mom, Luke and Cale chatted quietly.

"You think those shots were them?" Cale asked.

"Could be, but why?" Luke asked. "Fredricks wouldn't shoot the kid. That would ruin his big payday. I guess the kid could have shot Fredricks. That's more likely to me if it was them shooting. And it could just as easily have been someone spotlighting deer or shooting at coyotes."

"Yeah, you're probably right."

"I hope my mom gets the text soon," Green said as he went over, sat down next to Jack, and started to scratch his ears. "I know she'll be glad that you've found me and I'm okay."

"I bet she will," Luke said.

Fifteen minutes later, Luke saw Jack lift his head and look up the hill into the darkness. He knew the Chelan County deputies were getting close. A minute later, they heard footsteps coming down the hill. Luke put his hand on his pistol, and Cale grabbed his rifle, just in case.

"Chelan County sheriff," a man's voice came from out of the darkness.

"Come on in," Luke said. "Luke McCain and Cale Harris, state police."

The two sheriff's deputies came down the hill into the light of the fire.

"You guys made good time," Luke said.

"We weren't all that far behind you coming out of Stehekin," the older of the two deputies said.

"Speaking of making good time," the younger deputy said. "You were tough to keep up with."

"Assume you saw Skip Harvey?" Luke asked.

"Yes, he's doing fine. He's staying there at his camp in case we need him. Another deputy will be there with him soon."

"Where are the folks with horses coming from?" Cale asked.

"They're coming around from Chelan on the road below," said the older deputy named Juarez. "But it's a pretty good drive, so it'll be a while before they get here."

Rogers, who had been sleeping near the fire, moved a little and moaned.

"You need some pain medicine, mister?" Juarez asked.

"Yes, please," Rogers said. "Or you could just shoot me."

"We need to get back on the trail of the other man," Luke said.

"There's a faster way down to the main trail at the bottom," said the younger deputy named Larson. "I know this country pretty well. You have to climb back up onto that hogback ridge, but there's a good trail up there that'll take you right down to the main trail."

"Jack here has been tracking them," Cale said. "We'd hate to lose their trail."

"If they're going down to the road to meet someone, like you think they are, they'll need to hit that main trail first," Larson explained. "Going up to the trail on the hogback will save you a half hour anyway, and it's way better than breaking trail through some of them hell holes down there."

Luke really disliked hell holes.

"Great, thanks," he said to Larson. And then to Green, "Listen, Tory, you'll be good with these guys. You might even get to ride a horse out of here. We're going to get Skyler, and you guys will be back together soon."

"Thanks Officer McCain," Green said as he petted Jack. "Go find 'em, boy."

"Officer McCain," Juarez said as he handed Luke a radio. "Sheriff wanted me to give this to you. You should be able to get us and the Okanogan County Sheriff's Office if you need us."

"Thanks deputy," Luke said. "Come on, Jack. Let's go."

Cale was already two hundred yards up the hill, headed for the hogback trail.

*

Sloan was watching the man closely by the light of his headlight. The shot next to his foot had definitely gotten Fredricks' attention. But when the fright of the shot wore off—and it wore off quickly—Fredricks smiled at Sloan like he knew something that no one else knew.

"Two fingers," Sloan repeated, pointing the pistol at his chest. He'd already decided where he would shoot the man if he tried doing anything other than pulling his pistol with two fingers. Sloan still hadn't come to grips with killing a person. So, even though the shooting instructor who had worked with him always said, "If you have to shoot someone, shoot to kill. It will probably save your life," he just couldn't shoot to kill. He would shoot for the man's upper leg or hip. He knew that if the bullet hit the major artery in the leg, the man very well could bleed to death, but he was willing to take that chance.

Fredricks held up his hand, making a pinching motion with is forefinger and thumb. Then he slowly moved them down to the butt of his pistol. He gradually pulled the pistol up, but when the barrel cleared the holster, Fredricks, with surprising speed, brought his left hand across to hold the gun, so he could reposition his right hand to shoot.

Despite Fredricks' speed, Sloan was ready, and he fired almost immediately. He missed where he wanted to hit by a few inches, but as luck would have it, the bullet hit Fredricks' pistol and ricocheted into his upper thigh. Fredricks went down like he'd been hit by a thirty-six-ounce Louisville slugger, the pistol flying from his hand at the impact of the bullet.

Sloan ran over and picked up the pistol. He walked back over to Fredricks, who was lying on the trail, trying to stop the blood coming from the wounds. The leg was bleeding from the front and back of his leg, meaning the bullet had gone through without hitting any bone. But it wasn't spurting. Sloan had learned in health class that spurting blood was bad and needed a tourniquet immediately. Fredricks' leg was just bleeding steadily.

Sloan's left hand was shaking like a maple leaf in a gale. But his right hand, securely holding Harvey's .45 caliber Glock, was as steady as a surgeon's. The adrenalin was rushing through him, but he had learned to take deep, slow breaths to control his body. The breathing control was working pretty well, but his mind was an absolute freeway, including about seven cloverleaf exits and overpasses, with everything going eighty miles an hour.

"You gotta help me, boy," Fredricks said. "I'm going to bleed to death."

"I don't think so," Sloan said. "Just keep pressure on the wound, and you'll be okay."

"I can't believe you shot me. What the hell?"

"You were going to shoot me."

"No, I wasn't. I was just going to scare you a bit."

"See where that got you? I'm taking off. I hope I never see you again."

With that, Sloan turned and headed back the way they came. He figured it would be light before too long, then he'd climb back up to where they had left Tory. And once he found his friend, they'd head to the camp where they'd left Skip.

*

Bakshi and the boys had driven up and down the road near the campground where they were to meet Fredricks and Rogers every half hour since four o'clock in the afternoon. Patel wanted to abort the plan, drive back to Vancouver, and catch the first flight home. He was of the belief that every hour that this wasn't working out was an hour closer to spending time in federal prison for a very long time.

"They have no idea who we are. They do not know our real names. We are just three businessmen from India, on holiday, visiting the wilds of America," Bakshi reasoned.

"We do not look like your average campers," Singh said. "But I agree. There is no way they can arrest us for being on this road. As the Americans say, 'This is a free country, and we can do whatever we please.'"

"Except for hiring two Americans to kidnap a multi-millionaire's son and hold him for ransom," Patel said. "That, we cannot do, whether we look like campers or not."

They had seen some other vehicles driving up and down the road, but nobody paid them much attention.

After one SUV went by with what looked like a family in the car—adults in the front, kids in the back—Singh said, "See there. Those people never even gave us a second look."

"That is because the sun was in their eyes," Patel said. "We are lucky they did not crash into us."

Well into the night, on what seemed like the twentieth time up the road, Patel said, "Let me out. I need to urinate."

Bakshi slowed the Ford to a stop, and Patel jumped out. Except for the thirty-foot cone of light in front of the vehicle where the headlights mostly illuminated flying insects and the occasional mouse scurrying across the dirt road, the rest of the surroundings were extremely dark.

"I think bears are attracted to the smell of human urine," Singh said as Patel was exiting the Explorer.

"Let them come," Patel said, hurrying to get his zipper down. "I really have to pee, and being consumed by a bear would be more pleasant than spending the rest of my days in prison. At least it would be over quickly."

Those words had barely left the man's mouth when two gunshots rang out in the darkness. The first was muffled. Then, thirty seconds later, there was another that included what sounded like a ricochet.

"Those were fairly close," Singh said. "Do you think it is the men?"

"Ssshhh," Bakshi shushed. "Listen."

Each of the men strained to hear something, anything, that might tell them the origins of the gunfire.

"All I hear are the insufferable crickets," Patel finally said after listening so hard he was getting a headache.

"I thought I heard some voices," Singh said. "Right at first. But nothing after that."

"Get your guns," Bakshi said. "We will go check it out."

"I would prefer to stay here," Patel said.

"You will come with us," Bakshi said. "Get your pistol. And your pack. Put some water in it. And get our flashlights. Hurry."

After the men had their weapons and lights, and Patel had his pack, Bakshi got in their SUV and moved it into a turnout just up the road. He walked quickly back to the men, took a flashlight from his cousin, and led the way into the dark trees.

"The shots originated from this direction," Bakshi said quietly.

Singh, who was following Bakshi closely, agreed.

Patel, who was following Singh so closely he was bumping his toes into Singh's heals, was too busy looking behind him to even think about what was ahead.

Two hundred yards into the trees, the men hit a very well-used trail. They stopped for a minute and heard a thump, then a noise that sounded like a person moaning. Or was it a wild cat yowling?

Thump, moan. Thump, yowl. Thump, moan.

The sound was getting closer, so Bakshi turned off his flashlight and motioned for the other two to follow him into the darkness of the trees at the side of the trail. They would wait to see who or what was approaching.

Thump, moan. Thump, moan. Thump, crack. "Ouch. Shit!"

Definitely not a wild cat yowling. Bakshi inched forward and turned his flashlight on the person moving slowly down the trail. He was surprised to see Fredricks, leg covered in blood, hobbling down the trail with a stick as a cane, taking one step with his good leg, and then dragging the bloody one, moaning as he did.

Fredricks looked up at the three men and said, "Fancy meeting you here. Can you please get me to a hospital before I bleed to death?"

"Where is the boy?" Bakshi asked.

"Where is your partner?" Singh asked.

"What attacked you?" Patel asked.

"Let's see," Fredricks said. "The boy just left me up the trail about three hundred yards away. Last time I saw him, he was headed back up the mountain. My partner broke his leg up there somewhere and may have been eaten by a mountain lion by now for all I know. And nothing attacked me. The kid shot me. Can you believe it?"

With that, Fredricks sank down onto the trail.

"Seriously, can someone please get me some medical attention? I've lost a lot of blood."

"Ok, this is what we will do," Bakshi said to the others. "Darsh, you take him to the nearest hospital. Rishi and I will go after the boy. He cannot be that far ahead. We should be able to apprehend him."

Bakshi grabbed Patel's backpack and put it on his back. They would need the water.

"Better take a gun," Fredricks said as Patel was assisting him to his good leg. "The little shit can shoot."

"Come back here as soon as you can," Bakshi said to Patel. "Hopefully, we will be waiting here for you with the boy."

"Good luck," Patel said. "See you soon." He didn't say, "I hope." But he certainly was thinking it.

CHAPTER 33

The first hint of morning light came in the form of a line of gray on the eastern horizon. The robins, always eager to start their day, took the cue and started chirping from the tree branches. In short order, Western tanagers and mountain chickadees were sounding off too.

Luke loved being in the mountains when the woods were waking up. Soon, the squirrels would be chattering and skittering around. The animals that fed at night, including elk and deer, would still be up and about. It was the perfect time to see them as they wandered back to their bedding areas.

This new morning, though, Luke had other things on his mind. He and Cale had discussed the gunshots they had heard just before leaving the fire. They were of the mind that the shots very well could have come from the man that had Skyler Sloan.

"I think you're right," Cale said as they worked their way down the hogback trail. "But that guy wouldn't kill the golden goose."

"Unless Skyler pulled the pistol out of his pack," Luke said.

Since they weren't on the trail used by Skyler Sloan, Jack's nose wasn't needed. He was happy to lope along through the woods in near proximity to Luke and Cale. The two men moved along at almost double their normal walking speed. Going downhill helped.

If they'd have gone down the mountain the way Fredricks and Sloan had gone, they would have run right into Sloan as he worked his way back up. It was bad luck all the way around because Skyler Sloan was definitely not out of danger.

Sloan moved quickly back up the trail. As he went, he tried to remember exactly where they had come down off the hill earlier when they hit the trail. He hoped he could see his boot tracks in the dirt. His boots had a unique tread pattern that included four four-leaf clovers in the heel and front pad.

He felt bad about shooting the man. Well, he felt sort of bad. The guy was a jerk. The gunshot wound was not fatal. Or he didn't think it was. It didn't matter really. There was nothing he could do about that now. He needed to find Tory. He needed to get him away from the dude with the broken ankle.

Sloan was watching the trail closely in his headlight when he came upon a trample of boot prints. In amongst them were his. He backtracked them about a half mile to the spot where he and Fredricks had come out of the brush. It wasn't going to be easy, hiking back up the mountain. But he had to do it. He put his head down, pushed through some head-high brush, and started hiking up the hill.

After zigzagging up the hill for a half hour, with just a few short stops to catch his breath, Sloan turned and looked back. He was impressed by how far he had come. The first light of morning was just starting to show in the east. As he looked at it, breathing hard, he suddenly realized he was incredibly hungry.

It had been hours since he last ate anything, and with the miles he had walked, he surely had burned all those calories, plus who-knows-how-many more. So, he pulled his backpack off, sat down and started digging for something, anything, to eat.

Luckily, Skip had several high-protein energy bars tucked into one of the side pockets of the pack. Sloan ate two of those in rapid succession and washed them down with his last bottle of water. He still had some water in his camel bladder, but he made a mental note to fill up the bottles when he passed a spring or creek.

As he finished his second energy bar and drank the water, he tried to remember if they had passed any kind of a water source coming down the mountain. It was dark, so he hadn't been able to see very far, but he didn't remember seeing or hearing any creeks or springs. He knew they hadn't stepped over or walked through any. Oh well. He'd pay attention going up the hill. There had to be water somewhere.

What Sloan didn't realize was that even though he kept the growing daylight mostly at his back, having to go up and down through ravines and over small ridges was gradually pushing him to the northwest. If he kept on that heading, he would miss Tory at the fire by a half mile.

He didn't think the man he'd shot would be following him, but he didn't know that for sure. So, Sloan kept pushing up the hill. And he kept drifting farther off-course.

*

They followed the bloody drag marks left by Fredricks up the trail until they hit the spot where the shooting had occurred.

"There is a spent cartridge casing," Singh said as his light flashed off the small brass casing in the dirt.

Bakshi looked for boot prints, and after following Fredricks' tracks a short way back in the direction they had just come, he was able to determine which print was Fredricks' and which was the boy's.

"The track with the round clovers is the boy's," Bakshi said. "They should not be too difficult to follow."

"If the dirt is soft," Singh said. "But if he gets up into that rocky hillside, it will become much more difficult."

They walked up the trail slowly, searching for and then following Sloan's waffle stomper footprints.

"There," Bakshi said, shining his light on the tracks moving into the brush. "This is where he left the trail."

The men pushed through the brush and started up the hill. They didn't notice the light was changing until they no longer needed their flashlights to see the ground.

At first, the tracks up the hill were easy to follow. The freshly broken ground told them the boy had climbed up the hill this way. But as they hiked, they started losing the tracks in the rocks and dried grass, just as Singh had predicted.

They were getting winded very quickly. The men were out of shape, and the increase in elevation was making it more and more difficult to keep going.

Bakshi stopped, sucking for air.

"We will rest here," he said as he pulled the pack off his back and handed it to Singh. "Get the water. We need to stay hydrated."

Singh looked in the pack. There were two twenty-ounce bottles of water inside.

"We don't have much water," Singh said. "We better conserve this. Drink sparingly."

Bakshi was looking up the hill, trying to locate the boy walking above them, in the trees or on an open hillside.

"I do not believe he is that far ahead of us," Bakshi said. "We will catch up to him and then worry about water."

Singh did not say anything. He was remembering a story he had once read about a Pope in the eighteenth century who had sent some princes on a fool's errand so the Pope could steal their land while they were gone. He was of the belief that they were now on their own fool's errand.

If Bakshi had just a little better eyesight or the aid of binoculars, he might have seen Skyler Sloan cutting up the hill eight hundred yards above them.

*

Sloan spotted the two men during one of his quick stops to catch his breath. They were a long way below him, three quarters of a mile maybe. He pulled the binoculars from the pack and took a look at them. He didn't recognize either man. Could they be part of a search party? As that thought came to him, he almost started yelling. But, as he looked closer at the two men, they didn't look like they were part of any rescue party. They looked like foreigners. Their attire was totally wrong for hiking in the mountains. With the binoculars, he retraced his path up the hill, realizing the men were right on his tracks.

Sloan watched the men for another two minutes. He could tell they were out of shape. They stopped often to breathe. Even if they had been two hundred yards below him, they would never catch him. He turned and kept moving up the mountain.

*

When Luke and Cale hit the trail, they immediately spotted the blood and the drag marks.

"Someone is walking along, helping the person who is injured and bleeding," Cale said. "But neither track is from the boy's boots."

"Let's follow them and see where they go," Luke said.

They did just that. Right out to a Forest Service road and over to where a vehicle had been parked.

"They're gone," Luke said. "Let's backtrack the blood trail and see what we can see."

They did that too. They saw where three different tracks met the tracks of a person—most likely a man by the size of the boot—who was bleeding. Then two sets of tracks went up the trail, following the bloody drag to where the shooting occurred.

"Here's some waffle stompers," Cale said.

Luke bent down and picked up a brass shell casing. "And here is a casing from a forty-five."

The two men looked at the prints and ciphered out what had happened.

"Looks like Sloan shot Fredricks," Cale said.

"And then two men backtracked the blood trail and now are following Sloan back up the trail," Luke said.

"That's not good," Cale said. "You think it's the guys from India?"

"I don't know who else it would be. Rogers said there were three men who hired them. Could be one of them went with Fredricks to get him some medical help, and the other two went after Sloan."

Luke pulled the backpack off his back and grabbed the radio the deputy had given him.

"This is Wildlife 148, Officer McCain."

"Go ahead, 148," a male's voice crackled back.

"Hold on," Luke said. He pulled the GPS unit out of the pack and handed it to Cale, saying, "Get our coordinates." Then to the dispatcher, he said, "We're on the trail of a kidnapped young man named Skyler Sloan. We believe he shot one of the men who had abducted him. Please let all LEOs in Chelan and Okanogan counties know to be on the lookout for two men, one native of India, in a late-model, white Ford Explorer."

"We're already looking for that vehicle."

"Good, and let all hospitals and emergency care facilities know to be watching for the men. Again, one with black hair, possibly from India, and the injured man, white, age 35, GSW, possibly to a left leg or hip."

"Ten-four, 148. Do you need assistance?"

"Not at this time, but here are our current GPS coordinates."

Luke got the coordinates from Cale, and after giving them to the deputy on the radio, he signed off, pulled his sat phone out, and called his captain.

"What's going on up there?" Davis asked.

"Let's put it this way," Luke said. "We're not getting a lot of sleep."

Luke told him about finding Tory Green and having one of the kidnappers in custody.

"We knew that," Davis said. "I've been in contact with Chelan County and McCarthy at Region Two."

"It looks like the Sloan boy may have shot the other kidnapper, and now he is headed back up into the mountains."

They talked about that for a minute, then Davis asked, "Okay, so what are you going to do?"

"We're going after Sloan. By the tracks we have found, it looks like two other men, possibly the men from India, are pursuing him. We need to find him before they do."

They talked for another minute. Luke gave the captain their coordinates and then ended the call.

It didn't take them long to find where the tracks exited the trail. Luke, Cale, and Jack dove into the brush after them and started up the hill.

"Let's keep a good eye on the hillside above us," Cale said. "We might be able to see the men, and possibly even Sloan."

They pushed up the hill, looking for tracks, and watching for anyone above them. The tracks in some places were pretty evident. In others, they were non-existent. But always they found more headed in a northwesterly general direction.

"If Sloan is trying to get back to his friend, or to Skip Harvey, he's going to miss both going the way he's going," Luke said as he looked up the hill.

While Luke looked for tracks and led the way, Cale followed, watching for any movement up ahead of them.

The first indication that they were closing in on someone was by the blood-curdling scream that came from the rocky bluffs above them.

CHAPTER 34

Patel had no idea where the nearest hospital might be. So, he just drove. And as he drove, Fredricks continued to moan and groan, and unfortunately, bleed.

When they had gotten to the SUV, Patel had opened one of the duffle bags in the back and found a T-shirt. He tore the shirt in half and tied it around Fredricks' leg. The man screamed with pain, so Patel tied it a bit harder. Even with the makeshift bandage, the wounds in Fredricks' leg continued to bleed. Not, oh-my-God-I'm-going-to-die blood, but enough to make a mess.

"We definitely will not be getting any damage refund back from the rental car company," Patel said to Fredricks as he looked at the blood on the floor mats and the passenger seat of the Explorer.

"I couldn't give a rat's ass about your damage deposit," Fredricks said.

"How could you let a boy shoot you?" Patel asked in a snarky voice.

"You know what, if I wasn't gun shot, I'd kick your ass."

Patel chuckled and patted Fredricks on his leg, right where the bullet entered, and said, "Right."

Fredricks screamed in pain. "You son of a bitch," he said and tried to take a swing at Patel. But the punch had no power behind it, and Patel swatted it away like he would have a bug.

The two men remained silent for the rest of the drive out of the mountains. When they finally hit a paved road, Patel turned right and let the Explorer run now that it had hit hard road. He wanted to get Fredricks out of the car, and out of his life, as quickly as possible. He slowed to round a slight curve, bumped the speed of the SUV up to sixty-five, and then saw a gray SUV with a light bar on the roof coming at them.

"Shit," Patel said in his native language.

"What?" Fredricks said. He'd had his eyes closed, praying to get to the hospital before he died of blood loss or a horrific car wreck. The Indian dude was a very bad driver.

The law enforcement rig flew by them, going in the opposite direction. Patel watched it in the rearview mirror go around the curve they'd just come through.

"That was a police vehicle," Patel said. "I was exceeding the speed limit. But I do not think he is coming back for us."

In fact, the Okanogan County sheriff's deputy was not a he, but a she. And as soon as she recognized the late-model, white Explorer that every law enforcement officer in three counties was searching for, she hit the brakes, executed a nifty U-turn, switched her lights on, and radioed it in.

"OCS Deputy Hankins in pursuit of a late-model, white Ford Explorer."

Hankins told the dispatcher the road she was on and the direction in which the Explorer was traveling. She'd only gotten a very quick look at the driver. She couldn't swear to it, but the man could be from India or Pakistan. He had black hair and brown skin. It was definitely the car they had been looking for. She hadn't seen who was in the passenger seat.

Thirty seconds after Patel said it didn't look like the police vehicle was following them, he looked back into his mirror and saw the gray SUV coming up fast behind them with blue lights flashing in the grill and atop the vehicle.

"Shit," Patel said again in Punjabi and pressed the gas pedal to the floor.

He almost lost control of the Explorer going through some gradual "s" curves, and then got totally blocked by a school bus stopped in the middle of the road, a line of six kids crossing to get on the bus.

Patel watched as the cop car ran right up to the back of the SUV and slammed to a stop. A petite blonde woman, dressed in tan pants and a green shirt with a shiny silver badge just above her left breast, hurried out of the car with a pistol in her hand. She was pointing the gun right at his head.

The line of school kids had stopped in the middle of the road, watching, most with their mouths agape. This was stuff they saw on TV, not at the school bus stop.

"Is there a problem, officer?" Patel said calmly after he rolled down the window.

"Hands on the steering wheel where I can see them," Hankins ordered.

Patel followed her orders and looked straight ahead. He started wondering again if prisons in the United States were like the Arthur Road Jail in his country, where daily beatings were quite common.

While still holding the pistol on Patel, Hankins grabbed the microphone attached to the epaulet on her shoulder and told the dispatcher she had stopped the Explorer. After looking at Fredricks, who was not moving and sitting in a puddle of blood, she said, "Send an ambulance as quick as you can."

The school kids had to be pushed along out of the road by one of the parents who was waiting for the bus with them. That was something parents did pretty much everywhere nowadays because there always was that one-in-a-trillion chance that some deranged pedophile might come along and snatch up one of their little darlings if there wasn't an adult present.

Hankins had Patel exit the vehicle and ordered him to lay across the hood of her rig, hands behind his back. She wanted to get him in handcuffs so she could go deal with the passenger who, if he wasn't dead, wasn't far from it.

Fredricks remembered seeing Patel put a handgun under the driver's seat when they first got into the Explorer. Now, while the cop was putting cuffs on the Indian, he slowly reached under the seat and grabbed it. He needed to get to the hospital immediately, and dealing with the law was just slowing them down.

Hankins had just got the handcuffs on the driver when she noticed the wounded man in the passenger seat sit up. She saw the pistol in his hands, coming up to point at her, and without so much as a second thought, she pulled her side arm and shot at the man through the windshield.

As was the case with most police officers in America, Hankins had never shot her weapon at another person while on duty. She and her fellow officers trained weekly at the gun range to be ready, just in case, but few of them had ever shot at another human being. During those practice sessions, Hankins had regularly whipped the male deputies in shooting accuracy, so it wasn't surprising to anyone who heard about it later that both of Hankins' bullets hit Rod Fredricks center mass.

As he lay there in the white Ford Explorer, quickly losing what little blood was left in his body, Fredricks started to regret his decision to get involved in this craziness. He'd regretted it earlier, when the kid shot him, but now he was really regretting it. All for a measly ten thousand dollars, he thought. Wasn't his life worth more than that? Yes, it was. But still, the money sure would have been nice. He smiled at the thought of all that dough, and then he was gone.

CHAPTER 35

Bakshi and Singh had been climbing up a slope with rocks of all sizes and shapes scattered around, as if some mythical giant had sprinkled them around out of a huge shaker like sprinkles on a bowl of ice cream. The men wormed their way through the rocks until they hit a steep incline, composed almost entirely of big boulders.

The two men took yet another breather and drank the last of their water. Singh wanted to tell Bakshi that they should just turn around and figure out how to find the kid another time, but he knew it would do no good. The man was on a five-million-dollar mission, and he was not to be stopped.

Wasn't it just a couple weeks ago that they were in Mumbai, drinking beer, eating pani puri, while coercing old people in America to send them money? Now look at them. Here they were in a foreign land, hiking up mountains the likes of which they had never seen before. To Singh, it was almost like a dream. More accurately, a bad dream that was about to turn into a nightmare.

"Do you see anything?" Bakshi asked as he finished his water.

"No, nothing."

Bakshi climbed onto a huge flat rock, and Singh was about to follow when they heard a strange buzzing. Singh slowly looked over the edge of the rock and saw a snake coiled next to Bakshi's leg. Its tail was shaking so quickly, it was a blur.

"Do not move," Singh said.

"What is it?" Bakshi asked.

"It is a rattlesnake. They are poisonous."

Bakshi started to step back slowly when a second snake started rattling from behind him. Trying to watch the snake in front of him, and the one behind him, he stepped to the side, right into a third rattler. Unwittingly, he'd stumbled onto a rattlesnake den.

Bakshi felt the strike of the rattlesnake in his calf and instantly jumped back. In doing so, he caught his heel on the corner of a boulder which caused him to trip and fall on the big, flat rock. His fall put him eyeball-to-freaky-snake-eyeball with the first rattlesnake. The viper apparently took umbrage at having a human being invade its personal space and, with lightning quickness, bit Bakshi in the cheek. Upon being bitten, Bakshi screamed, fearing the worst. In India, snakes kill nearly sixty thousand people a year, so it was natural for Bakshi to believe he was not long for this world.

He rolled away from the snake that bit him in the face and immediately bumped into the second snake on the rock. It was the only snake that hadn't bit him. Yet. When that rattler struck him in the side of his throat, Bakshi became paralyzed. Not from the venom, but by fear.

While Bakshi was being attacked by the snakes, Singh was pulling his pistol out. When he saw Bakshi just frozen, lying there on the rock, he didn't know quite what to do. The snakes, seemingly done with their attacks for the time being, slithered off into a crack in the rocks.

"Are you okay?" Singh asked.

"I have just been bitten by three venomous snakes. Do you

think I am okay?"

"Well, no, probably not. What would you like me to do?"

"First, make sure there are no more snakes around. Then, crawl up here and assist me. We need to seek medical assistance immediately."

*

"That sounded like someone being murdered," Cale said to Luke when they heard the crazy scream. "We better get up there."

Luke put his binoculars to his eyes and scanned the area where he thought they heard the scream.

"It sounded like it was up in those rocks," Luke said. "But I don't see anything."

Cale pulled his rifle out of the scabbard attached to his backpack, and they began working their way up the hillside slowly, watching the rocks. When they were about a hundred yards from a big, rocky outcropping, they caught movement. Two men, one assisting the other, were coming down slowly.

"Just for the heck of it, cover me," Luke said to Cale.

He saw that both men were thin, with brown skin and black hair. The slightly taller man had a beard. They fit the description given to them by Bart Rogers at the fire of two of the men who had hired him and his friend to grab Skyler Sloan.

"State police!" Luke yelled, holding up his badge. "Stay right there."

Luke and Cale carefully watched the men look down at them and then sit in unison. Cale stayed back and kept an eye on the men as Luke and Jack climbed the rest of the way up to them.

"So, what's going on here?" Luke asked as he got to within ten yards of the men. He noticed that the man with the beard was not looking well. His face was a sickly shade of gray.

"My friend has been bitten by some rattlesnakes," Singh said.

"Well, that's not good," Luke said. "Where'd they get ya?"

"In the face, the throat, and the leg," Bakshi said in a scratchy, shaky voice.

Luke turned and gave Cale a head nod to come on up. Then he took his pack off, grabbed a bottle of water, and a small first aid kit. From the kit, he pulled some gauze and walked over to the man with the bites.

"Is your name Dinesh?" Luke asked.

There was a hesitation as Bakshi and Singh looked at each other. They now knew the lawmen had identified the men who hired Fredricks and Rogers. Luke caught the hesitation.

"Listen, we know you're the guys who are after Skyler Sloan. I don't know what your real names are and don't care at the moment. We'll figure that out later. Right now, you need someone to treat these bites, and we need to figure out how to get you out of here."

While Cale cleaned the snake bites on Bakshi, Luke radioed into whoever could hear him.

"This is wildlife 148, Luke McCain. We have another medical emergency."

Luke had also pulled the GPS out of the pack and was waiting on it to acquire the satellites.

"Go ahead, Officer McCain," a female voice said.

"I'll get you coordinates as soon as the GPS links up, but we have a man with multiple rattlesnake bites, one bite on the face and another on the throat."

"Copy that," the woman said.

"I think we can get him to a flat spot where a helicopter can pick him up, but I don't know if this is a life-saving emergency. You'd need to consult a physician."

"Copy that."

"Do you know how the horse riders are doing on the rescue of the man with the broken leg?"

"They're heading up the hill. Should be there in a half hour."

"We're probably only a mile from the other man, as the crow flies. Maybe they could swing over and pick our snakebite victim up on the way back down the hill."

"Copy. We'll check on that. We have some other news

regarding this case."

"Go ahead."

"An Okanogan County deputy made a stop on the white Explorer. One of the men in the car, who was already wounded, pulled a gun. She shot him."

"Is he dead?"

"As disco."

"Copy that. Assume the other man was apprehended as well."

"That's an affirmative."

Luke looked at the two men sitting a short way away. They'd heard the whole conversation.

"Let us know what is decided on the pickup here," Luke said and gave her the GPS coordinates.

"Copy. We will let you know as soon as we know."

"So," Luke said as he turned to the two men. "Sounds like your partner is in custody, and one of the men you hired has been killed. Was it all worth it?"

Bakshi thought about the five-million-dollar ransom he had planned on getting. He would have to say it was. But he would not tell anyone else that. He was glad his cousin was alive but knew he would probably not fare well in prison.

It had been over twenty-four hours since Luke had talked to Sara. He'd gone longer periods without checking in with her, and she seemed not to worry too much about him. Jack, on the other hand, she worried about constantly. Since they needed to stay there until they heard back from whichever county was in charge of the rescue operations, he decided to call her.

It took almost a minute for the connection to go through.

"Hey, how are you?" Sara asked.

"Tired and hungry. How are you?"

"Okay. I've been catching bits and pieces about what's going on up there from Bob Davis. Sounds like you have a real rodeo on your hands."

"Yeah, it's been pretty crazy, and it's not over yet. We have to get one of the suspects to a hospital. He has multiple rattlesnake bites."

"That sounds horrible. Is he going to be alright?"

"Don't know. I think so. And we still need to find Skyler Sloan."

"Is Jack able to track him?"

"No, not really. He's helped some, but it's mostly Cale and me doing the tracking."

"I hope you find him soon. His folks must be beyond worried."

"We will. Listen, I need to go. I just thought I'd let you know that Jack is doing great. I know how you worry."

"I worry about you too, you know."

"Good to know. I'll call soon. Love you."

"Love you too. Give Jack a hug," she said, and then she was gone.

Luke put the sat phone back into the pack and walked over to Cale.

"We need to stay on the kid's trail while it's still hot," Luke said. "What do you think about one of us staying here with these two until we figure out how to get them down the mountain? And the other will go after Sloan."

"I was thinking the same thing. You and Jack should keep after the boy. I'll stay with these two."

"Okay, here's the radio. I'll keep the sat phone. That way we'll both have some communication."

Luke looked at the man with the snake bites. He was still ashen and seemed to be having some difficulty breathing. And the right side of his face had puffed up to about twice its normal size.

"Hope something happens soon," Luke said. "I don't like the looks of him."

"I agree," Cale said. "If I don't hear something pretty quick, I may try to walk him down to the road."

"Not sure that's the best idea on a snakebite victim, but it might be better than sitting here and watching him die."

"I'll figure it out. You go. Hope you catch up to Sloan sooner rather than later."

"Me too," Luke said. "I'm about to fall asleep just sitting here. He's got to be tired too."

Luke pulled his pack over his shoulders, called for Jack, and off they went up the hill, avoiding the flat rock and the scene of the rattlesnake encounter.

CHAPTER 36

Skyler Sloan had heard the horrible scream in the rocks well below him. He had no idea what caused the person to scream, and he didn't want to find out. He'd been checking on the men with the black hair following his tracks. Each time he saw them, they had fallen farther and farther behind. Then, after the scream, he didn't see them again.

His body was running on empty and he'd begun taking longer breaks. He was also running low on water, which concerned him. He needed sleep, and he needed food to fuel his climbing. When he was totally out of gas, he walked over to a small grove of aspens and pulled out the backpacker's stove and pot. There were several packs of freeze-dried food in the backpack, so he decided to cook two pouches. He poured just enough water in the pot to make the meal, lit the stove, and waited for the water to boil.

As he sat watching the pot, his eyes closed. The bubbling of the boiling water on the stove woke him up a minute later. Sloan shook his head to try to stave off the slumber, opened the pouch of beef stroganoff, and poured the water in.

After waiting for the meal to cool, he took a bite. It was so good he devoured it in seconds. He opened the second pouch of mac and cheese and proceeded to devour it too. Something about the warm food in his stomach made him that much sleepier. He laid back in the grass, with the full intention of sleeping for just a few minutes.

*

Luke looked for anything that would tell him which way Sloan was going. He'd find a track here and there, telling him Sloan was still on a northwesterly heading. The few tracks he found were very fresh, and Luke was of the mind that he was closing on the young man. He wanted to stop and rest and eat something, but the idea that he was getting close kept him moving.

Ultimately, it was Jack who found Sloan. The boy had diverted off his line to the northwest and had turned due south into a grove of aspen trees. Luke probably would have kept walking and would have never noticed the change in direction—for a while anyway. But Jack, like most Labradors, enticed by the smell of food, veered in the direction of the aspens and wouldn't come when Luke called.

*

He'd been asleep for thirty-five minutes when he heard a man's voice calling for someone named Jack. Sloan was so tired, he thought he must be dreaming when he first heard the voice. He lay there for another minute, and the voice came again.

"Jack! Come here!"

Sloan sat up slowly and saw a yellow dog looking right at him. The dog was twenty yards away and just standing there. It looked like the dog that had come up to him and Tory at the boat launch two days before. What was that dog doing up here?

Then, he saw a man behind the dog. It was the man they had chatted with at the boat launch. He was going hunting, Sloan remembered. Maybe he was hunting up here.

"Hi," Sloan said, waving his arm.

As soon as he said something, Jack ran to Sloan and started licking his face.

"Hey, boy. What are you doing up here?"

Luke was now walking quickly to Sloan and heard him ask Jack the question.

"We're looking for you," Luke said. "I'm a state police officer—game warden actually—and we've been tracking you ever since those two men grabbed you up on the ridge when you were with Skip Harvey."

"I was hoping you weren't with the men who took us. I saw some other guys tracking me. I couldn't figure out why, but they didn't look right, you know what I mean? So I kept walking. I was trying to get back to Tory."

"I know what you mean," Luke said.

Then he told Sloan about how they had located his friend. There was a rescue party coming for the man with the broken leg. Then Luke told him about how one of the men Sloan had seen following him had been bitten by three rattlesnakes, and they were now in custody.

"Wow, I haven't been watching for snakes," Sloan said. "What happened to the man I shot? Did you find him?"

"No, I didn't, but the county sheriffs did. He pulled a gun on a deputy, and she shot him. He didn't make it."

"So he died from the deputy shooting him and not from the wound in his leg?"

"That's right, yes."

"I'm glad to hear that. Not that I'm glad he is dead. It's just good knowing I didn't kill the guy. He was a jerk, but I'm not sure he needed to die."

Luke decided to change subjects. "I haven't eaten in, well, I don't know how long. You have any more of those food pouches with you?" he asked as he pointed to the two empty packages next to the little burner stove.

"I sure do, but I'm pretty low on water."

"I have plenty of water," Luke said. "So whatcha got?"

As Sloan boiled water, Luke used the sat phone to call John McCarthy at the WDFW Region 2 office and asked him to notify all the other agencies involved in the search that he had found Sloan and they were about to enjoy a much-needed freeze-dried lunch.

"I need to see where we are on the GPS," Luke told McCarthy. "Depending on our location, we'll either go back down to the trail on the east side of the ridge or we'll go on up and find Skip Harvey's camp."

"Ten-four," McCarthy said. "Let us know."

Once he was done talking to McCarthy and his lunch was ready, Luke handed the phone to Sloan and said, "Here. You better call your folks and let them know you're okay."

Sloan walked twenty yards away and called his parents. They talked for only a few moments, but Luke could tell it had been emotional.

"How'd that go?" Luke asked after the phone conversation was over.

"There were a few tears, mostly from my mom."

"I bet," Luke said, but he could see two little tear trails down the dusty cheeks of the young man.

"They want to see me get home as soon as possible, but I told them my week of survival school isn't over yet."

Luke looked at him to see if he was serious.

"As weird as this has been, it also has been kind of fun. I've learned a lot being out here, and I'd like to learn more. In fact, tell me a little about what it's like to be a game warden?"

When they were finally done with the cooking, Luke had eaten a package of spaghetti and another of mac and cheese. Sloan ate another mac and cheese, and Jack got to enjoy a beef stroganoff. After they ate, they sat back and just rested. Jack rested too, falling fast asleep in the shade of the aspen trees.

*

Their rest turned into a major power nap. The warm September sun made it almost impossible to stay awake. And, with some food in their bellies, sleep was unavoidable.

Their slumber was interrupted by the thumping of helicopter blades. As soon as Luke figured the helicopter was coming their way, he was up and looking for it.

"Are they coming for us?" Sloan asked.

"No, I think they are going to pick up the man with the snake bites. He didn't look too well when I left them."

Luke looked at his watch. They had slept only twenty minutes, but it seemed like hours. He actually felt somewhat rested.

As they watched the chopper hover below, sending a stretcher basket down on some cables, Luke's sat phone rang.

Luke answered the phone. "This is McCain."

"Hey, Luke," Bob Davis said. "It's taken a bit, but there is a helicopter headed your way to pick up the guy with the snake bites. Harris radioed in and said the guy is having some issues and needs medical attention right away. Harris is going to go with the two men, as he has one in custody and needs to figure out what to do with him."

"Yeah, we're watching the chopper now."

"If you're that close, you want me to have them pick you and the Sloan boy up too?"

"I don't know. I'll ask him."

After a quick conversation, Luke got back on with his captain and said, "We haven't quite figured out what we're going to do, but no, we don't need a lift."

"Ok, keep in touch. Oh, and the search and rescue people on horseback got to the guy with the broken leg, and they have the Green kid with them too. They're riding out now."

"I'll let Skyler know," Luke said, then he told the captain goodbye and hung up.

"Let me know what?" Sloan asked.

"That your friend is riding out of the mountains on a horse right now."

"That's good. I know his mom was really freaking over this whole deal. He's all she's got, so she worries quite a bit."

"I think that's natural. I know your parents were worried about you too."

"What I don't get is why they picked me and Tory to take? I'm pretty sure I saw the two men who grabbed us at the boat launch where we saw you. And I know I saw them in a boat at Stehekin."

"We believe they weren't really after Tory, just you. They were going to hold you for ransom once they had you."

"My folks have some money, but they're not rich like Bill Gates."

"The men with the black hair who were trailing you at the end, they were the masterminds of the abduction. The two men who actually took you at the camp with Skip were just hired hands."

"I was thinking about that too. How'd they know where we'd be camped? We never saw them following us."

"That's a good question. But you definitely were the one they wanted." They both sat quietly for a minute or two, and then Luke asked, "So where'd you learn to handle a pistol?"

Sloan told Luke about the gun training classes he had taken and about the range where he practiced. "My dad's not much of an outdoor guy. He's busy at work pretty much all the time. But he's been cool about getting me the shooting lessons and this survival school. Tory and I were really looking forward to this."

"Everyone should learn gun safety," Luke said. "Knowing how to handle a pistol may have saved your life."

"That man, Fredricks, had a gun on us most of the time. And he had it on me after we separated from Tory and the guy who broke his leg. Fredricks slapped me once, which pissed me off. I had no idea where he was taking me, but I knew I had Skip's gun, so I took a chance."

"You did the right thing," Luke said. "Where were you aiming?"

"Right about where I hit him, though I think the bullet glanced off the pistol and into his leg." Sloan pulled Fredricks' pistol out of his pack and handed it to Luke. "See there. I hit the side of the barrel. His gun went flying when I shot."

"You probably should have aimed for the chest, but it all worked out."

"I just didn't think I could kill someone. But I had my chance to get away, so I took it."

Sloan asked if Luke had ever shot anyone, and Luke told him about how he and Jack had tracked down a serial killer and how Luke had shot the guy with his rifle.

"Did you kill him?" Sloan asked.

"Almost. Like you, I wasn't wild about killing him, or anyone else for that matter, but I was tired of chasing him. He started shooting at me, so I took his leg out."

"Wow, that was kinda like me."

"If you're serious about staying up here, continuing with the school, I think we can make that happen."

"I'll have to do some more convincing with my mom and dad, but I think I would really like to."

"Let's see what we can do," Luke said and pulled his sat phone out again.

*

Luke made a couple calls and received a couple more. When it was all said and done, the deputy who had stayed with Skip Harvey was able to confirm that Harvey would stay at the camp until Luke and Sloan arrived. Skyler could stay with Harvey for the rest of the week if he still wanted to.

"You think Tory can get back up here?" Sloan asked Luke.

"If he wants to, I'm guessing it can be worked out."

"I think he'll want to, but his mom may have something to say about that."

"You need to clear it with your parents too," Luke said and handed him the sat phone.

After some serious discussion, Sloan's parents finally gave in. Part of the deal was he would call home every night on Harvey's sat phone.

Luke and Sloan sat and rested and talked for another hour. Then, Luke pulled his GPS out of his pack and turned it on. In two minutes, he had the map up and located Harvey's camp.

"It says we're a little over two miles from Skip's camp," Luke said.

"You think we can make it tonight?" Sloan asked.

"I think so, if you're up for it."

"Let's go!" Sloan said, grabbing his pack, throwing it on his back, and heading up the hill.

"This way," Luke said, pointing to the southwest.

"Oh, yeah, it would probably be good to go the right direction," Sloan said, moving in the direction Luke was pointing.

CHAPTER 37

They arrived at the camp where Skip Harvey was waiting for them at just after six. Harvey had a fire burning in the ring Sloan had built two days before and was happy to see them.

"Man, I was worried about you and Tory," Harvey said to Sloan after he and Luke got settled in. "I'm sorry for letting them grab you."

"I don't see how you could have done anything other than what you did," Luke said. "Best to not push it when you have two handguns in your face."

"You really shot that guy with my gun?" Harvey asked Sloan.

"Yeah, I don't know what would have happened or where I'd be right now if you hadn't switched packs with me."

"That was quick thinking," Luke said to Harvey.

They talked about all the things that happened over the past two days. Harvey was especially interested in hearing that the two men that had come to their camp the night before were hired by another group of men.

"And their reason for doing all this was to get a ransom payoff from Skyler's dad?" Harvey asked.

"That's what we believe," Luke said. "In hindsight, it wasn't a very good plan."

"They didn't factor in the wilderness," Harvey said. "Out here, everything can be hunky-dory one minute and life or death the next if you're not paying attention."

Luke agreed. Skyler Sloan might have too, but he had fallen asleep on his sleeping bag.

"I feel bad for the guy who got bit in the face and the neck," Harvey said. "I got bit by a rattler when I was guiding some fishermen down on the Deschutes River a few years ago. Got me right on the ankle. It was painful, and I was pretty sick for a couple of days."

"They airlifted him to the hospital in Wenatchee," Luke said. "Haven't heard how he's doing."

"I can't image what he's been through," Harvey said as he nodded at Sloan, asleep on his bag.

"Smart kid," Luke said. "Even though it was only for a day, I think it was being with you that helped save him. He knew what he was doing out here, although he got off track a bit. Definitely getting that gun to him saved him from who-knows-what."

"I'm surprised he used it, but I'm glad he did."

About then, Luke's sat phone rang. It was Sara. He told her about Jack helping to locate Skyler Sloan and that they were now back at the camp where the boys had been taken the night before.

"Jack and I are going to go down to Stehekin and get Cale's boat in the morning," Luke said. "Can you call Cale and have him meet us at the boat launch in Chelan about noon? Tell him I'll stop and pick up his deer meat on the way down."

"Will do," Sara said. "Glad to have you coming home."

They said their goodnights and hung up.

"I'm beyond beat," Luke said to Harvey a few minutes later. "I'm going to hit it."

He dug his sleeping bag and pad out of his pack, rolled out the tiny pad in the tent, threw the sleeping bag on it, stripped to his shorts and a T-shirt, climbed in the bag, and was asleep in less than a minute.

Harvey stayed up and watched the fire until the last few remnants of daylight faded to dark.

*

Several happy robins started chirping at the first hint of the day to come, waking Luke and Harvey. Sloan slept away soundly.

"He'd probably sleep through an earthquake right now," Luke said.

Sometime during the night, Jack had snuggled up next to the young man, and he didn't move either.

Harvey got the fire going and soon had water boiling over the crackling flames.

"I have some instant coffee," he said to Luke. "It's not great, but if you absolutely need some caffeine in the morning, this will take the edge off."

"Naw," Luke said. "I'm not much of a coffee drinker. Thanks though."

"How about some breakfast then?"

"I'll take you up on that, if I'm not leaving you short."

"Since Tory isn't here, we have plenty. And if he decides to come back up, I'll have him bring more."

After a quick breakfast of freeze-dried scrambled eggs for Luke and two high-energy doggy bars for Jack, Luke loaded up his pack and got ready to leave.

"I'm going to leave your pistol with you," Luke said to Harvey. "In case you should need it. But I'm sure the sheriff will need it for evidence when you get back to Chelan. I'll take the gun that Fredricks was using and hand that over to him today."

"And," he continued, turning to Sloan, "they'll want to talk to you about exactly what happened with Fredricks. I told them you would come see them as soon as you got back to Chelan."

Sloan, who was sitting up in his sleeping bag, blond hair sticking up everywhere, said, "I'll be happy to tell them everything."

"C'mon, Jack," Luke said as he threw the straps of his pack over his shoulders. "You guys have a fun and safe rest of the week."

Sloan got up, walked over, and shook Luke's hand.

"Thanks so much, Luke. I owe you, big time."

"Holler if you want to learn more about becoming a game warden," Luke said. "You know how to reach me."

Luke nodded a so-long at Harvey, and he nodded back. Then Luke patted his thigh, bringing Jack to his side, and they headed up the trail to go over the ridge and down to Lake Chelan.

✻

It was a perfect late summer day when Luke and Jack crested the ridge and looked down at Lake Chelan. The sky and the water were as blue as could be. The morning sun had not yet warmed the air in the mountains, so it made for perfect hiking weather.

As they dropped into Stehekin, two gentlemen approached Luke and Jack.

"We heard what happened up there," one man in a button-up red sweater and a fisherman's cap said. "We're glad those boys are safe, and you caught the bad guys."

The man who was walking with him had on a crimson and gray Washington State University ball cap and a purple and gold University of Washington sweatshirt. Luke wanted to ask him what was up with that but decided the man couldn't be all bad if he had a Wazzu hat on.

"Figured you'd be coming through," the conflicted state university man said. "The deputy said you'd be with a yellow dog. We just wanted to say thanks for helping keep this area safe."

"Well, I didn't do much. But you're welcome."

Then he turned and headed toward the boat launch and docks.

"Come on, Jack," Luke said. Then he said, "Go Cougs," just to see what kind of a response he'd get.

The old boy in the WSU hat said, "Go Cougs."

Cale's boat was right where they had tied it up two days before. Cale kept an extra key hidden under the dash, and Luke found it, fired up the big Yamaha, and let it idle for a few minutes to warm up. Jack was over peeing on the same tree he'd hit when they'd arrived.

"Let's go," is all Luke had to say, and the yellow dog loped down the dock and jumped into the boat.

Luke climbed back onto the dock, untied the ropes holding the bow and stern tight in the slip, threw the ropes in the boat, and jumped in.

Jack was sitting in the passenger seat, tongue hanging out, watching some seagulls sitting on the next dock over.

They slowly motored out of the mooring slips and away from Stehekin. Pushing the throttle handle down slowly, Luke brought the big aluminum boat up on plane, and off they went, headed to Lucerne.

There was no wind, the water was like a mirror, and the run down-lake was beautiful. Luke didn't push the boat, to save fuel and also so he could just enjoy the scenery. He passed three different boats that were trolling for kokanee or lake trout. He wished he could stop and join them.

As he got close to Lucerne, he saw Cale and Earl standing on the dock. Luke slowed the boat to an idle and eased up to the dock.

"Hey there, Luke!" Earl said like he'd just found a long-lost friend. "And Jack. Boy, don't you look good."

Jack wagged his tail, anxious to get out of the boat.

"Hi, Earl. And hello, Cale. Didn't expect to see you here."

"I called Earl last night when I heard you'd be stopping by to pick up the venison, and he invited me up for breakfast. I caught a ride on the express boat. Got here fifteen minutes ago."

"You mean, I'm not late for breakfast?"

Earl laughed a hearty laugh. If he had a white beard to match his snow-white hair, he might make a good Santa Claus, Luke thought. Except he'd have to gain about a hundred pounds to really be believable.

"Joyce baked up some coffee cake just for you two," Earl said. "She can't wait to see you. And she's really looking forward to seeing Jack."

They tied the boat off at the dock and went to Earl's truck. Luke and Jack jumped up in the bed.

As they bounced up the road to Earl and Joyce's place, the warm morning sun hitting him in the face, Luke closed his eyes and smiled. It had been a crazy few days, but he wouldn't have missed it for anything.

CHAPTER 38

Nine days after Luke had returned home from Lake Chelan, he was driving to work when his phone started buzzing. He looked at the caller ID. It was Skyler Sloan.

"Hey, Skyler," Luke said into the Bluetooth. "How did the rest of the week go?"

"It was awesome," Sloan said. "I pretty much slept the first day, but the rest of the time Skip had me doing all kinds of things. I really learned a lot."

The young man thanked Luke again for helping get him safely back to Skip Harvey. As it turned out, Tory Green didn't make it back up to the camp. His mother wanted him home.

"We saw some more bears and a cougar and a bunch of deer," Sloan said. "I'll never forget it."

He asked about Jack and told Luke a little about school. He said he'd only had one nightmare about the man he shot.

"My folks want me to talk to a counselor, but I think I'm fine."

"Might not hurt to give it a go," Luke said. "And if you ever want to just talk, I'm here anytime."

"That would be cool. Thanks. Well, I better get going or I'll miss World History."

Luke said goodbye and ended the call.

Two days before, he had heard from Cale who had been following up on the arrest of the three men from India. Evidently, it had been touch and go for a while, but the man with the snake bites was going to live.

"If he hadn't been airlifted to the hospital, he probably would have died," Cale said. "The snake venom ate up a bunch of flesh on his face and neck. He's in for a long recovery and some serious plastic surgery. Not to mention some prison time."

"Like Skip Harvey said, there are all kinds of things that can happen in the wilderness."

"I guess so, and we saw a bunch of it up there," Cale said. "Let's do it again soon."

They both laughed.

Luke was thinking about his conversations with Skyler and Cale as he pulled into the office. He was about to climb out of the truck when his phone rang again. He clicked on the Bluetooth button to answer the phone.

"Hi, Luke. Oxford Smythe calling."

"Hey, Ox. What's up?"

"My girlfriend's daughter just called. You'll never believe it, but there's another gator in the lake by her apartments. She says it's much bigger than the last one."

"Oh, I believe it. I'll be right over there," Luke said. He put the truck in drive and headed that way.

ACKNOWLEDGEMENTS

Thanks to the following people for their assistance in the writing of this novel. For their technical assistance: Gene Beireis, retired Washington State Department of Fish and Wildlife enforcement officer; Jeff Witkowski; and Merle Shuyler.

And thanks to my advance readers: Kyle Phillips, Kevin Phillips, Terri Phillips, Doug Phillips, Sue Durr, and Rob Robillard.

ABOUT THE AUTHOR

Rob Phillips is an award-winning outdoor writer and the author of the bestselling and critically acclaimed Luke McCain mystery series set in the wilderness of Eastern Washington and featuring a fish & wildlife officer and his yellow Lab, Jack. Rob and his wife, Terri, live in Yakima, Washington with their very spoiled Labrador retriever.